FAUN Over Me

B.L. BROWN

Cover Art by The Caprica

Illustration by Lindsey Staton

ISBN 979-8-9879716-9-7 (pbk)

ISBN 979-8-9879716-8-0 (ebook)

1st edition 2024

If you see something in the woods, no, you didn't

To every daughter told to speak softly and dress pretty: I hope you burn brightly and love loudly.

Content Warnings

While the tone of *Faun Over Me* is lighter in spirit than *Witch of the Demesne* and *Witches of C.R.O.W.*, the characters in these pages live in a world much like our own. As such, there are references to and instances involving the following topics and potential triggers. Please take care of yourselves.

XO – B.L. Brown

Religious trauma, Evangelicalism, dead-naming, emotionally abusive parent, on-page sexual acts (consensual), conscious and unconscious biases, homophobia, queerphobia, racism

Elkwater Music Camp

Elkwater, WV

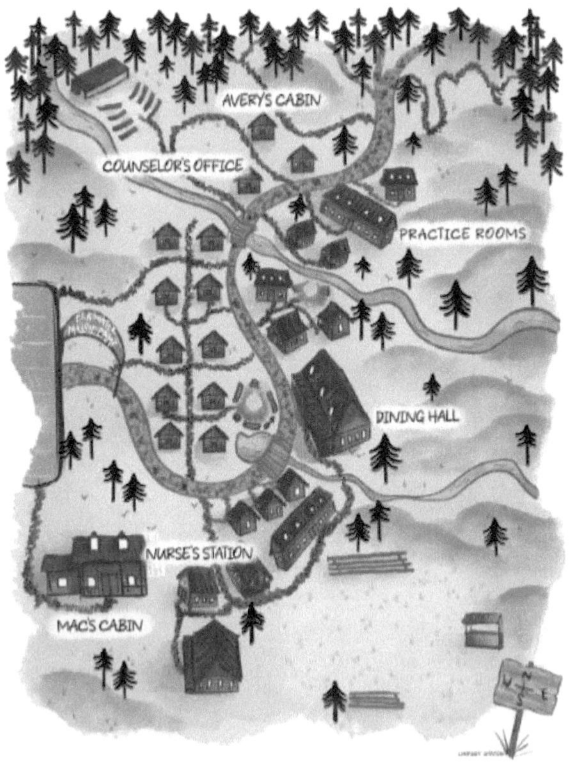

1

CRICKET

Sweetgum and mountain ash bowed and tussled, their branches creaking and groaning beneath gale-force winds. Rain fell in heavy sheets, obscuring the deer trail, and the only light came in intermittent bursts as lightning cracked overhead.

An exceptionally bright flash revealed the snaggled, clawed ends of a branch, and Cricket ducked low, narrowly avoiding having her eyes gouged out. She stumbled over a root, pin-wheeling her arms to stay upright.

"Oak and ivy!" Her hoof came down on a mud slick, and Cricket skidded forward, barely grasping the thin trunk of a sapling cottonwood to stop her fall. She raised her free hand, shielding her eyes from the rain and squinting through the dark. She had to keep moving; had to get to the camp and out of this storm. Had to get walls and a door between her and whatever it was that stalked her through the woods. Her ears swiveled, seeking the sound of snapping twigs and thudding footfalls over the howl of the wind and pouring rain.

Nothing.

Nothing but the rain and the wind and the thudding of her heart in her ears.

She pushed off the cottonwood and darted across the clearing. Lightning cracked, illuminating the woods in an all-too-brief flash of white light—not so brief that she missed the looming shadow in the trees.

"Fuck." Her ears snapped back. Adrenaline surged through her legs, sending her bolting across the tiny hollow. She ducked under branches and leaped over boulders and roots, running on sheer instinct alone.

Gods, she had to be close. *Please*, let her be close. She'd been running for hours, ever since that argument with her parents. As the crows flew, the camp was only eighteen miles away, an easy distance for a faun in good weather. And the trail well-known: up the ridge to Bald Knob, north for a ways, then down into Shavers Fork Valley before summiting Barton Knob and descending into Elkwater. Two hours on well-traversed deer trails frequented by their border patrol.

But in the rain? And with a monster snapping at her heels?

Gods, please, please let me be close.

She launched herself at a boulder blocking the path, grabbing onto slick, moss-covered roots dripping down the granite side. The flat hammered points of her fingercaps pinched the roots, her hooves scrabbling against stone as she hauled herself up.

Thunder rolled, a deep, visceral rumble Cricket felt in her gut, and a series of staccato lightning flashes followed, strobing across the sky and casting long, dreadful shadows over the stone. Jagged, bent shadows like fingers, or claws, or ...

Antlers?

She jerked her head around, her grip on the roots failing at the sight of a beast looming at the edge of the hollow. Coarse stone scraped her arms as she fell, landing hard on her ankle. Pain barked up her leg, and she bit her tongue to keep from crying out.

Taller than an elder faun, the beast's shoulders filled the space between the trees. Lightning illuminated a bone-white brow half hidden in the branches crowning its skull, giving the illusion of eight-point antlers.

Cricket bleated, fear pressing her back against the boulder. She couldn't look away. Logic told her to run, to bolt, to use the adrenaline burning in her veins to escape, but she was caught by the same prey instinct that kept her family hiding in the woods. Frozen beneath the direct glare of a predator. Unable to act. Unable to move.

"Please," she whimpered. Granite dug into her back, and her hair whipped in the wind, lashing against her cheeks and brow. Thunder rolled and rumbled, joining the trembling in her limbs, and only when the accompanying lightning sizzled away did she realize it wasn't thunder she heard but a low, warning growl.

She should have listened to her mother. She should have stayed home and tried to reason with her parents when they had all calmed down, but *no* – she had to do what she always did and act rashly, and now she was going to be mauled to death by the same monster that had been terrorizing the people of Green Bank.

So many people had left, so many homes and properties snatched up by some company out of Georgia, and with every sale, the faun were pushed into smaller and smaller areas, forced out of the woods they had made their home over the last fifteen years. Seeing the county assessor tromping through *her* woods was the last straw. With his clipboard and surveyors' maps, his presence and the little strips of neon pink he tied to branches could only mean one thing: the little sliver of the Monongahela her family called their home had been sold, and Cricket had had enough.

Enough packing up her den, enough rolling the reed mats and disassembling the thatch roof. Was it too much to ask to live somewhere and put down roots? To live somewhere long enough that she knew every trail and hollow in the wood with her eyes closed?

She'd begged them to consider living in a house with a foundation and walls, to become part of something instead of staring in through the windows. Instead of being forced out, she wanted them to elbow their way in, and they refused time and time again until Cricket had had *enough*.

Her cousin had left. Ten years ago, they had wandered into the woods and found all the things Cricket wanted for herself: a home, a place where they could live and breathe and grow. A wife. A *life*.

And now she'd have none of that because, like a doe-eyed dumbass, she'd run out into a storm and gotten herself chased by the very monster that had started all of their problems.

"Oh, Gods," she blubbered.

"No Gods," a voice rasped, brought to her ears by a sharp gust of wind. Musk and the faint scent of wintergreen tickled her nose as branches snapped, trees groaning and bending in the storm. "Not in this world."

"Please," Cricket begged again, eyes stinging from the rain and unshed tears. "I don't want to die."

"Then run."

Lightning flashed, half-blinding Cricket and freeing her from the predator's spellbinding gaze. She launched to the side, hissing at the pain in her injured leg as she darted through the trees. A cruel snapping of teeth clashed at her back, the monster giving chase.

This was stupid, this was so stupid. Every faun knew you never ran from a predator once sighted. It only delayed the inevitable. Still, Cricket ducked under branches and leaped over roots, tripping over her own hooves and splashing across flooded streams. She didn't risk looking back, didn't want to see how close the monster may be, or worse, find that it had vanished altogether, returned to stalking her silently and unseen. So she ran through the pain in her leg, scrabbled upright when she fell, and let thin, whip-like branches snap at her back.

Rocks and stones scraped her knees; her denim jacket snagged on twigs and thorns. She shrugged it off, wriggling free from brambles and lurching forward. The metallic tang of blood rose over the aether of the storm, and Cricket mentally cursed the trail she was no doubt leaving behind. She should stop and find a place to hide. Wait out the storm and the monster, but to stop now meant certain death.

The rain halted abruptly, the wind died down, and another roll of thunder rumbled ominously overhead. Silence followed, the woods utterly still and calm. Only her rasping breaths and stunted hoof beats punctuated the night.

The dim glow of electric light sparkled through the trees—a house or a gas station.

Humans. Help.

Cricket risked a glance back, missing the upturned root. Her hoof caught, and she tipped off balance, landing hard on her shoulder and rolling down a hill. The lights whirled and spun, trees twisting as lightning strobed across the sky.

Her head jolted against a fallen trunk, and the last thing Cricket heard before the darkness closed in was a single, mournful howl.

2

AVERY

"THEY'RE JUST KIDS, AVERY." Director Murray leaned back in her chair, the wicker creaking as her weight settled. "Treat them like you would any other band geek battling acne and raging hormones."

"I do!" Avery leaned forward, wringing her hands together in her lap. "I mean—I'm trying to. I've just never been around this many mons-" At Director Murray's raised eyebrow, Avery caught herself. "Inhumans."

"See? You're getting better already."

"But that's the problem, Director Murray," she whined. "I keep slipping and offending them, and then I second-guess myself for the rest of the class. How am I an effective teacher if I can't even speak appropriately to them?"

"Well, first of all, stop thinking of our campers as a 'them.' We're an 'Us' at Elkwater Music Camp." Director Murray spun the gold ring on her finger, frowning slightly. "Second of all, you're an incredible teacher and an even better musician. I wouldn't have offered you the job if you weren't; and *third*, for the love of God, stop calling me Director Murray."

Avery opened her mouth, closed it, then muttered, "I still don't know why you hired *me*."

"Because you were the best-qualified candidate." Director Murray's frown deepened. She sat forward and placed her elbows on the desk between them, hazel eyes pinned on Avery. "Because you applied."

"But—"

"No more *buts*, Avery," she sighed. "You graduated from the composition track at Messiah. You're a poly-instrumentalist who spent the last four summers counseling at a band camp in Virginia, which, come on. You couldn't have applied to work for me earlier?" Avery opened her mouth to argue, but at the director's pointed look, she decided the question was rhetorical. "I should probably be asking why you finally did decide to apply for a job here."

Avery's only response was a quiet squeak.

"You knew we were an integrated camp when you applied, Avery, and that told me you were the right person for the job." Director Murray smiled and eased back, gesturing to the framed pictures decorating the walls. Happy teens grinned in one photograph with their arms slung around wolven and naga. In another, gnomes sat on the shoulders of human boys, tiny fingers poised on piccolos and flutes. A group of musicians—furred, scaled, and fleshy—perched on logs and tree stumps around a fire, mouths frozen open in song. Photograph after photograph of musicians of multiple species marching in a field, collaborating on music, and grinning in the dining hall. So unlike the childhood she had known and entirely the one she had desperately wanted. "Stop being so hard on yourself and focus on what's most important: these kids are here to learn. From you."

Avery smoothed the front of her skirt and scuffed the toe of her white tennis shoe along the worn woven rug, feeling the weight of Director Murray's gaze on her. "I'm just scared that I'll—"

"Ah." The director stood, setting palms on the desk and leaning over the paperwork she had been reviewing when Avery knocked on her door. "There it is." Her eyes narrowed, darting over Avery in quick assessment. "That's your father talking, Payne. Not you."

"I—"

"There's nothing to be afraid of in this camp. Everyone here earned their spot through talent and hard work. It's what we all have in common. Think about that, yeah? These kids earned a place, just like you earned your job as my Assistant Director."

Avery dropped her eyes to her lap, staring at the grass stains on the knees of her skirt and biting her lips to keep from blurting the truth: that she'd only applied for the job after an argument with her dad. That she was piggybacking on Director Murray's reputation for churning out top-tier musicians and using this job to get a spot in Carnegie Mellon's graduate program. That she was using this camp and the director's goodwill to further her own aims, and was using this summer to live the life she never got to. That she couldn't sleep at night because of the guilt and fumbled chords during the day because she was drowning under the pressure. That the storm last night had seemed to mimic her own inner turmoil until she thought she was going to burst. That she—

"I know you grew up in an area that was ... affluent," Director Murray continued. "I did, too; I know how close-minded it can get, but you're here, regardless of your reasons for applying. That matters."

Avery swiped the back of her hand under her nose, blinking tears away before raising her head. Director Murray had resumed her seat, fingers laced on the desk. Though her face was calm, her mouth closed but soft, there was a tension in her arms and shoulders. From her years spent as a camper, a counselor, assistant director, and finally director, Director Murray was tanned and lean, toned in the way of an Appalachian thru-hiker. She kept her shaggy pixie cut swept back from her face, the ends of the short style bronzed from the sun. Small lines clung to the corners of her eyes and mouth, earned from summers on the field and evenings spent laughing and smiling.

Avery wondered what it was like to be so carefree when surrounded by so many mons—*no. Inhumans.*

Back home, in Harrisburg, it wasn't exactly rare to see them, but just as Director Murray said, she had grown up in an affluent area, surrounded by people who looked, spoke, and existed like her: human, white, and Christian.

Elkwater Music Camp was the furthest from home Avery had ever been, not in terms of distance but in lifestyle and culture. Messiah wasn't an integrated campus, and whenever she traveled to Philly or New York with her family, they were ushered from their car to the hotel, paraded about like a Christian Right Von Trapp Family, and ushered out of sight. The most diversity Avery had ever experienced was from playing softball as a teenager. Even then, the team was entirely human, as were those of the other private schools they played against.

Sure, she had *seen* inhumans. She wasn't a flower in the attic or anything weird like that. It was just that people like her didn't associate with inhumans like them ... until now.

"I want to be here," she said. "I want this job, I want to teach these kids, but I—"

"There's those buts again," Director Murray smiled. "The campers have only been here for two weeks, and you did great during onboarding with the counselors and staff. Take it each day at a time, pick a different kid in each class, and give them some special attention. Learn how the unique qualities they each bring can help them excel in music, and you'll have done your job."

Avery exhaled, blowing a stream of air at a curling wisp of her hair. "Okay."

"And maybe sit with the other counselors at dinner?" Director Murray added. Avery straightened, a tendon in her neck pinching. "It hasn't gone unnoticed …"

"They don't want to sit with me."

"Says who?"

"I—no one." She dropped back in her chair, arms crossed. "But—"

"No more buts, Avery, Jesus." Avery flinched, and Director Murray dropped her head back, groaning. "Ugh, sorry. Look." she rose and stepped around the desk, cuffing Avery on the shoulder with a loose fist. "I know this is a lot, and I respect how you addressed this in your interview, but don't give up after two weeks. A lot of these kids and counselors have grown up in this camp. I marched at OSU with Nurse Almaden, and your roommate has been a counselor here for as long as I can remember. We've got you at a disadvantage, but it's not one you can't overcome. You're *here*, and you're coming to me when you need to talk it through. Keep doing that, and next summer this'll be as common as a chord progression in C."

Avery huffed. "You're saying that like you know I'm coming back next year."

"You haven't run screaming for the hills yet." Director Murray smiled. "That's a good sign."

"There's still twelve weeks to go," Avery replied as she stood, adjusting her skirt. "Plenty of time."

"There's that can-do attitude I hired you for." She sighed and straightened the papers on her desk. "I could use a little of that, I think."

"Still no takers?"

Director Murray shook her head, lower lip thrust in a pout. "Not yet. My mom is gonna talk to a few of her associates in DC. Hopefully, someone will be interested in investing, but it feels like cheating."

"How so?"

A bell rang before she could answer, the electric tone buzzing through the open window and calling the camp to breakfast. Director Murray checked her watch and tipped her head at the door, gesturing for Avery to walk with her.

"I can't even get investors to call me back, much less answer the phone. Growing Elkwater to welcome more students feels like something I should be able to do without relying on my parents' connections," she said.

"It'll happen."

Director Murray snorted quietly and bounced her shoulder against Avery's. "Where's that confidence when it applies to your job performance?" Avery opened her mouth to argue, holding her tongue when Director Murray sighed and shoved her hands in her pockets. "Let's talk about this later; if you don't mind channeling some of that Payne knowledge, I'd like to pick your brain on how I can better approach sponsors."

"Sure thing." She sent her boss a weak smile.

Director Murray jogged up the stairs to the dining hall, pausing at the door when she realized Avery had not joined her. "Not hungry?" she asked, offering an easy out.

"I had cereal in my bunk," she lied.

"Right." Director Murray nodded and hit her with a direct stare. "I'll see you at dinner, then."

"See you at dinner."

Not a request, but then again, Avery couldn't really blame her. She was the Assistant Director. It was her job to be present and available for the campers and counselors, and she couldn't do that by hiding in her bunk and eating alone.

"At the counselor's table," she added. Avery bit her lips and nodded, sagging with relief when Director Murray slipped inside the dining hall.

Embarrassed and not yet ready to be immersed in the bustle of a band camp in full swing, she took a narrow trail around the side of the dining hall, cutting onto a well-used path through the woods. Twigs, leaves, and fallen branches from the previous night's storm cluttered the trail. Her conversation with Director Murray rambled over and over in her head as she kicked the mess aside, clearing the path for others. It helped to hear she was coming into this at a disadvantage, and yet, it didn't. Avery was raised to do the good thing, to love thy neighbor, and all that, but nowhere in the doctrine of her congregation had they allowed space for those who *weren't* her fellow man.

But being a good neighbor was about loving those around you, regardless of creed or color.

Right?

"Right. Of course, that's right," she muttered, hitching her skirt to swing a leg over a recently fallen tree trunk. The storm the night before had been wild, blowing in from the west without any warning. It was a wonder they hadn't lost power in the camp, so Avery was hardly surprised to find a tree blocking the path. The sweet scent of rotting wood tickled her nose and she rubbed it with her palm, peering at the dark hollow of splintered oak and churned earth at the base of the trunk. "Why else would they be here if we weren't supposed to share this earth with them?"

She straddled the tree, enjoying the quiet of the wood and the peace that thought brought. She could do this—get over the biases of her upbringing and be *better* before starting a graduate program at a fully integrated university.

Avery slid off the trunk and started down the trail feeling lighter. It all seemed so *easy* now that she'd argued her way out of a legalistic trap. Every living thing was on the earth for a reason that she, a single human, wasn't in a place to question. All she had to do was accept it and be kind. Easy.

She ducked under a low branch, and a thorny bush snagged her skirt. Grumbling, she stooped and tugged at the fabric, yanking it free with a tearing sound that didn't bode well for the fabric.

"Great. Just great." She inspected the inch-long tear, tossing the fabric aside as she rose, took two steps, and stopped at the sight of a skinny, haggard form leaning against a tree less than six feet away.

"Hel—" the figure wheezed, raising a filthy, shaking arm. Sunlight glinted off of the tips of three trembling fingers. "Help me."

"Ohmygosh." Avery rushed over, stopping short when the figure lurched away from the tree and practically threw itself at her.

"It's in the woods," they gasped, gripping Avery's shoulders. Sharp points pinched her skin and raised goosebumps. They drew close, blinking at her with wide and wild, coppery eyes. Mud caked their arms, masking their face and matting the curls clinging to their head. "It followed me, I ran, I—"

"Are you okay?" Avery circled her fingers around their thin wrists—they were covered in a soft, delicate down, she noticed—and gently pulled them away.

"It followed me; it's out there. I ran as fast as I could."

"Hey, it's alright." Avery raised her voice, using the "counselor tone" that worked so well on her campers. "Calm down, okay?" The creature's pupils tightened to thin, horizontal ovals. Every muscle went taut, and they held themselves so still Avery wondered if they were breathing at all.

They weren't a camper; she knew that much. As Assistant Director, it was part of her job to know every kid in their bunks, if not by name, then by sight, and this figure with their mud-caked clothes and soft downy fur, was neither a camper, counselor, or staff member of Elkwater Music Camp. "Where are you from?"

Those narrow pupils pulsed, and they twitched to meet Avery's gaze. "Monongahela."

And with a tight exhale, they collapsed.

Avery stood there, biting her lower lip and weighing her options. Nurse Almaden would be on the field this time of day, ensuring none of the wolven collapsed from heat stroke. Her roommate would be goodness knew where, and even if Avery could find her, what would Sanoya do? This wasn't a camper; they didn't *belong* here, which meant there was only one person to go to for help.

Avery turned and ran, scrambling over the tree trunk and hitching her skirt to lengthen her stride. In half the time it took to reach that part of the wood, she was back with Director Murray in tow.

"They said they ran here," she panted, hitching forward and gripping her knee with one hand, pointing to the figure lying crumpled in the dirt with the other.

Director Murray skidded to a halt, the flush in her cheeks from their run fading as she stared down at the creature in shock. "She ran here?"

"How do you know it's a she?" The figure was a mess, all torn clothes, mud, and twigs. If she'd learned one thing over the last month of being thrown feet-first into integration, it was that one never assumed gender. That was an easy way to earn the hatred of a skunk ape, and she was still apologizing for making that mistake by calling the camp cook, a rat-like inhuman with four arms and too many tails to count, "ma'am."

Director Murray glanced at Avery and then crouched beside the figure, brushing matted curls away from its face. Her shocked expression eased to worry. "I just do."

"Do you know...her?"

Director Murray tensed, working her jaw before speaking again. "Go back to camp."

"What?"

"Go back to camp, grab Nurse Almaden, and send her to my cabin."

"Do you want me to help—"

"*Go*, Avery," Director Murray snapped, angrier than Avery had ever heard her. "Go and get the nurse; I'll handle this." She gathered the figure in her arms, struggling to her feet and turning to head back to camp. The creature hung limp, her head lolling and feet dangling.

No. Not feet.

Avery startled back, pressing against a tree as she tried to make sense of what she was seeing. The torn hem of filthy yoga pants gave way to delicate, lean calves covered in more mud, and where she would have expected shoes or toes, the creature's ankle tapered into a cloven hoof.

"Avery," Director Murray's voice was calm and even. It was the voice she used whenever a counselor called her to a particularly rambunctious bunk after lights out. "Go get the nurse."

3

—·—

CRICKET

A CURLING WISP OF steam rose from the teacup, tickling Cricket's nose with dandelion and lemon—her cousin's favorite blend. She hunkered down in her blanket, gritting flat teeth as her cousin's wife tugged on a bandage, wrapping it tightly around her hoof.

"Ow," she said. It didn't hurt, but aside from the intermittent chirps from a walkie-talkie on the table, the kitchen was too damned quiet. Her cousin's wife had barely spoken a word to her, at least not directly. She'd had a full-on conversation with a tall, bird-like woman who introduced herself as Nurse Almaden and helped Cricket into a bathtub, gently scrubbing her clean before prodding her ankle and hoof. For the nurse, her cousin's wife had loads to say, most of it concerning care for Cricket's hoof and not to tell anyone she was here.

But for Cricket herself? Only terse commands like, "get dressed," and "drink this," and "stop moving."

So she said, "Ow," trying to get something other than cold anger out of Mac.

"Sorry." Mac tugged on the bandage and pressed the edge down with her thumb. "She said to wrap it tightly."

"Any tighter, and you'll cut off blood flow," Cricket grumbled.

Mac glanced at her, and her features relaxed. She gently lowered Cricket's hoof to a footstool. "Sorry, Crick. I just—you scared the hell out of me. What are you doing here?"

"I'm looking for my cousin," she said, raising the teacup and inhaling the herbal scent. A hint of peach teased beneath the lemon and dandelion, adding a subtle sweetness. She took a sip, letting her eyes drift closed as warmth rushed down her throat. Oak and ivy, she was tired. "Tried to get here last night, but that storm blew in, and I had to take the ridgelines to—"

"What was so important that you ran the ridgelines in a storm?" Mac shot up straight in her chair.

"I need to talk to my cousin." Cricket set the teacup down a little harder than necessary, sloshing hot liquid onto the table. "Someone keeps buying up the land in Green Bank and forcing us out of our dens, but no one will listen to me when I suggest moving. They're happy to get shoved into less and less space until we're forced out altogether, and yesterday, I saw the assessor out there marking trees."

"Trees."

"Yes, *trees*. They only do that when the land has been sold, which means we have to move a*gain*, but there's nowhere else to go. And the noise!" She rose to her feet, wincing as the weight came down on her injured hoof—a small sprain in her ankle, the bird nurse had said, and smaller injuries along with a crack in the hoof wall. Gripping the chair back, she glared at Mac. "They start up before dawn and work into the night. We can't even leave to forage or patrol the border without risking getting run down by their trucks, and they're not even *from here*. They're all outsiders thinking they can move to our mountains and–"

"Cricket."

She sighed, glaring at the table. "I thought if I brought my cousin back, maybe they could talk to the family. You know how they are; they don't listen to anything I say. My parents still think I'm the little doe that fell through with them fifteen years ago. I thought, with my cousin, we could prove it's safe outside of Green Bank and, I don't know, get everyone to move away."

"Ramble's not here," Mac said, naming Cricket's cousin as her attention drifted to the window. "They went down to Elkins yesterday morning for supplies. No idea when they'll be able to get back; the roads are closed from that storm."

"They go into town?" Her ears pricked forward in surprise.

"Of course, they go into town; we've lived here for a decade."

"How long did it take for people to ... to ..."

"Get used to them?" Mac finished. A soft smile overtook her face, and she patted the table, urging Cricket to sit back down. "A summer."

She eased herself into the chair, blinking her eyes at an unfamiliar burn. "And no one tries to hurt them?"

"Why would they?" Mac asked.

"Because we're different," she mumbled. And they were. Others had dropped through to this earth at the same time as Cricket's family: wolven and naga, thunderbirds and gnomes. A hundred different creatures, all of them integrating with the humans and finding a place for themselves while, for whatever reason, the faun had kept to the woods, cloistering around Green Bank and befriending the locals—people who had clung to the Monongahela Hills since settling there centuries prior, or the kinds of people who sought the peace of the radio-free zone and an escape from the noise of modern living.

Mac chuckled and shook her head. "You came here asking for help to prove it's safe. How can we help if *you* don't even think it's safe?"

"It's not my fault I've been stuck in Green Bank!" she protested. "And you've met the family; they won't move."

"Always wondered why," Mac said. "Every time we asked, Ramble's dad said they weren't old enough to know."

"My father says the same thing." Cricket released the chairback and knocked it with a fist. "But I can't just wander off and leave them there. The assessor is already out marking the trees, which means it's only a matter of weeks, maybe days, before they start clearing the woods. I need everyone to be somewhere *safe*, and Ramble's letters talk about how safe it is here." She waved her arm toward the gingham-curtained window and the camp beyond. "I just need them to come back and talk to our parents. "

Mac stood and crossed the kitchen, grabbing a towel to clean the spilled tea. "Well, I'm glad my wife thinks our home is safe."

Cricket pointed at her. "That's sarcasm. I know what sarcasm is."

"Clearly," Mac replied. She tossed the towel on the counter and leaned against the edge, arms crossed. "It's not just Elkwater, you know. A lot has changed since your family got here. Maybe it *is* time you wandered out of the Monongahela."

"Now?" Cricket straightened, her ears pressing tight against her head. "I *just* said I can't leave—"

"No, not now, dingbat." Mac rolled her eyes and waved a hand at Cricket's hoof. "You're not fit to go anywhere. Ramble would kill me if I let you wander off on an injured hoof, and I can't drive you until they get back with my truck." She pressed her lips in a line, gaze dropping to the bandage wrapped around Cricket's ankle. "How did you do that, by the way? Aside from being dumb enough to run the ridgelines in a storm."

"Oh." She stretched her leg out, gripping her calf with her fingers, absent the metal caps. Half of them had fallen off in her tumble down the hill, and the rest sat in a pile on the kitchen table. Her felt-covered fingertips pressed back slightly, the flexible extra knuckle all faun had giving way under the pressure. "Something chased me."

"*What?*" Mac hollered. "Why didn't you start with that?"

"Because it's the Monongahela, there's loads of monsters out here," Cricket argued. "I told that camper, the one who found me." She racked her brain for any details she could remember, but her head had been foggy, pain and exhaustion overriding any sense. What she did remember was crystal clear: sky-blue eyes ringed in dark eyelashes and a reddish-orange halo of bright auburn friz escaping from a long, thick plait. "The fox-haired one, didn't she tell you?"

Mac pinched between her eyes, lips moving silently in what Cricket realized were numbers. She was counting numbers to calm herself down before talking again. Like Cricket was some hours-old doe staggering in a field.

"It's not a big deal."

"Yes, it's a big deal, Cricket." Mac tore her hand away, glaring at her. "I run a camp with *children* in it. I have a responsibility to keep everyone here safe, and you're telling me something chased you all the way from Green Bank?"

"Not all the way," she protested. "I think I lost it when I fell and twisted my ankle."

"Did you get a good look at it?" Mac asked. "Some of the staff are from the hills; maybe they'll know what it was."

Cricket shook her head. "Not a good one, no. It was real dark; I only caught glimpses in the lightning."

"And?"

"Big." She shivered involuntarily, recalling how tall the thing had been—tall and broad and *fast*. "Like Kane big."

"I have no idea what that means."

"Kane? WWE Wrestler? The guy is huge." At Mac's blank look, Cricket laughed. "And you're telling *me* I need to get out more?"

"If your sole knowledge of modern pop culture is the WWE, then yes, I am."

"And the Spice Girls."

"*Christ*, Cricket." She shook her head, but a tiny smile curled the corner of her mouth. Static crackled from the walkie-talkie, and a gravelly voice came over the speaker.

"Hey, Murray, you're needed on the field."

Mac groaned, grabbed the walkie-talkie, and pressed the button on the side. "Be right there, Aksel. Do I need the Gator?"

"Uh…" Aksel responded. Discordant blurts followed, drowning out a second voice bellowing angrily. "Yeah, probably. One of the naga got tangled in a Sousaphone."

Mac pressed the walkie-talkie to her forehead, once again counting silently before responding. "On my way." She clipped the walkie-talkie to her belt and pointed at Cricket. "Get some sleep. There's food here, but if you get bored and want something other than granola and peach rings"—Cricket's ears perked at that—"the dining hall is the long green building at the center of camp, and Almaden left you a crutch." She gestured vaguely in the direction of the front door where a crutch was propped and, Cricket assumed, the camp beyond. "Dinner bell's at six; Cooky preps for all diets, so you won't have a problem finding something you can eat."

She grabbed a set of keys from a hook and pulled a baseball cap on over her short, shaggy hair, hesitating at the door. Rapping knuckles against the frame, she twisted at the waist to address Cricket. "You can stay here as long as you like. You know that, right? We'd love to have you."

Cricket could only nod, caught off guard by the offer. The welcome. Not that it was unexpected from Mac. The woman had always been so easy-going around Cricket's family, and she'd seen first-hand how Mac doted on her wife. The two were still crazy about each other a decade into their relationship. It gave Cricket a thrill of hope that maybe, *maybe*, if she brought her cousin home to talk to their parents and the rest of the family, they could convince the faun to leave Green Bank before they were pushed out altogether.

"I'll, um, consider it," she mumbled, offering Mac a weak smile as she stepped onto the porch, pulling the door shut behind her.

Sleep came easy once Cricket had assembled a pile of blankets and pillows and beat them into something resembling a nest. In no time at all, she was startled awake by a loud, electronic blaring through the camp. She shot upright, bleating as pain ribboned up her injured leg, and collapsed against the side of the guestroom bed. Scrabbling nail-less fingers against the mattress, she hoisted herself onto the bed, gawking out the window as human and inhuman alike tore down the center path of the camp.

They manifested from the woods and filed out of cabins and buildings. A lumbering, bipedal figure in gym shorts sauntered across the green, chatting with the gnome on his shoulder while a young woman jogged up beside them. Three human boys spilled out of a tan building, the last one holding the door open for a dusky-furred creature with gossamer wings tucked in close. A pair of shifted wolven leaped over one another, yipping at each other's heels and barreling into a naga and another human. The boy wrapped his arms around his serpentine companion, sweeping her out of harm's way as the wolven yowled their apologies and darted into a long single-story green building halfway down the center path.

She watched in awe as the display of full and healthy integration played out before her. No one was staring. No one was pointing or threatening the inhumans. They were ... together, coexisting in a way her parents told her the faun never could. Seeing it play out before her, Cricket had to believe there was a place for her family. If this is what Mac had achieved and what her cousin so staunchly defended, why couldn't Cricket have it, too? Why couldn't she live with humans and others like her? Why not move from Green Bank and—

A figure caught her eye, walking paces behind the crowd. A long plait of fox-red hair hung down her back, swinging lightly with the sway of generous hips in a floral skirt. Arms tightly folded and shoulders hunched, she waited at the base of a short flight of stairs as the last of the campers entered the green building—the dining hall.

Once alone, the camper dropped her arms and rolled her shoulders in a gesture Cricket recognized—she was preparing herself to deal with something, but what? What could anyone have to be nervous about in a paradise like Elkwater Music Camp?

4

—·—

AVERY

"Brush your index finger against the D string like this."
Avery angled the neck of her guitar, showing the class the placement of her fingers. "Otherwise, you'll muddy the scale with ringing from the rest of your strings."

"I thought you said we had to maintain finger posture," a young man with coal-black eyes whined.

"I did, Tom, yes." She acknowledged his question with a nod. "But once you've mastered finger posture, you can let it slip, as long as it's intentional." Putting her money where her mouth was, Avery straightened her seat on the tree stump and played a rapid pentatonic scale, demonstrating first with the muting technique, then a second time without. Tom's eyes widened, intent on Avery's fingers as she repeated the scale, again with the technique. After a third pass, she gestured for him and the rest of the class to try.

Notes thrummed out, some in perfect pitch, others a little flat. "You need to build strength in your pinkies," Avery advised. "Reverse the scale and pay attention to your fretting."

A series of discordant notes followed. Avery paced the circle, stopping by each student to correct their finger posture and placement and, in the case of the stubby-fingered howler, correct his grip altogether.

Guitar lessons were a new offering at Elkwater Music Camp, an idea floated by Director Murray after Avery missed the deadline to accept. The next day, Director Murray called her house and offered the idea of a guitar track to be taught by the Assistant Director.

It felt like bribery, especially when her father scoffed and told her they were "sweetening the pot," but Avery hadn't even waited a day to accept and begin drafting a lesson plan. Being wanted so *badly* for something had been too tempting to pass up. So she had accepted and, upon arriving in Elkwater, sought out the perfect place for her guitar lessons: a circle of stumps and sanded logs in an idyllic glade down a fairy-tale path leading away from the camp.

The students were clumsy, many of them learning the pentatonic scale on guitar for the first time, but they were bright and quick to grasp the concepts of composition and the theory behind the instrument. She kept her focus there: on the commonality of passion for music and the desire to create glorious sound together. They were a chorus of people weaving a song regardless of creed, color, or species.

"Ugh." Tom played a sour chord and all but throttled the neck of his guitar. "This is dumb."

"It's not dumb." Avery moved beside him. The boy was the youngest in her class by a few years but had become her most eager student in the last two weeks. "It's a new technique, is all, and you've been playing guitar for how long?" He mumbled something, his head hung low, and Avery nudged him with her elbow. "What was that?"

"I said two weeks." He raised his head, black eyes glinting with a sheen of frustrated tears. "But it's not fair. How are any of us supposed to get anywhere when people like *her* exist?" He pointed across the small circle to a young woman with long, silken black hair parted down the middle. A series of tattoos, deep black against stone-gray skin, bisected her face from forehead to chin, and she played with her eyes closed, swaying in time as she played the scale to perfection in both forward and reverse. Avery's lips parted in surprise, and she scrambled for a way to bring Tom's focus back in line with the lesson when he continued. "What's even the point? I'll never be as good as a Spearfinger."

At his accusation, the young woman opened her eyes and grinned fiercely at Tom, agile fingers continuing their dance over the strings, save for the wickedly sharp blade where her right index finger would be. It took Avery a second to recognize what the young woman, Kola, was doing—she was using her spearfinger to mute the strings, altering the placement to achieve a pitch-perfect pentatonic scale without the previously played strings ringing out.

The other students took note, their excitement and determination fading as Kola continued to play. Where before they had been smiling and focused, now they grumbled and set their guitars down—the magic broken by an inhuman.

"Kola, cut it out," Avery barked. The scales faded away, along with the young woman's triumphant smile.

"I'm sorry," Kola said, glancing around the glade. Pink crawled into her cheeks, and she dropped her gaze. "I was just playing with the placement and I realized—"

"That wasn't the exercise. If you're going to learn to play guitar, you're going to learn to play it *correctly* before you start to improvise."

"Correct for who?" Another camper, a naga, asked. They raised their head, stretching their fingers wide. "Because I can tell you right now, my fingers are too long for half the placement you want us to practice."

"Mine too," Jared, a swamp ape, added. "And the guitar neck is so thin, I feel like I could crush it if I'm not paying attention."

"Must be nice," Eddie, the Howler, whined. "My fingers are too short for a power chord."

"So we'll get you a ukulele," Avery snapped before she could think better of it. A quiet fell over the glade, the eyes of every student trained on her. "I mean, no. Not a ukulele, but we can—" Eddie set his guitar down and nudged it away with a claw-tipped, furred foot. "I didn't mean—" She'd lost them. One look was enough to see that. Even the human students were eyeing her with distrust and leaning closer to their camp mates. "I-I can see we're frustrated; why don't we call it for the day? You all can practice on your own time, and we'll pick the lesson back up in two days. Alright?"

The campers muttered their agreement, gathering instruments and leaving the glade in pairs. Eddie took off down the short trail to the camp before Avery could grab him to apologize, and she stood alone, fists clenched and shoulders hitched. Pinching her eyes closed, she willed herself not to cry, knowing she was utterly and irrevocably in the wrong.

He hadn't deserved her anger; none of them had, but what was she supposed to *do* when they raised such solid points? How were any of them to compete when inhumans clearly had the advantage? It wasn't *fair*.

"No," she forced through her teeth. "No. That's dad, not you." And *wow,* was it her dad. She'd heard him go off on tirade after tirade against inhumans at the dinner table, in the club, and on the golf course. She had overheard him speaking with his colleagues over cocktails in their front room while Avery helped her brothers and sisters with their homework in the kitchen. She had heard, and she had answered her siblings' questions, emphasizing that they ought to love thy neighbor as they love themselves, to love their enemies. To be gracious and kind. Teaching them all the ways they could be anyone but Nathan Payne. "That's not Avery Payne."

"They didn't deserve that." A warm, raspy voice broke through Avery's thoughts, flying her eyes wide open. Beyond the circle of stumps and tree trunks, on the trail leading away from camp, stood an inhuman.

Their posture was odd, hunched to the side, but it did nothing to draw attention away from their figure. Willowy and lean, they wore an Elkwater Band Camp t-shirt that had been modified into a muscle tank, leggings cut off at the knees, and a flannel tied around their very narrow waist. Wild blonde curls framed their face, drawing attention to the high cheekbones and delicate chin dusted in sandy tan fur, and bright, wide-set coppery eyes were trained on Avery.

She swallowed, embarrassed at having been caught in her poor behavior. Heat flooded her cheeks, and when the figure hobbled forward, revealing a bandage-wrapped ankle and crutch, that heat rose to an outright burn as she realized who they were.

The mud-caked inhuman from the woods.

"Are you spying on me?" she blurted, too horrified to mind her words.

"No."

"Good." She spun away, hands shaking as she gathered her guitar and fumbled with the latch on her case. "I don't need your judgment."

"From what I just saw, I'd say you do."

Avery sent a glare over her shoulder. "So you were spying on me."

"Just seemed like for someone who doesn't want any judgment, you were awfully quick to do so."

"No, I—" She slammed the case closed and jumped to her feet, wanting—no, *needing*—to explain what had happened, that she didn't mean to snap at Kola or imply Eddie couldn't play the guitar. That she was *trying* even if she was failing, but it had to count for something. "I didn't mean—"

"Nevermind." The inhuman sighed and shook their—*her*. Director Murray had said she was a her—head. "I'll just continue my hobble through the woods, where you decided to set up your lesson where anybody could come limping by." She gestured at the trail with her crutch and hopped around, heading back the way she had come.

Avery watched her go, eyes drawn to the flex of muscle in her arm as she gripped the crutch, dropping to her long, lean legs and the bandage-wrapped ankle. Muted music from the field wove through the trees, brassy blurts and the call of a bugle, the driving tempo of snare drums, and still Avery didn't look away. She chewed her lower lip, guitar case in one hand, as she replayed their brief conversation.

It was like being a living broken record, repeating the same groove in the vinyl over and over again. Unable to break free of the cycle until something, or someone, jostled the turntable, giving the nudge necessary to move forward.

And maybe ...

A cymbal crashed and Avery took off at a jog, legs catching in her skirt. "Hey, wait up!" The inhuman kept hobbling along, neither faltering nor glancing back. Avery fumed and matched her slow-going pace, switching the guitar case to the other hand and reaching for her elbow. "Let me help you."

"Don't touch me." She jerked her arm away, swaying off balance.

"You're hurt," Avery pointed out.

"I don't need your pity," the inhuman retorted.

"It's not pity; I just want to help you." She reached again, determined to help, to show she was good and kind—not a bigoted specist but someone who was trying to do the work to be better.

The inhuman leaned away, setting her injured hoof on the ground. She bleated in pain, waving an arm as she teetered backward. Avery acted without thinking, dropping her guitar case and snagging the only part of the inhuman she could reach. Her fist closed around the knotted sleeves of the flannel at her waist, and she tugged with all her strength. A bony, lean body far heavier than it looked collided with her, knocking Avery off-balance, and they went down in a heap. Her back hit the ground, and the air was forced from her lungs with a pained "oof."

Spots danced in her eyes as the backlit treetops slowly came back into focus, and she gasped, struggling to fill her lungs. A heavy weight shifted, metal clanged against a tree stump, and a curly head rose, wide-set copper eyes glaring at Avery.

This close, she could make out the amber and gold shards in her pupils and each individual little bump on the dark tip of her nose. Avery had read somewhere that each dog's nose was particular to the dog, the pattern as unique as a fingerprint, and her oxygen-deprived brain wondered if it were the same for whatever this inhuman was.

And then she acknowledged it was a very cute nose. Or was it a snout? Was it even polite to ask?

A thin upper lip curled back, splitting slightly in the middle and revealing blunt, white teeth. Avery's eyes dropped to the inhuman's plump lower lip as she snarled, "What in the hells was that about?"

"I was ... trying to ..." Avery wheezed, flicking her gaze away from the inhuman's mouth only to be caught by that angry glare. Reality rushed in, and suddenly, she was all too aware of how their legs tangled together. Hyper-aware of soft downy fur and an ACE bandage rubbing against her shins. Of the scent of meadowgrass and peach, and the comfortable weight of the inhuman who had fallen on top of her. Her body heated from the roots of her hair to the tips of her toes. "I just wanted too …"

"Help me, I got it." She grunted and wriggled onto her knees, groping for the crutch and using it to hoist herself from the ground. "Please, don't."

"But I—" She scrambled to her feet, unsure how to finish that sentence. The inhuman had said no, and she wasn't helping anything or anyone by pressing the point.

She cocked her head, gaze flicking over Avery before stabbing her crutch into the ground and swinging around. "If that's what passes for your help, trust me, I don't want it." And with that, she hobbled away, still somehow graceful in the swing of her free arm and sure step of her uninjured leg.

As if sensing Avery's lingering stare, she hesitated at the intersection of two trails and angled at the waist to meet Avery's gaze. It was a beat. A moment. A rest in the score, stretching on, awaiting the conductor's signal for the song to continue. Avery's cheeks burned, her lips parted and dry, and with the crash of a cymbal from the field, she glanced down. When she'd recovered herself, she flicked her gaze up and found the trail ahead empty and quiet, as if the inhuman had never been there at all.

5

— · —

CRICKET

Fox fur.

That was the only thing Cricket could focus on, and it was driving her insane.

Fox fur and a pale blue morning sky.

She'd been hobbling around the woods for an hour, trying to clear her head and figure out which trail would take her back to the camp. She should be focusing on disturbances in the brush, listening for the blare of a horn or the laughter of human and inhuman voices, but all she could think about was fox fur, a pale blue sky captured in wide eyes, and soft curves.

"Gods dammit." She smacked her crutch against a tree, dropping her head back with a groan. Not like the camper … counselor? She was teaching those kids, albeit poorly, so she had to be one of the counselors. She certainly didn't *look* like a teenager, and Gods knew she didn't feel like one.

"Not helpful, brain," Cricket muttered.

Still, it wasn't like she was helping matters any, standing there staring after Cricket with a look of … longing. That's the only way Cricket could translate that expression—soft lips parted, eyes wistful, her shoulders dropped in defeat. She'd expected anger, maybe even disgust, when she'd looked back, and the stricken, wanting expression she'd gotten instead had scrambled something in Cricket's head. All she could think about was red hair, blue eyes, and how easy it would have been to sink into the girl's body and just … stay there.

"Think about other things," she told herself. "Like this trail. This trail could *clearly* use some work. Why did they even put it here?" She gestured to a matted, you'd-miss-it-if-you-weren't-looking-for-it path jutting into the woods as if someone else were present to hear her diatribe. "That deer trail offers way more cover. It's like these humans don't even know how to *find* trails, much less know how stupid it is to hold a class in the *middle* of one. At least it's not raining, that would suck. Then I'd be hobbling in the mud on a trail without cover, which is just dumb."

A twig snapped. Cricket froze, ears jolting upright. She scanned the trees for any movement or shadow out of place. Dust motes and tiny gnats hovered in sunbeams. A slight breeze rustled the leaves, and a quiet shuffle told her a rabbit was nearby, but otherwise, all was as it should be. She relaxed, easing into her hobble and keeping her thoughts to herself.

The roads had to re-open soon. Once they did, her cousin would be back, and they could head to Green Bank and begin Cricket's petition for the family to relocate before they were forced out. She'd already lost a day to her stupid ankle; how much longer before the sale was finalized and the trees were cut down?

A flicker of shadow had her stopping again, staring intently into the wood. Her ears twitched, swiveling to catch any sound. Nothing. Not a whisper of wind or the shuffle of critters in the undergrowth. Even the marching band on the field had gone quiet, leaving the woods still and calm.

Too calm.

Cricket hitched her shoulders, the down on her neck prickling at the sudden feel of eyes on her back.

"Oak and ivy, you're being ridiculous," she whispered to herself. "It's probably that human girl. Woman. Whatever."

A twig snapped as if in reply, a shadow twitched, and every prey instinct took over. She bolted, discarding her crutch in favor of running full out. At the first step, white-hot pain shot up her leg. Stars burst in her eyes, but the panic was all-consuming. Branches groaned, and leaves rustled furiously at her back. There was something in the wood. Something that had her scent, and Cricket had no idea where to go. Was the camp to the left? Did she take a turn on the trail?

Oh, Gods.

She couldn't remember which way she'd come; she didn't know these woods like she knew the woods around Green Bank. She was lost and being chased, and she couldn't even *run*.

Every step was a nightmare, her speed hindered by the sprained ankle and split hoof. Still, she darted through the trees, leaping over tiny runnels in the forest floor and skidding under branches, gritting her teeth against the pain as tears streamed from her eyes. She stumbled over a loose stone, grasping for anything to keep her upright.

Thorns bit into her palm, and Cricket could have wept for relief. Thorns *sucked,* but their bushes were thick, sturdy, and predators hated getting caught in them. Dropping low, she scuttled into the thicket, biting her lower lip to keep from crying out as sharp pinpricks tore her borrowed shirt and drew blood.

Heart pounding in her ears and ankle, Cricket curled into a tight ball, blinking away tears to keep an eye on the wood. The rustling rose, and a stream of rabbits and rodents darted past the hiding place seconds before a massive, furred paw slammed into the ground. Heat and musk filled the air. Musk and a fresh wintergreen scent at odds with what she was seeing. Unable to scooch forward, she squinted through the thick branches, catching glimpses of a broad, muscular back covered in dark fur—humanoid in build, an inhuman for sure.

It let out a low, rumbling growl that Cricket felt in her bones. Claws dug into the dirt as the creature's paw twisted, scoring the ground.

A wolven?

She craned her neck, trying to see more clearly through the thick, thorny patch. It was too tall, too broad to be any wolven she'd ever seen. A bear shifter, maybe? Did they fall through with the rest of the creatures from her home world?

She had no way of knowing. How would she, when she'd been secluded in Green Bank her entire life on this insane earth?

The distant blare of an electronic bell drew the creature's attention. It spun around, the movement revealing the pale orb of the moon hovering in the morning sky, and sent a rush of musk and wintergreen into Cricket's face. She slammed a hand over her nose and mouth, eyes burning and nose tickling. A sneeze built, her nose twitching furiously under her filthy palm, and right when she knew she wouldn't be able to hold it back any longer—

The creature darted into the wood, back the way it had come.

Cricket sneezed in shock, blinking rapidly and ready to scurry deeper into the thorns when a new sound caught her attention.

"Hello?"

Her ears shot forward, catching in thorns, and she whimpered, smoothing them back before pressing a hand into the dirt and leaning forward.

"You dropped your crutch!"

Gods dammit.

It was the human girl. Woman. Whatever. What in the hells was she doing here? The creature couldn't have gotten far, and Gods knew the idiot counselor was easy prey.

"Hello?"

"Get out of here," Cricket yelled in a whisper.

"Is that you?" Two tennis shoes stepped into view, scuffed with dirt and grass stains that matched the hem of her skirt. "Are you ... are you in the bush?"

"Seriously, you need to leave."

"What are you doing in there?" She crouched low, blue eyes searching the thorns and shadows for Cricket.

"I like it," she deadpanned. "What do you think I'm doing in here?"

She blinked, and a flicker of surprised amusement raised her eyebrows. "You like ... the bush?"

"This one."

"You are so difficult." She dropped onto her knees, placed her hands on the ground, and peered into the thornbush, eyes going directly to where she had heard Cricket's voice. "If I asked if you were stuck, would you tell me the truth?"

Cricket scowled and wriggled forward, careful of her ankle, and stopped almost immediately. Thorns scraped her arms, her scalp pinched from her curls tangling in the branches, and even without putting weight on her leg, the pain had her seeing stars. Begrudgingly, she sighed and met the girl's totally-not-judgmental gaze. "Maybe."

"'Maybe' you're stuck, or 'maybe' you'll tell me the truth?"

Cricket shrank into herself, biting her lower lip before muttering, "Both."

"What was that?"

"I said *both*," she raised her voice, and something about that made the girl smile. It struck Cricket momentarily dumb, that smile. Every time she had seen the girl, she seemed so somber. So sad and uncertain. Like she thought she'd made a mistake or wanted to be anywhere but in this incredible camp. But that smile ... it rounded the apples of her cheeks, spreading lovely pink lips to put a mouth full of pearly white teeth on display. Even worse, it made her blue eyes sparkle, and *that* Cricket could not deal with.

"Are you going to help me out of here or not?"

The smile fled, and with it, all sorts of super confusing flutters in Cricket's belly. "Right."

She hopped to her feet and walked away. Cricket's ears perked, catching the sound of her footsteps just out of sight, the rustle of something being picked up, and then she was back with two pieces of crutch in her hands. "You dropped this." Cricket stared at her. "It broke."

"I can see that."

The girl huffed and shoved the crutch pad into the thorns, grunting as she used it to pull branches aside. "Can you get through?"

Clenching her jaw, Cricket struggled forward, wincing again as more thorns scraped across her arms and back, tearing her leggings. The flannel caught on the thicker thorns closest to the trunk of the thicket, and she paused. "Hold on a sec."

"I need to let this go."

"Alright, just—" Cricket glanced at the crutch and the bush. "Um, carefully, okay?"

"Okay." She eased the branches back, sighing with relief when she set the crutch down. Cricket took note of that, tugging the knot in the flannel undone and balling it as tightly as she could. Finding a fist-sized gap in the thorns, she pushed it through. "Can you grab that?" The flannel was whisked away, and the crutch again worked through the branches.

"On three?"

"Sure." She closed her eyes, willing herself to ignore how the throb in her ankle had risen to a constant scream of pain. The girl must have heard it in her voice because she held for a moment, giving Cricket more time before starting her count.

"Now?"

"Yeah."

"One." Cricket clenched her teeth. "Two." Told herself this was going to hurt, but only for a moment, and then it would be over. "Three." And shoved forward. At the same time, the other half of the crutch was shoved through the gap in the bush. "Grab on," the girl demanded, her voice dropping and becoming surprisingly authoritative.

Cricket did as she was bid, grabbing the rubber knob and bleating in surprise when she was hauled forward by deceptive strength. In one tug, she was halfway out of the bush. The girl grunted, sweat beading on her brow, and then tugged again until Cricket cried out with pain.

"Sorry!" She dropped the crutch and grabbed onto the other half, pulling the thorn bush further aside with both hands. "I don't want to hurt you."

"I've got it," Cricket gasped, army crawling forward on her forearms and one leg. "I think."

"What the heck happened?"

"Something chased me," she said, clearing the bush and rolling onto her back, panting as she spoke in short sentences. "Was walking. Stalked me. Chased me here."

"That explains the crutch." She gathered the two pieces, tucking them under her arm and extending a hand for Cricket. "Come on, let's get you to the nurse."

She stared at her hand. "What are you doing?"

"I'm helping you."

"I don't need your help," she argued.

"Right, so that whole thing with the bush just now was part of your plan?" At Cricket's silence, the girl snorted. "Thought not, come on." She waggled her fingers—slender with neatly manicured nails— and Cricket took her hand. "Up we go." With a tug, again displaying a deceptive strength she never would have expected from the soft-looking girl, she hauled

Cricket from the ground. Just as easily, her arm was slung across the girl's shoulders, and she slid her arm around the middle of Cricket's back. The difference in their heights—the girl was at least four inches shorter—made it oddly comfortable. Still, she grunted, staggering under Cricket's weight before starting them into a slow, hobbling walk. "You're heavier than you look."

"So glad we ran into each other. Really, this is a delight," Cricket muttered.

"No! It's just that you're so lean." As if to demonstrate, the girl curved the flat of her palm around Cricket's ribcage. The press of her fingers did something funny to Cricket's chest, and she bit her tongue, pinning her eyes on the trail ahead. "I didn't expect—"

"Me to be a real, live, breathing inhuman?" She glared at the girl, and her ears, flattened against the side of her head, twitched in anger. "Guess I shouldn't expect anything more from a human."

"Avery," the girl said in a low voice. Her fingers twitched, and Cricket was suddenly hyper-aware of everywhere their bodies touched: how the softness of Avery's upper arm cradled her back, the cushion of her rounded shoulder, and the smooth, supple feel of her skin. "If you're going to insult me when I'm trying to help you, you can at least use my name."

Cricket's ears pressed harder against her head, and she pinched her lips together, her nose uncomfortably dry. They shuffled in silence, save for intermittent grunts whenever her hoof was jostled and the ragged sawing of their breaths. When the camp buildings came into view, she said, "Crick."

"Not for a few more feet, but there's a bridge," Avery answered.

Cricket glanced at her, beyond confused, and held her tongue until, sure enough, they came across a small, arcing bridge over a gully and narrow creek. "Oh," she said dumbly. "No, I mean, my name—Crick. Cricket."

Avery glanced at her, the hard expression she'd worn since leaving the wood softening. The crease between her eyebrows eased, and if Cricket didn't know any better, she'd say the edge of her mouth curled up.

She readied herself for a barb or a joke, but instead, that ghost of a smile broke into a full grin.

"It's nice to meet you, Cricket."

6

Avery

"You were where?" Nurse Almaden's beady eyes widened. She blinked, and then twitched her head to the side in a very birdlike manner, assessing the pair.

"The woods," Cricket muttered. She gripped the edge of the counter and slid her arm off of Avery's shoulders. Soft, downy fur tickled the base of her neck, and she shivered, hugging her arms around herself. "I went for a walk."

"You split your hoof!"

"That happens all the time."

"And sprained your ankle," Almaden squawked.

Cricket shrugged and made a soft sound that sounded like "meh." She hobbled to the chair and collapsed into the cracked, worn leather. Dropping her head back with a relieved sigh, she stretched her arms and groaned in a way that had Avery spinning to stare out the window.

Classes and practice were done for the day, and campers wandered through the middle of camp, laughing with their friends and fiddling with instruments as they made their way to the cabins. In the hour before dinner, Avery usually headed to the practice rooms and lost herself in music, dancing her fingers over a keyboard or chasing a melody on her guitar, working out all the tension of her day in a melodic world of her own. Any filing or scheduling she needed to do for Director Murray could wait until after lights out when the camp was quiet and the night calm, but she found herself antsy to complete something. Anything. To achieve *something* instead of wandering aimlessly in the chords of an unnamed song.

"Sss, *ow*." Cricket hissed behind her, that raspy, rusty voice sizzling in Avery's ears.

"Apologies," Almaden muttered. "But you did this to your-self."

"I was bored."

"Your cousin gets bored, but I never see them being stupid about it," the nurse clapped back.

Cricket muttered something Avery couldn't catch, and she twitched her face to the side, catching the inhuman from the corner of her eye. Nurse Almaden perched on a stool in front of Cricket and was unwrapping the filthy ACE bandage from her ankle. She'd pulled a rolling service tray up beside them, the surface loaded down with antiseptic spray, gauze, gels, and a fresh bandage.

Cricket's leg stretched between them, the nurse careful not to pinch her calf with the neatly filed points of her short talons.

Her upper lip was curled back, blunt teeth clenched together. She gripped the armrests, the tips of her fingers bent slightly backward. Sunlight glinted off of the metal caps she wore on half of her fingers—three on her right hand, covering her thumb, index, and middle fingers, and two on her left, capping her index and middle finger. Avery turned all the way around, puzzling the purpose of the caps.

"No nails," Cricket gasped. She hitched in the seat, shoulders rising as the nurse sprayed antiseptic on her hoof. Avery flicked her gaze up to the inhuman's, heat burning her cheeks as she realized she'd been caught staring. Cricket waggled the fingers of one hand as Almaden prodded her hoof with a Q-tip. She hissed, eyes clenched in pain, arching her back in the chair. Her head fell back, and Avery's gaze was drawn to the long line of her throat. She coughed lightly into her fist and aimed for the door. "I should go start the paperwork."

"No need," Nurse Almaden called out.

"No need?" Avery whirled around. "Cricket was hurt on camp property; I need to file a report."

"That's not necessary." The nurse didn't bother looking up from her task. She poured a measure of hydrogen peroxide on the hoof, and Cricket grunted as white foam rose, squirming but managing to remain in the chair.

"What if she sues?" Avery gestured at Cricket, who cracked open one eye.

"I live in the woods; how would I retain an attorney?"

"Okay, so you know you'd need to retain an attorney, which suggests a certain amount of risk."

Cricket snorted, and twin patches of blonde curls on either side of her head danced. "I'm not going to sue the camp, but I do need to talk to 'Director Murray.'" She crooked an over-long finger on each hand, palms still flat against the armrests, as she said the director's name. "Need to tell her about what chased me."

"Why don't you fetch the director, Avery," Almaden said, beady eyes intent on Cricket's hoof. "I'm sure she'll echo what I've said."

Avery left without a word, jogging down the stairs and charging across the center promenade toward the director's cabin. The lights were off inside, save for the small lamp on a table beside the door. The light Director Murray always left on.

"To keep my wife from tripping," she'd explained. "They're an early riser."

Turning on lights as she went, Avery headed to the office where the filing cabinet with the insurance forms lived. Despite Nurse Almaden's instruction, she had every intent of filling out the appropriate forms and maintaining a record of events. *Just in case*, she told herself.

Settling at the desk, she glanced over the form, hesitating with a pen poised over the line asking for Species.

What *was* Cricket? Avery had never seen an inhuman like her. Granted, she'd never seen half of the inhumans at Elkwater

Music Camp before starting this job, but still—what had long graceful legs and cloven hoofs. A satyr? Were those even real? Inhumans had only come around in the last fifteen years; the news reports of the sudden influx of mythological and fae creatures were some of Avery's oldest memories, but satyr had been depicted in ancient art. Had inhumans always been here, only just now deciding to come forward?

And if so, why?

She scanned the desk as if Director Murray's papers held the answer. Grocery and supply lists submitted by the dining hall and counselors were strewn across the surface, along with bills, marketing proofs, and a blueprint for the proposed renovation and expansion of the camp. Additional bunks, a second marching field, an acoustic dome for the amphitheater, a theatre complex, and a chorus room—all the dreams Director Murray had for the camp that would never be realized if she failed to find investors and sponsors.

Avery set the blueprints aside and frowned at the yellow notepad with her name scrawled at the top.

She snagged the notepad, deflating in the chair with a sigh as she read the message:

"Avery – your dad called. Call his office. –M"

She sighed again, setting the paper down and pinching between her eyes. There was no time listed to tell her when her dad had called, but knowing Nathan Payne, he'd be in his office for another few hours until her mom had finished putting the youngest kids to sleep.

Steeling herself, Avery pulled the phone closer and dialed his work number, silently praying for the line to keep ringing and clenching her jaw when her father's secretary answered.

"Payne Strategies," Mrs. Jones greeted, her voice crisp yet kind. "How may I direct your call?"

"Hi, Mrs. Jones. Is my dad available?"

"Eliz—Avery!" She corrected herself, the formal tone giving way to what sounded like a smile. "Hey honey, how are you? How is summer camp?"

"It's good. Busy, but good."

"They feeding you enough?"

Avery laughed, her apprehension put at ease by the middle-aged woman's care. Mrs. Jones had worked for her dad for close to a decade and for the lobbying firm her dad had inherited for a decade before that. Her cheerful, kindly nature hid a cunning secretary with a steel-trap of a memory that had put no small amount of politicians in their place. "Almost too much, but nothing's as good as your tater tot casserole."

"And that is how you get yourself a care package of cookies," Mrs. Jones said. "You calling for your father, honey?"

"I am, had a message that he called the camp earlier."

"Got it; he's just finished with a meeting. Let me patch you through."

"Thanks, Mrs. Jones," Avery said. "It was nice to chat with you."

"You too, Avery. One sec."

The line went silent, long enough for Avery to take a deep breath and center herself in a place of calm before her father picked up.

"Elizabeth! How's my eldest daughter?" Nathan Payne's voice boomed as loud and forceful on the phone as he was in person. Avery drew in a quick breath, tensing at the sound even though miles separated them. His office was in the heart of Harrisburg, and Avery was safely tucked far and away in the Appalachians. He wasn't here; he wasn't anywhere near her, and yet the crushing weight of her father's personality had Avery wanting to shrink against the wall to avoid his notice.

"Good, Dad. You called?"

"Right to the point, that's my girl," he chuckled. "I was beginning to think you weren't going to call me back. Doesn't your last class end at three?"

"There was an issue with a camper," Avery mumbled. "I had to take her to the infirmary."

"Is that what they have you doing up there? Babysitting monsters and applying Band-Aids?"

"No, Dad, it—" Avery exhaled, dreading the coming argument. "I'm the Assistant Director, it's my responsibility to—"

"You told your mother and I that this was a stepping stone, Elizabeth. A strategic choice to further your career, not an Inhumanitarian Aid Mission."

"It is, Dad. I mean, it isn't—"

"You need to keep your focus, Elizabeth," he stated, launching into the tirade Avery had heard numerous times throughout the weeks leading up to the day she left for Elkwater Music Camp. "Carnegie Mellon isn't going to want someone who gets easily distracted. They want students in their program who are focused. No matter how many musicians Murray has churned out over the years, you're still just a girl. Integration has only made it harder for humans to succeed. Affirmative Action, my ass."

"Dad!"

"It's an overreaction from bleeding-heart liberals thinking equality means leaving our children behind."

Avery closed her eyes, inhaling through her teeth. "Was there something you wanted to talk about, Dad? The dinner bell is going to ring any minute."

"Wouldn't want to keep the monsters waiting." He chuckled as if it were a joke and not how he actually thought and felt about inhumans. Avery pressed her lips together. "So much like your mother. Listen, kiddo, I've got to run, but I wanted to let you know I'll be in the area later this week."

Avery's eyes flew open at that, dread curling in the pit of her stomach. "Why?"

"Meeting with a business partner up from Atlanta. US Petrol has an interest in the Monongahela; you know how it is. Got to get to Green Bank and put eyes on the property. Thought I'd swing by and take my little girl out to lunch. Mix a little pleasure with business. Think you can step away from babysitting the monsters for an afternoon with your old Dad?"

"I mean..."

Avery fumbled for an excuse not to see him. She might be struggling to fit in at Elkwater, fighting every day against lifelong lessons and biases, but the camp was still a respite. An escape from her father's views and loud opinions. She would have to return home at the end of the summer, living back under her father's roof until it was time to move to Pittsburgh. Avery refused to think about what would happen if Carnegie did not accept her. She didn't want to think about the pressure he would place on her to marry a Penn State boy and pop out more little Paynes. Her time at Elkwater may be fleeting, but it did not make it any less of a haven.

A haven she didn't want poisoned by his presence.

"Um, I think the roads are still closed. There was a storm that—"

"They'll be cleared by tomorrow. Given the amount of money my client is throwing at the towns up there, I'm surprised they're not already cleared for their trucks. Day after next, Elizabeth. My associate and I will pick you up."

The line went dead, and Avery stared at the desk, eyes burning. Road closures or not, there was no way her dad wouldn't follow through on a promise to US Petrol. They'd engaged Payne Strategies when her grandfather was still in charge, and the firm had built its reputation on that relationship, lobbying for pipeline expansions and barrel rates for the last fifty years.

She exhaled and pressed the tips of her fingers against her hairline. She knew it was too good to be true. Knew her parents would never let her have this summer for free. There was always a cost with Nathan Payne. Always a hoop to jump through and a dance to perform. That he was meeting a business associate told Avery everything she needed to know: her role wasn't to enjoy lunch with her dad. It was to smile and be silent, the perfect Christian daughter upholding the image of fine, upstanding American values that Nathan Payne had launched his career on. God and country. A Family man. Human.

The dinner bell rang, and she jumped from the chair, tearing Director Murray's note from the yellow pad and crumpling it in her hand. Her skirt tangled in the legs of the chair, and she gave it one strong tug, clenching the fabric in her fist.

What was done was done. Her mother always said that whenever a decision was made that Avery and her siblings disagreed with. Whether it be the location of the family vacation or the toppings on their pizza, what was done was done, and there was no use wallowing in it.

"Lift your chin, bite your tongue, and act with grace."

Nathan Payne was coming to the camp. Avery could suffer one lunch. She could act with grace for a meal, and then he would be gone.

Easy.

7

—·—

CRICKET

From her table at the far end of the dining hall, Cricket watched the campers with a mounting sense of awe. Her cousin had written about the camp, and for years, Cricket had read descriptions of human and inhuman kids sitting together, laughing together. Forming friendships and romantic involvements. But to see it firsthand was something stellar indeed. Where else could a naga and a gnome share a piece of cake? Where else could she watch a teen girl teaching a skunk ape how to twirl spaghetti with his fork?

Gods, she wished her parents were here to see what she did: a future, hope, a world outside of Green Bank and its ever-shrinking forest.

A plastic tray slapped against the table, and a figure slid into the seat opposite Cricket, obscuring her view of the campers. She blinked, gaze refocusing on the pale, freckled face and frizzy red hair of Avery.

She offered a tight-lipped smile as she settled, placing her hands in her lap and bowing her head.

"What are you doing here?"

Avery snapped her head up. "Eating?"

"Yeah, no duh. I mean here." Cricket waved her fork over the table, where she'd been perfectly happy sitting alone. "Don't you have campers to sit with?"

"That's not ... that's not really how it works." She raised her hands from her lap and straightened her fork. "I'm the Assistant Director. I'm not in charge of a singular cabin; it's my job to make sure the campers are comfortable and having a nice time, dinner included."

Cricket stabbed the bowl of sprouts, grains, and roasted vegetables Nurse Almaden had put together for her at the buffet. "I'm not one of your campers." She pointed the bite at Avery before shoving it in her mouth.

"No, but you're in the camp, and you're eating our food, so for all intents and purposes, you're one of us."

"Right." She shoved another forkful into her mouth, chewing loudly before asking, "Did you get your filing done?"

Avery, who had bowed her head again, peered at Cricket beneath thick lashes. For the briefest instant, she thought she tracked annoyance in her expression, and then the girl dropped her gaze away, mumbling something unintelligible.

"What was that?"

"I said, '*no*'," Avery snapped. "I didn't."

"I thought you had to submit an insurance claim."

"I did. I do, but I ..." She glanced side to side, cheeks flushing a sweet shade of pink.

Cricket set her fork down and laced fingers under her chin, lips curling in amusement. "Oh, this is gonna be good."

"I don't know what you are," Avery squeaked. The pink blazed hot, cherry tomato red. "The form asks what species you are, and I don't ... I'm not ..."

"Woooooow." Gripping the edge of the table, Cricket leaned back, drawing out the moment with feigned shock. Of course, the human wouldn't know what she was. As far as Cricket knew, *no one* did. The faun, at least, her family unit, had dropped through the veil fifteen years ago and remained hidden.

Not even the people of Green Bank spread the word of their fae friends in the forest. The faun kept the predators away, planted produce, and tended the earth, and the people of Green Bank bought their vegetables and thanked them for the lawn care. Being an isolated town smack dab in the middle of a radio-free zone, the people were almost as technologically adverse as the faun. Just like the song said, their little patch of West Virginia was almost heaven. Until recently.

But *apparently,* Avery had no idea the faun were unheard of, and the opportunity to watch that lovely blush color her cheeks was too good to pass up.

"You're the Assistant Director of an integrated camp, and you can't tell one inhuman from another?" Cricket clicked her tongue, ears twitching underneath her curls. "What, do we all look alike to you?"

"No!" Her eyes bugged, and her lips formed a plush, lovely circle. "Oh my goodness, not at all."

"Oak and ivy, your *face*." Cricket pealed with laughter, wrapping arms around her stomach as the human turned deeper and deeper scarlet. She didn't even care that her laughter came out in short, bleating bursts. "I'm totally messing with you."

She grinned at the human, tears limning her eyes from the laughter, and then froze at the new look on Avery's face. Her eyes were wide but reddened and sheened, her brow wrinkled and lower lip trembling. In that look, Cricket knew she'd gone too far, teasing someone who took herself far too seriously.

"Hey," she said in a low voice, reaching across the table. Without giving thought to the gesture, she pressed two metal-capped fingers lightly against Avery's hand. She stared down at the touch and then jerked her arm away as if she'd been burned. Cricket kept still, taking the insult in stride. "I'm sorry, I didn't think—"

"No, it's my fault," Avery whispered and transformed before her very eyes. She sat up straight, rolling those soft shoulders back and raising her chin. In a blink, her eyes were dry, if still red. She gave a curt nod and plucked her napkin from the tray as Cricket shoved a forkful of food into her mouth, chewing in silence until Avery asked with all the poise of a hostess, "What brings you to Elkwater Music Camp?"

Cricket, hunched over her meal with both elbows on the table, looked up from her vegan bowl. She finished chewing, swallowed, and blew a curl out of her eyes. "Came for help."

Avery's cold expression eased, and she leaned slightly forward. "Help?"

"Someone keeps buying up the land where we live—faun, by the way."

She blinked.

"Kind of related to satyr, but also, like, deer?" Did Cricket imagine it, or had Avery's shoulders relaxed as well? "So, add that to your form."

"They want to push you out?"

It was Cricket's turn to blink, taken aback by her sudden interest and the hint of concern in her voice.

"I-I don't know," she admitted. "That's what it feels like. Every time we settle in a new part of the woods, the land gets bought, and we get pushed out. Used to be we could spread out, but now the dens are getting closer and closer."

"Why don't you move?"

Cricket huffed a laugh, shaking her head. "I wish it were that easy." She poked the food in her bowl. Gods, why was she even telling Avery all of this? She didn't even know what faun were and was clearly out of her depth in dealing with inhumans. But there was something about how she leaned forward, completely engaged in Cricket's story in a way no one in her family had been for years.

She knew why; it wasn't hard to figure out. They were tired of her pestering the family to move. Tired of her wild claims and cries of evil real estate developers. Tired of her criticisms. When she was younger, her mother and father would humor her, nodding and smiling and placating her with repetitions of "one day," and "wouldn't that be nice," and "you will understand why we stay when you are older."

When her cousin married, Cricket was hopeful they would see how integration was possible beyond Green Bank. See how the faun could have more than their ever-shrinking patch of woods, but the elder faun, like her father, Bosk, were immovable, and Cricket was desperate.

"It's complicated," she said, those two words failing to sum up the last decade of her life. "Anyway, I came here to find my cousin; they've lived at the camp full-time for the last eight years."

"There's no one here like you."

The words were spoken quietly, almost reverently. Cricket snapped her gaze to Avery, who was prodding the food on her plate, cheeks once again flushing the lovely pink of a mountain laurel in late spring.

"I ... thanks?"

"I mean, I've never seen another, um, faun. We have naga, wolven, gnomes, and all sorts of campers in the Sasquatch family, a few lizard people. There's a satyr around here somewhere; he's in the woodwinds, but I haven't seen another faun."

"They're here," Cricket stated. "Just got stuck out of town with the road closures."

"Oh, those should be cleared in the next day or so." Avery twirled her fork in the air. "Still, I've never seen another faun in the camp."

"How do you know?"

"I'm the Assistant Director." She raised an eyebrow, blue eyes intent on Cricket. "It's my job."

"No," she shook her head. A half smile quirked her mouth, and, to her surprise. Avery's delightful blush returned. "How do you know the roads are re-opening?"

"My dad has a meeting in Green Bank, over the ridge. Some business deal. He wouldn't make the drive from Harrisburg if he thought he couldn't get to the real estate his client wants him to inspect."

Cricket stiffened at the name of her small town. Her ears pressed flat against the side of her head as a new suspicion about Avery, or rather, her family, arose. "What does your dad do?"

"He's a lobbyist." She set her fork down at a perfect ninety-degree angle, then straightened her already straight tray. "His firm has worked with US Petrol forever. They've been pushing for a new pipeline." Avery folded her napkin into a perfect rectangle and ran a finger along her knife and spoon, ensuring they were parallel to her plate. Cricket wiped her mouth with the back of her hand, watching the performance with interest. "Before I came up here, my dad was pretty deep into the project; they're purchasing the land on behalf of US Petrol using a third-party firm in Atlanta."

"Atlanta?" Cricket's ears perked up, and Avery's gaze lifted, dancing from one side of Cricket's face to the other. "Like, in Georgia?"

"Where else?"

At Cricket's lack of response, Avery again lowered her head, hands disappearing under the table. She exhaled, shoulders dropping, and Cricket's ears pricked forward at the sound of low mumbling. She ducked to the side and caught sight of Avery's lips moving. It was hypnotic how the plush pads formed each silent word. Her gaze drifted over Avery's face, lingering on her eyelashes, long and curled in a delicate arc so much darker than her hair and skin, the contrast beautiful and alluring.

That thought straightened her back. Unsure of what to do, she grabbed her glass and swallowed the last of her water before asking, "What are you doing?"

"Praying."

"Why?"

Avery cracked open one eye, peering up at Cricket. "Because it's what you do."

She glanced around the dining hall at the other counselors and the campers. Chatting, eating, laughing. "No one else is doing it."

Her head jerked up, neck crawling red. She flipped her hand at the dining hall at her back. "No, they aren't, okay? They think it's weird, too."

Cricket glanced around their table, shoved in the furthest corner of the room and curiously empty when she'd taken her seat only moments before Avery joined her. Her stomach dropped, and she took in the human girl with fresh eyes.

"I didn't say it was weird," she said. "I just asked what you were doing."

"You ... don't think it's weird I pray before my meal?"

She gave the question a beat, feigning thinking about it before responding, "I mean, I didn't say it *wasn't*."

Avery's chin tucked, her head tremoring in tiny surprise, and then she unleashed a peal of giggles that rang like a bell. "I knew it! You do think I'm weird."

"Yeah, well, tomato, lycopersicum."

⁂

Campers streamed past, chatting and laughing, some holding hands and scurrying into the dark. The sun had set since she entered the dining hall, and now, in the dark and alone, Cricket had no idea where to go. She leaned on her new crutch as she scanned the crowd for a counselor or Nurse Almaden and found neither.

"Need help?" Avery skipped down the stairs, skirt flouncing around her ankles and twisting between her legs. She scowled, tugging the fabric free and tossing it aside with a huff.

"Do you?"

"What?" Avery's eyes widened. Lights strung along the central path of the camp reflected in the blue, bringing to mind planets gleaming in a spring dusk sky. "Oh, no. It's just the skirt; it gets in the way."

"Then why do you wear it?"

"You are full of questions tonight, aren't you?" Avery smiled as she walked by, stopping after a few paces to call back. "Are you coming?"

"Depends. Where are you going?"

"Shortcut to the Director's Cabin." She pointed at a trail running along the side of the dining hall. "It's about a ten-minute walk if you take the main trail, but if we shortcut behind the field, it's closer to five."

Cricket flexed her hoof, swallowing a wince as a sharp pang warbled up her shin. "Okay then." She followed Avery around the building and out onto a large grassy field. In the low light bleeding from cabins and the dining hall, she could make out bleachers and light poles black against the sky. Avery kept close to the low-lying building running the length of the bleachers, walking at a hurried pace that Cricket struggled to match.

"Hey, slow down."

"What?" The human glanced over her shoulder, slowed, and then stopped, waiting for Cricket to catch up. "Sorry, I didn't want to bother anyone."

"Bother who?" She glanced around, ears pricking at the quiet. The purposeful quiet. She peered under the bleachers, picking out shadows that were deeper than they ought to be. Avery cleared her throat, the sound coming from much closer than Cricket anticipated. Less than a hand-span away, Cricket could *feel* the girl warming as if she were blushing from head to toe, the heat of her embarrassment radiating off of her in waves.

Her ears pricked, shooting upright from her curls and swiveling toward the sound of a low moan coming from the shadows. Realization struck, and she laughed. "Oh, my Gods."

"Ssh!" Avery grabbed her wrist lightly, tugging Cricket into movement.

Her grip was strong, not soft like she would have guessed from Avery's appearance and demeanor. But then again, she *was* a musician. Cricket only played panflute, but a few members of her family had branched out to other human instruments. Guitar and banjo were the most popular—their extra knuckled fingers lent the faun an advantage, and the hours of practice strengthened their hands. The lack of fingernails was a bit of a hurdle at first. To get around it, the faun who had picked up those instruments wore metal caps on the tips of their fingers, the ends hammered to a nail-like point, and the necessity had become a fad among Cricket's generation.

"It's a shortcut, I promise," Avery muttered over her shoulder.

"And a well-known one at that." Cricket snickered, craning her neck around to spy on the lovers under the bleachers. "How many are down there?"

She thought she heard Avery grumble, "I don't know," but whatever she said was lost as she cut between two buildings. The narrow width of the breezeway forced them to walk single file. Avery dropped Cricket's wrist, and she adjusted herself to face forward rather than hobble at an angle. The wood panels of the buildings brushed her shoulders on either side, and she shuddered.

"It's really tight."

"Claustrophobic?" Avery asked.

"Yes."

"I'm sorry." Avery looked over her shoulder. "I didn't know."

"It's alri—"

Avery stopped abruptly, spitting and swiping at her face with both hands. Cricket bumped into her, something wispy tickled her ears, and Avery screamed. Every hair rose along Cricket's neck and shoulders, the sensation of that scream like that of metal tips scaling down the strings on a guitar. Avery darted down the breezeway, spinning in a circle once she had the space to do so. Her hands flew down her front, batting at her skirt, then returning to her face as she chanted, "Ew. Ew. Ew."

Cricket hobbled out of the breezeway and into a small back-yard. A soft yellow glow spilled onto the lawn from the light on a wrap-around porch, illuminating a small grill, two lounge chairs, and a picket fence. Flowers she recognized from growing up in Green Bank hugged the fence, and in the far corner of the yard, beneath a Mountain Ash already blooming with berries, was a hammock and a soft, welcoming bed of pine straw, grass, and all-weather pillows.

A small breeze wafted through the yard, tickling across the back of Cricket's neck.

Wait.

Was it the wind or a ...

"Oh, Gods." She copied Avery's awkward dance, dragging spiderweb away from the back of her neck and out of her hair. A swipe at her throat brought away something with structure, and Cricket shot her hand out, whimpering at the sight of an orb-weaver spider scurrying up her arm.

"Oh, gosh, are there *more*?" Avery shrieked and pulled at her hair, loosening the long, frizzy ponytail. A cascade of fire poured down her back, tiny curls crowning her brow as she shoved her hands into the mass and shook it out. Cricket stood transfixed by all of that hair. Porchlight danced in the strands, illuminating golds and oranges. Just as quickly, it was whisked away, pulled into a messy bun on top of Avery's head. "I swear that web wasn't there yesterday."

"You have beautiful hair," Cricket replied. Avery stared at her, eyes wide, lips parted. *Oh, Gods.* Cricket scrunched her eyes, pinching the bridge of her nose. "I mean, I believe you."

She opened her eyes to find Avery staring at her, lips now pursed as if she were about to speak. Instead, she coughed into her fist and faced the stairs. "This way."

The back porch was cluttered in the way of frequent use. A basket of shoes sat by the door, and two rocking chairs flanked a small wood-burning stove and a metal barrel of logs. Flannel blankets covered a wicker loveseat, and she caught the undeniable scent of her cousin woven in with the fibers.

Avery tested the knob on the backdoor, nodding when it proved to be unlocked and facing Cricket. Again, she noticed the human's height—the perfect height for Avery to rest her head on Cricket's shoulder.

Her ears twitched, and she tucked her chin.

Where in the hells did that come from?

The gentle brush of Avery's fingers startled her from the thought. They plucked at her sleeve and the soft down on her shoulder before lifting away, flicking something from the tips. "You've got some ..." Avery looked up, brows bunching together as her eyes darted over Cricket's face, her hair, like the faun was a puzzle she couldn't figure out.

Her tongue darted out, moistening her lower lip and drawing every iota of Cricket's attention to her mouth.

Oh. Oh no.

She knew herself well enough. Had known for years where her interest lay, and it always started like this: noticing the little things like the strands of gold woven into fox-fur hair and how that tiny line appeared when Avery was considering something.

I need to go inside. I need to get away from her. This is a terrible idea. She doesn't even like me. I'm not even sure she likes girls or females or …

Her hooves wouldn't move, and Avery's eyes were impossibly large in the low light, her upturned nose giving her a fae, other-worldly appearance, like one of the fair folk from her mother's books but far shorter and with more curves and—*oh, Gods.*

"You have something …" Avery reached up. The movement startled Cricket enough that her instincts took over. Rooted in place, eyes pinned on Avery, her ears shot straight, intent on every sound on the porch and in the woods beyond. Trapped by the glowing reflection of the porchlight in Avery's eyes. "Here."

Her fingers lightly brushed the tip of an ear, and a thrill of pleasure shot straight down Cricket's spine. She bit her lip, barely halting the whimper that a single touch elicited.

She wouldn't know. She couldn't know. She said there's no one here like me, and she's clearly never been around inhumans before this summer. There's no way she could know.

Still, she screwed her eyes closed, forcing slow breaths through her nose as Avery's fingers continued their soft, teasing touch. Gods, the light pinches were beyond teasing. This was *torture.*

Her nipples pebbled all the way down her torso, and she thanked the Gods she'd worn a shirt that covered her body, even as a low, heated throb began in her core.

Avery's fingers scaled the inner curve of Cricket's ear, and a sound rose in her throat. She darted her hand up, grabbing the human's wrist. "Please," she managed. "Please stop."

"I'm sorry. I—" Muscles flexed beneath Cricket's palm, and she let go, finally zeroing in on what Avery held pinched in her fingers. "Spiderweb." She smiled sheepishly. "It was caught in your hair and your ears."

"Yeah." Cricket swallowed, body burning from the echo of that soft, teasing touch. "Yeah, I need to go."

She rushed inside, leaving Avery in all that soft, invitingly low light, and let the door slam behind her.

8

AVERY

SHE TOOK THE LONG way to her cabin, winding around the band rooms and back onto the field to holler at the counselors and older campers beneath the bleachers. Couples scampered away, giggling hand in hand, and Avery found it hard not to smile. There was something special about summer camp. Something magical about being out under the stars, far from the home you knew. It allowed an escape of self, a chance to explore and determine the sort of person you wanted to be.

At least, that was how Avery felt, and with each passing day at Elkwater, she felt herself becoming ... not a different person, but *more*. A truer version of herself than she could ever be at home. She only hoped she could hold onto this New Avery when she was.

Humming quietly, she walked the track around the field to check the second set of bleachers backing up to the woods. Intended for family members when the marching band students performed at the end of each session, it was smaller than the main bleachers, and its compact build allowed for more shadows. Few couples wandered across the field to use the shadows, less now considering half of the stand had collapsed in the storm, but it was still a good idea to check, especially after an incident ten years prior with a human oboist and her wolven lover.

She ducked under a bent metal support, squinting in the dark before knocking on the joist. "Hey, anyone still out here?"

Silence met her question, and Avery waited, listening for any held breath or whisper. Hearing nothing, she nodded and hoisted her skirt, stepping over a fallen beam and onto the track ringing the field. The silence was thicker out from under the bleachers. Avery shivered, berating herself for not bringing a flashlight as she quickened her pace. It would be quicker to cross the grass, but the field was pockmarked from practice and ground squirrels, and she had no desire to join Cricket on crutches with a sprained ankle.

Cricket.

The thought of the faun sent another shiver down Avery's spine. A shiver that churned into a flurry in her belly. She'd looked so peaceful, so soft, with her eyes closed and lips parted as Avery plucked spiderwebs from her hair. And those *ears*. Even now, she could feel the tempting, velvet-soft down against her fingertips.

I wonder if the rest of her is as soft.

Avery stutter-stepped to a stop, startled by the thought. It wasn't the first time her mind had wandered and wondered about other girls, and it certainly wouldn't be the last, but ever since she'd decided to pursue music over softball, it was the kind of thought she kept tucked away and locked in a box in the back of her mind. Out of sight and never addressed.

To have a thought like that about an inhuman, about *Cricket* … she held it there, cupped in her mind like a treasure in the palm of her hands. Examining the thought with a new curiosity.

"Hey!"

Avery tensed, breath caught in her throat. She craned her neck toward the sound of the call, wondering if she'd been so lost in her thoughts that she hadn't heard a camper approach. Silence and shadows clung to the woods, the field and track empty.

"Hey!"

The call came again, and every hair on her neck and arms stood straight. She squinted, making out the narrow trunks of the trees, the hollow where a deer trail wound into the woods, and a bulky, shifting shadow.

Stories from childhood crept to the forefront of her mind. Legends and "Jack Tales" her grandmother used to tell Avery and her siblings. An Appalachian woman, born and raised a coal miner's daughter in Fairmont, West Virginia, she wove them stories of moon-eyed people and caverns running the length of the mountains. She taught them to hang a broom over their doors and never to do their laundry on a Sunday. But at this moment, one of her grandmother's most frequent lessons screamed across her mind:

If you see something in the woods, no, you didn't.

The shadow Avery absolutely *did not see* shifted again, and she hitched her skirt and ran.

Moonlight crept across the floor of her cabin, falling in cracks between beams and casting long, unwanted shadows. Avery pulled the blanket tighter around her shoulders, wanting to roll over but too afraid to take her eyes off the door. Something had been in those woods; she was sure of it. Something big, watching her.

She shivered, creeped out anew, and rolled onto her back, eyes tracing the ceiling. Sleep had been impossible. By the time she reached her cabin, Avery was wide awake and jumping at every little sound. It would have helped if her roommate were there, but Sanoya had spent a grand total of zero nights in the cabin with her since the start of camp. They'd met, shaking hands and making small talk at move-in, but the pale-haired, willowy Life Sciences Instructor preferred to keep to herself and slept ... somewhere in the camp.

Or maybe she was nocturnal. Though human-appearing, the long-limbed woman with her wide, dark eyes was otherworldly—so much so that Avery scrunched her face and groaned.

Of course, Sanoya was inhuman. Why the heck had she been so quick to assume otherwise? Avery's assumption was probably the reason Sanoya wanted to keep space between them, just like Cricket, with her terse words and eagerness to get away.

And what had *that* been about? During dinner and the walk to Director Murray's cabin, it felt like they had found an easy middle ground—not a friendship, but something warmer than strangers. Cricket had seen Avery in a way the other inhumans at camp hadn't been able to, and Avery, in turn, had seen her.

But then she'd darted away so quickly as if Avery had spooked her.

She played through the moment again, trying to pinpoint her misstep. They'd entered the yard, Avery had walked up the stairs, and in the porchlight, she saw the spiderweb on Cricket's shoulder and tangled in her hair, and yes, *maybe* she'd been looking for an excuse to touch the faun again, so she had. Simple as that. She plucked the spider web away, content with one last brush of her fingers against the soft down on her arms. In that low light, she'd noticed tiny white flecks on Cricket's shoulders, like little inverse freckles, and the desire to count them all had been overwhelming. She'd pulled her hand away, showing the faun the spiderweb, and then spotted more in her hair.

Had that been it? Her ears had shot straight up. Delicate, conical ears that had been hidden beneath the short mass of curls. Dusty brown at the base, they lightened to an enticing snowy white at the tips, softer even than the velvet-down on Cricket's wrists.

The image of the faun frozen in front of her, large, liquid eyes intent on Avery, made her belly swoop. She lightly curled her fingers, nails tickling the skin above the waistband of her shorts.

At that first touch, Cricket had bit her lower lip between her teeth, trying in vain to stop the tiniest, sweetest whimper from escaping. But escape it had, and that sound now rang in Avery's ears. That, and each tight, almost panting breath that followed. She couldn't have imagined that, just like she couldn't have imagined how the peaks of Cricket's nipples had hardened beneath the thin cotton of her shirt.

Avery was no fool. You didn't spend the entirety of junior high and high school playing on a championship softball team without learning a thing or two about girls, their bodies, and how they responded to certain ... stimuli, and Avery had learned that lesson well, time and time again exercising that knowledge.

Her dad always joked she only played softball because it was the only time she was allowed to wear shorts or pants. Avery had bitten her tongue, refusing to correct him. What was the point? To admit what she got up to on travel weekends or when one of her teammates came to spend the night would be to ensure she never got to enjoy the escape of a tournament and sharing a hotel room with Stacy. Or Erica.

Instead, she smiled and feigned laughter, and when Erica came over for a sleepover, she thanked God for her Mom, who only ever said, "I love you, make good choices."

Her thumb brushed over her nipple, and she gasped at the surprising sizzle of pleasure, sweeping the hard peak again as she kept Cricket's face clear in her mind. Thick, short lashes dusting her cheek, those wild curls springing every which way. How her plump lower lip looked juicy enough to bite. To tug.

"Oh." Her hand slipped beneath the waistband of her shorts, driving between her legs, while the other cupped her breast, pinching and teasing her nipple.

Would Cricket make those sweet little pants if she touched her like this? Would she call out Avery's name in that raspy, throaty voice? Or would she curse?

Her fingers trailed through her curls, nowhere near as soft as Cricket's hair—oh, wow, was she that soft all over?

She circled her clit, hips twitching. The tiny flurry that had begun at that first accidental brush of her nipple blazed into an outright fire. She dragged a finger through her folds, teasing the slick flesh and circling her clit again, drawing closer and closer until the image of Cricket in her mind morphed and shifted. It became Cricket's teeth pinching her nipples. Cricket's long, soft fingers teasing Avery until she felt she would combust.

She drove two fingers deep, eyes flying wide as they crooked against a spot that made her see stars. Abandoning her breast, she pressed down on her hand, applying pressure to her clit until her toes curled and the sensation became too intense, too delectable to restrain any longer. She came with a silent scream, whipping her head to the side and burying her face in the pillow until each lapping wave of pleasure receded into her core.

Panting and, finally, exhausted, Avery lay on her back with her hand cradled on her chest, waiting for the guilt that usually followed. She wasn't supposed to think about girls. She wasn't supposed to want them, but she had, and she did, and even more surprising and no longer deniable, was that she wanted Cricket.

9

— · —

CRICKET

Dawn in the woods had once been her favorite time of day. The world was mostly sleeping, the roads and villages were quiet, and the woods were the playground of the faun. She remembered traipsing after her mom, Thicket, when she was young, following deer trails only she knew into new, exciting corners of their old world—remembered being bedded down when the sun fully rose and spending those long days in a space between waking and dreaming until her mom and older siblings returned at dusk to rouse Cricket and begin the journey home to their den.

And then the world split, they fell through, and Cricket's mother kept her close and safe. As the only one of Thicket's children to fall through, she spent her doehood in a den with other young faun, given only a tight radius to wander that her parents considered "safe." She was only allowed into Green Bank proper when her cousin returned to be married in the Faunish style with her human wife.

So it was little wonder she found herself hobbling the paths and deer trails running along the backside of the camp a little after dawn, leaning on her crutch and cursing under her breath whenever the knobbed end got stuck in a patch of mud or tangled in ivy. Which was exactly why she was bent at an awkward angle, tugging ivy off of the aluminum leg, and stopped long enough to catch the delicate, dancing melody floating through the trees.

Her ears swiveled in the direction of the sound, and her head followed as she straightened. The edge of a building was just visible through the trees, painted a lovely, deep shade of green. Jerking the crutch free, Cricket stepped off a path that could hardly be considered a trail and followed the sound. She hopped one-hoofed over a runnel feeding into a larger creek and swung around a tree, stopping beside a half-opened window.

Lovely piano music spilled out, a song Cricket had never heard before. She leaned against the wall, closing her eyes as the melody poured over her like warm, sweet honey. There was a hopefulness to the song, a whimsy tempered by a longing that tied itself to Cricket's very soul. Gripping the window sill, she peered in, jaw-dropping at the sight of Avery lost in her music.

Eyes closed, body moving in time to the sound she produced, she was without care, without worry. *This* was Avery, plying her passion on the keyboard and baring her heart to an empty room. Her expression shifted with each measure, the human feeling every beat, every emotion evoked by the music written by her very soul.

Cricket was again caught by the puzzle of this human girl. Mesmerized, hypnotized, whatever it *was*, it held her in place like ... a deer in headlights.

The song petered to an end. Avery exhaled all of that passion in one long sigh, releasing Cricket from her spell. She spun around, out of sight, frantically smoothing her ears down while imagining those graceful fingers—long, lean, and strong—brushing along sensitive down. The memory shifted, Cricket's imagination taking full control, and those fingers brushed lower, trailing along her jaw and down her throat. Heat flooded between her hips, and she shot away from the building, catching herself with the crutch before faceplanting in the pine straw.

"Oak and ivy, you're being stupid."

Picking any direction that led her away from the building and Avery, Cricket followed one of the well-trod paths into the woods, careful to keep the camp on her right, though just out of sight. The morning bell rang, and muffled voices filtered through the trees as campers headed to the dining hall for breakfast. Her stomach grumbled, but the last thing Cricket wanted to deal with right now was sharing a meal with Avery. What if she asked about her hasty exit two nights prior? What if she had to admit that a faun's ears were, like, *super* sensitive? Oh, Gods, what if Avery had *seen* her in the window?

Her ears flattened against the side of her head, and her face flushed hot. Gods, she needed to get out of this camp. Avery was running a number on her, emotionally and physically. She'd all but run up the stairs to Mac's guest bedroom that night, needing to take the edge off after the incident with the spiderweb, but even then, it wasn't enough. No matter how wild her imagination was, no touch or caress she gave herself could match the arousal she'd felt at those light, careful touches.

"Gods damn." Cricket hobbled to a halt, shaking her head to rid herself of the memory. There was only one way out of this: distance. She needed her cousin to return so they could go to Green Bank and convince their family to move.

Her stomach growled again, and she raised her head, catching the scent of bacon, eggs, and—"Waffles, awesome." Working around, she caught another scent in the air—wet and musky, with the faintest hint of wintergreen.

Her ears shot straight up, every muscle in her body going taut as instinct took over. The woods fell still, birdsong dying along with the quiet rustling in the undergrowth. It was here. Whatever had chased her over the ridgeline and stalked her through the wood was here.

Fighting her instincts, Cricket grit her teeth and spun around, nose twitching and ears swiveling, seeking any sound or scent or hint of where the *thing* was in relation to her. Just when she was about to give up, she caught it. A stronger, headier musk coming from the northwest. Abandoning her crutch against a tree, Cricket limped off the trail, wincing and hissing through her teeth. This was stupid; she was probably courting death, but she needed to know she wasn't crazy. That whatever had chased her was *real,* and it was here.

Bacon and blessed waffles grew fainter in the air, and a new scent joined the musk and wintergreen. Something metallic and sharp that turned Cricket's stomach, growing stronger with each step. She swallowed a sour mouthful of spit, ducked under a low-lying branch, and halted at the edge of a large, circular patch of churned and matted earth tucked up against a fallen tree. Flattened leaves and pine straw blanketed the bed, and her eyes easily picked out another trail leading away from the site.

She made it three steps onto the trail before the reality of that metallic scent smacked her in the face.

Blood.

"Oh, Gods." Cricket slammed a hand over her mouth, limping as fast as she could away from the kill site, the bed. Away from where that creature had slept and eaten. Gods, what did it *eat?* A deer, a rabbit? An inhuman like her?

Her stomach twisted, all desire for waffles erased under the unignorable need to vomit and scour her body, erasing the stink of the hours-old kill from her coat with lye.

The trail spat her out on the edge of the parking lot, and she hurried across the gravel, glancing at the luxury sedan parked beside the gate. Her gaze lingered on the license plate, a soft orange at the bottom fading up to white, a peach for the O in the state's name.

Georgia.

Cricket hastened along, following her cousin's trail around the cabin. She ducked into the yard and up the stairs, letting herself in the back door. Strong cologne damn near smacked her in the face and, stifling a gag that only sent the lavender, citrus, and wintergreen scents burrowing deeper into her sinuses, she backed out onto the porch and collapsed in one of the rocking chairs.

Her hoof and ankle throbbed, the bandage stained and unraveling. Nurse Almaden was going to have a fit, and yet Cricket couldn't be bothered to care. She dropped her head back, willing her heart rate to slow as she sipped the cool morning air, rocking the chair with her uninjured hoof. Voices drifted out of the kitchen window, muffled, and it took her a moment to realize they were coming from Mac's office at the front of the cabin.

"—aware she was expecting anyone."

"First, you don't know where my daughter is, and next, you don't know what your own employees are up to?" a male voice drawled. "What sort of freakshow are you running up here, Miss Murray?"

"Mrs.," Mac's voice, hard and cold, replied. "I don't appreciate your calling Elkwater Music Camp 'a freakshow'."

"And I don't appreciate your tone, ma'am," the voice turned snide. "Payne Strategies is an influential firm among certain parties in DC. Parties that have shown an interest in this … camp." He said the word like it was dirty. "Careful how you speak to me."

Cricket sat upright at that, her hoof thudding quietly against the porch and both ears swiveling toward the window.

"Speaking of donations," another voice cut in, slick and smooth like black ice. "Lunar Asset Management is always looking for a charity case to do a little pro bono work, and rumor is that you're looking to expand this quaint operation."

"I … yeah," Mac answered, sounding startled. "I am, how did you—"

"May I take your card?" A beat of silence followed, in which Cricket could easily imagine Mac nodding. But imagining the conversation wasn't enough. She wanted to see the faces of the men who talked to her cousin's wife so disrespectfully and called this wonderful place a *freakshow*.

As quietly as she could, Cricket limped to the door, turning the handle all the way before easing it open and slipping inside. There was no easy way to spy on the office, not if she wanted to remain unseen, but the guest bedroom overlooked the parking lot, and these dickweeds had to leave eventually.

Floorboards creaked in the office, followed by the sound of shuffling. As Cricket crept up the stairs, the second man spoke again.

"Murray? As in Congressman Murray?" He huffed a laugh. "I heard he had a philanthropic daughter."

"Something like that." Mac managed a laugh of her own, but to Cricket's ears, it sounded forced.

"Well, I'll be in touch, Miss Murray." Cricket frowned when Mac didn't correct him. "We'll set up a dinner. Here, I think. A decent amount of the team is in the area working on Mr. Payne's project. It'll be good to get a macroscopic view of what you're hoping to accomplish."

"Sounds wonderful." The floorboards creaked again, and the door to the office pulled wider. Cricket scampered the rest of the way up the stairs, diving into the guest bedroom before she could be seen. "Avery should be done with her morning classes by now."

"Avery?" she whispered to herself, head cocked and ears intent on the conversation. What in the hells did these men want with *Avery?*

"Shouldn't take me more than fifteen minutes to grab her," Mac continued. "You're welcome to wait here—"

"Outside," the first man barked. Footsteps charged from the room, and the front door creaked open. "We'll wait outside, in the parking lot."

"Great." Mac exhaled. "Let me walk you out."

More footsteps, on the front porch now. Cricket scrambled across the bed, peering over the window ledge and keeping as low as possible.

Mac led the way, dressed in her uniform denim button-down tucked into khaki shorts, her tan legs and running shoes churning across the gravel. Two men in suits followed, one of average height and build walking in a way that suggested he wore lifts in his shoes, and the other tall and broad in a perfectly tailored suit with slicked back, dark brown hair that oozed douchebaggery. Cricket's eyes locked onto the hair of the shorter man, a bright orangey-red like fox fur. Avery's hair.

Little pieces of the conversation she'd overheard clicked into place, and Cricket clutched the windowsill, startled and angered by the reveal. This man was Avery's *dad?*

She snarled as much as a faun could snarl, her lip curling and a low hiss slithering from her teeth. The second man twisted at the waist. Sunlight glinted off the silver frames of his Ray-Bans, temporarily blinding Cricket. She shut her eyes, rubbing them with her fists before opening them again and immediately spotting Avery's dad halfway to the luxury sedan she'd passed on her way in. Alone.

She scanned the lot for the second man and found him standing in the same place, staring up at her window with a slick, wolfish grin.

10

— · —

AVERY

THOUGH NOT AGGRESSIVELY WINDY, the drive down to
Elkins was nauseating. With her father in the passenger seat,
chatting business as his associate drove, Avery spent most of it
with her head pressed against the window and her eyes closed.
Were she her younger brother or had she any interest in Payne
Strategies as a future career, she would have felt pressured to
pay attention, absorbing all she could for the inevitable moment
weeks from now when her father decided to quiz her on the
conversation.

But Avery was neither of those things. Firstborn, yes; first
son, no. In a way, it made life easier. She felt none of the pressure
to follow in her father's footsteps that Michael did, but the
expectations leveled on her were different.

Old fashioned, she mused.

Avery was expected to be a Good Daughter. To be modest in
demeanor and dress, to pursue feminine hobbies, and, eventually, marry and produce more little Paynes for her father to use as

marketing and PR props. She supposed she ought to be grateful that America also cherished its athletes and that women of her mother's generation had fought for and earned the opportunity to pursue higher education and moderate independence so long as they eventually "settled down."

When Avery presented her case for working at Elkwater Music Camp, her father had vetoed the idea. It had been her mother's interference, pointing out how a Payne working at an integrated camp was good for optics, that led to his begrudging agreement.

Though Avery was grateful for her mother stepping in, she still fumed that she'd had to argue for her own future. Forgetting that she needed this summer, for Carnegie, for herself, that she had to present a business case to do something any other parent would be proud of, that it required his *buy-in*, was ridiculous!

It was no surprise, then, that he had wanted to make the hour-long drive to Elkins rather than eat at the camp and tour Avery's home for the summer. He brushed it off, as he always did.

"Business expense, kiddo, you know how it is."

And she did. With so many kids and a wife to provide for, it made sense Nathan Payne would cut corners where he could. Not that the family needed to cut corners. Her grandfather had built Payne Strategies from the ground up in a golden era of bootstrap sensibilities, taking on clients that represented the beliefs of a particular political party and riding that wave up until the day he handed over the reins to his son.

Still, Nathan Payne clung to his public image: businessman and father, family man, a man you could trust, but only so long as you didn't look too close. So long as you didn't peel back the shiny veneer and glimpse the nasty, bigoted man beneath the wide smile and styled hair.

The sedan slid into a parking spot, and Avery snapped out of her thoughts, sitting up and blinking out the window.

"Best this shithole has to offer, I'm afraid," her father's business associate, Troy, said. "The other options were McDonald's, a dago-run pizza joint, and a bar that likely serves tetanus along with your fries."

"This'll do nicely." Nathan shoved the passenger-side door open, sliding out of the sedan like a snake slithering from its burrow. "Nothing better than a stick-to-your-ribs Appalachian burger."

"If you want to have your Armani let out," Troy laughed.

Avery joined them on the sidewalk, biting her tongue to keep silent. Her father dropped an arm around her shoulders and tugged her close.

"Elizabeth certainly looks as though she's been enjoying the local fare." His fingers tightened on her upper arm, digging into the softness there. "Can't be that bad."

"She certainly does." Troy's smile turned leering, and he flicked his gaze over her in a way that made her skin itch. He spun and charged up the restaurant stairs, reading the name painted on the glass pane before holding the door open for Nathan. "We might as well meander in."

"Meander's," Avery corrected before she could stop herself, pronouncing the restaurant's name the way she had heard other locals say it. *Mean*-ders.

"Fitting in already." Nathan smiled down at her, his eyes cold. "Let's pretend we're civilized for a few hours, hm?"

And with that, he sauntered up the steps, nodding at Troy as he entered the restaurant. Avery lingered on the sidewalk, debating running for the hills.

"You coming?" Troy called from the door, that sharp, intense gaze leveled on her. She sighed and trudged up the steps, tugging her skirt from between her calves. He held the door for her, an innocent grin on his face, and followed Avery closely into the restaurant. She stopped a few feet away from her father, who was chatting with the hostess, and Troy stopped right behind her. She glanced back, hoping her annoyance wasn't too clearly written on her face. Oblivious, he swept the plackets of his tailored coat aside and put his hands on his hips. Eyes drifting closed, he inhaled deeply and exhaled with a sigh.

"Ah, now *that* smells like a full meal."

Avery frowned, sniffed, and had to agree. Meander's smelled amazing: burgers and fries, country gravy, and a hint of sweetness from the dessert display. Her stomach growled, and Troy chuckled far too close to her ear.

"Hungry, little girl?"

"Wilkolak!" her father barked, circling his hand in the air for them to follow. "Let's get this over with."

Troy shot Avery a tight-lipped smile as he slid past, following her father and the hostess into the dining area.

Wood-paneled and cozy, Meander's interior looked like it hadn't been updated since the restaurant opened. Taxidermied deer heads decorated the walls alongside sun-bleached photographs of the region and framed newspaper articles spanning thirty years featuring the citizens of Elkins.

The hostess sat them in a booth, Troy sliding in beside Avery on the cracked leather bench, and eyed both of the men warily as she handed out menus. Her hand lingered on Avery's, and when she looked up, Avery startled at the young woman's eyes—slitted like a snake and set in bold yellow pupils. She nodded once, eyes dropping to Avery's shirt, then let go of the menu. Avery glanced down, belatedly remembering she was wearing a green Elkwater Music Camp polo tucked into her tiered denim skirt.

Warmth kindled in her chest as she deciphered that brief nod into the acknowledgment of a sort of belonging. She sat straighter, scanning her menu as her father and Troy continued their discussion from the car.

It was about a real estate deal; she had gleaned that much. The same one her father had mentioned on their call.

"We have three properties set to close in the next week," Troy said. "And then I can get to work on the next batch of holdouts."

"Excellent," said Nathan. "I'm sure the fellas at the home office are pleased with the commission you'll be bringing in."

"They're not upset, I can tell you that," Troy replied.

"I was doubtful when Lunar Asset argued for 7%, but with the progress you've made, I can see your firm is worth every penny." He cleared his throat, jovial tone dropping. "US Petrol wants us to present our first case in two weeks; if we secure the properties before then, we can use that to pressure the local congressman."

"Y'all ready to order?" A heavily bearded waiter stepped up to the table. The Meander's t-shirt he wore strained against a barrel chest and massive, hairy arms. Nathan leaned away from their waiter while Troy turned that wolfish grin directly on him.

"I'll take the steak, rare, no potatoes, an extra side of au jus, and the house salad. Undressed."

"And to drink?" the waiter asked, seemingly blind to Troy's threatening smile and Nathan's obvious disgust.

"Tea, unsweetened, if that even exists in Elkins. If not, water."

"Unsweetened tea it is," the waiter replied, his friendly expression unfaltering. Avery was impressed. Just listening to Troy's order had her fingers trembling. She clasped them together in her lap, her head down to hide the angry purse of her lips. "For you, sir?"

"Club sandwich, bag of chips, bottle of water," Nathan answered, throwing the menu down on the table when the waiter held out his hand.

"And you, miss?"

"Cheeseburger," Avery mumbled. Her father cleared his throat, and she lifted her head. He glared at her from across the table, mouth turned down in a frown. "I mean, the cobb salad."

Without missing a beat, the waiter smiled, revealing a row of blocky yellow teeth that identified him as an adolescent sasquatch. "I can do the cobb as a side for the burger instead of fries. Sound good?"

"I, um." Avery glanced at her father, who shook his head. Heat built in her chest, and she sat up straighter, smiling at the waiter. "Yes, please. With blue cheese dressing, if you have it."

"We absolutely do." He grinned wider back at her, deep-set eyes twinkling as Avery reached across Troy to hand him her menu.

"Gluttony is a sin, Elizabeth." Nathan clicked his tongue, shaking his head in the way of a disappointed father. "Once you're home from Camp Cryptid, we'll discuss your behavior." Threat leveled, he faced Troy, effectively cutting Avery out of the conversation. It was a dismissal meant to make her feel small and useless, but to Avery, it was a relief. She let her eyes wander the street until their food arrived, and then she nibbled on her burger, watching the daily life of Elkins, West Virginia, pass by.

A man and a female-presenting naga wearing a baby in a sling crossed the street hand-in-hand. Outside the local bar, a moth-man leaned against the wall, smoking a cigarette and nodding to people as they passed by. A young woman hopped up onto the sidewalk, and the mothman's eyes lit up bright red, his smile widening as they embraced in a friendly hug.

"No one will even name the damn thing," Troy said with a chuckle, drawing Avery's attention away from the street. He shook his head, a disbelieving grin crinkling his cheek. "Can you believe these backwoods hicks? Getting stalked and terrorized by a mystery cryptid; it kills their chickens and livestock, and still, they won't sell. They won't even admit they saw anything in the woods."

"That's the problem with these hillbillies," Nathan grumbled through a mouthful of sandwich. "You saw that camp; they'd rather cater to monsters and bring them into the fold like we're all one big, happy family than face the truth: this nation is being overrun. Look at my daughter—" He pointed his sandwich in Avery's direction, frown deepening as his eyes landed on the half-eaten burger and untouched salad. "She's had to sacrifice her upbringing and morals in order to get ahead."

"Americans have no spine anymore," Troy agreed.

"We need to push these monsters out and take our land back," Nathan continued. "Not incorporate them into our society."

Avery shrank in her seat. This rhetoric wasn't new. Her dad had touted the same arguments for most of her life: America is for the Americans. This land was built by human hands. Why should they have to accommodate the arrival of monsters?

The one time she'd spoken up, arguing that they weren't monsters, they just weren't human, her father had slapped her across the cheek and sent her to her room for being impertinent.

"All it takes is a little push," said Troy. His eyes followed a woman as she walked by. Scales clung to her temples and trickled down her neck, and she flicked a forked tongue before commenting to her friend how good the food smelled. "We have to remind these hillbillies how dangerous the monsters are, and they'll sell. Once they do, Lunar Asset Management is poised to pivot directly into working with your client. Our team in DC is close to securing the votes we need to file for eminent domain."

"I've got a direct line on Congressman Murray, as you noticed," her father added. Troy smiled, a malicious light entering his eyes. "He'll come around soon enough."

"Your bill." The waiter returned, waving a vinyl billfold between Troy and Nathan. Avery's father grabbed it and, to her surprise, set the billfold down in front of Avery.

"Use the card I gave you," he instructed.

"The emergency card?" Sure, it was his credit card. He'd given it to her when she went to college, but why would he have her pay for a business lunch?

"You haven't used it this month. Even small purchases you pay off help build your credit, Elizabeth." He shook his head as if she ought to know better. "And we thought giving women credit cards was a good idea," he said to Troy. "You should see the bills my wife racks up."

"My girlfriend is just as bad. Does one woman *need* that many manicures?"

Avery scrawled her name on the customer copy first. Payne Strategies' accounting department wouldn't reimburse for a meal unless you submitted a signed receipt, and her father had already read her the riot act once before for submitting an unsigned copy. The inkball failed to roll, and she scribbled in the margin of the receipt to get the ink flowing, trying again and managing the latter half of her name. Her father glanced over, frowning.

"Pen's not working," she explained, pressing hard against the receipt to fill in the first letters of her full name. Nathan nodded, returning to his conversation with Troy.

Unobserved, Avery added a decent tip and signed the merchant copy. Setting it in the billfold, she slid the customer copy across the table. Her father broke away from his conversation long enough to drop his attention to the receipt, nodding at her signature and slipping it into the pocket of his coat. "That's my good girl."

11

—·—

CRICKET

CRICKET SLAMMED HER TRAY against the table, ignoring the pang of guilt as Avery startled at the loud slap of plastic against particleboard. "Where were you today?"

Avery narrowed her eyes, knuckles blanching white from her grip on the fork. "Excuse me?"

"You weren't around this afternoon. Where were you?"

She opened her mouth, closed it, and prodded the pile of minced meat and gravy on her plate. The corner of a thick piece of Texas toast peaked out from beneath the slop, and another piece was placed at a perfect ninety-degree angle on her napkin—which was aligned parallel to the table's edge. "Not that it's any of your business, but I had lunch with my dad."

"And his friend?"

"How did you—?"

"I saw them, your dad, you two have the same hair color." Avery's open expression shuttered at that comment, and she went back to poking her food but never actually eating it. "His friend, who is he?"

"A business associate."

"Sure, fine. Don't tell me." She stepped over the bench with her injured leg first, leaning on the table's edge as she put weight on the hoof to bring her other leg over and plopped down.

"I'm not sure what you want me to say," Avery said after a moment, her voice low. "My dad took me to lunch in Elkins. He brought a business associate, and they talked business the whole time. Then dropped me off here and drove to Green Bank."

"You drove down to Elkins?"

Avery's head snapped up, alarm making her blue eyes bright. "Why are you interrogating me?"

"Oak and ivy, just answer the question."

"No!" she raised her voice, drawing the attention of campers and counselors at the surrounding tables. Hunching, Avery flushed and whisper-hissed, "When did you see my dad?"

"He came by to talk to Mac." At Avery's blank stare, she amended, "Director Murray. That doesn't matter. You went down to Elkins. Are the roads open?"

"How else do you think my dad got here?" Avery rolled her eyes and shoved a forkful of ground beef into her mouth. Cricket's stomach twisted. She stuck her tongue out and fake-gagged. "What."

"How can you eat that?"

"It's meat."

"Exactly." She shuddered. "It's disgusting. The smell alone makes me nauseous."

"Then sit somewhere else," Avery fumed. "I was perfectly fine eating my meal in peace. Alone." She shoved another forkful of meat into her mouth, chewing noisily before swallowing. "But apparently, I can't even do that right." And another.

Cricket took a second to look at the human. Like, *really* look at her. Purple shadows clung to her eyes, her hair was pulled back tighter than usual, and she looked somehow … diminished. Or stretched too thin. It was one or the other, and Cricket couldn't quite decide which she thought it was. But *whatever* it was, it had put Avery in a foul mood, and something about that made her more real.

"Oak and ivy, fine." She slid on the bench, giving Avery a few more inches of space, and tucked into her salad.

They ate in angry silence, the cafeteria chatter humming like a beehive around them. Cricket was just debating hobbling to the buffet for a second helping when Avery cleared her throat.

"What does 'oak and ivy' mean?"

"You need me to explain basic botany to you?"

"No, just—when you say it, it's like a curse word?"

Cricket laughed, her ears perking in amusement. Avery's gaze tracked their movement, her slight embarrassment giving way to a curious tilt of her head. Self-consciously, Cricket smoothed one of her ears down, eyes dropping to Avery's hand, those long, strong fingers still curled around her fork. The down along her neck prickled, and she shifted where she sat. "Yeah, something like that."

"Why 'oak and ivy'?"

"Why 'Jesus Christ'?" Avery straightened at the question, and Cricket rushed out, "I'm not belittling your faith. I was just giving an example. Why do humans say 'Jesus Christ' when they're surprised or angry?"

"*I* don't," Avery blurted. "It goes against our teachings to take the Lord's name in vain."

Cricket exhaled, the curls on her forehead dancing in the puff of breath. "Okay, bad example." She tapped the fork against her lip, unable to ignore how Avery's eyes followed the gesture and then lingered. "It, uh, it's important. Like Jesus Christ is to you. I think. In my family, we hold the white oak in high regard. Faun are married underneath their branches, and pregnancies are blessed with their boughs. We make wine from the acorns for our festivals; it's—"

"Religious," Avery cut in. "I think I understand. And ivy?"

"It's sweet," Cricket shrugged. "Most faun have a sweet tooth."

"Do you?" A bit of minced meat gravy clung to the corner of her mouth. She swept it up with her thumb, the motion drawing all of Cricket's attention to soft, pink lips.

"Yeah," she rasped. *What the hells is wrong with me?* She couldn't pull her eyes away. Avery was staring at her, waiting for Cricket to elaborate, but all she could think was how stupid she was being. There was no way Avery was into females, much less inhumans. The girl would sooner take her god's name in vain than hook up with a *monster*. "And salt."

"Salt?" Her tongue flicked the corner of her mouth, and Gods *dammit,* Cricket needed to look away because the longer she looked, the more likely Avery would notice and—*oak and ivy*, now she was blushing.

"Yeah," she nodded tersely, shoving a cherry tomato into her mouth. "Was it a nice lunch?"

Avery leveled her gaze across the table, her fork hovering over sodden Texas toast. "What do you actually want to know, Cricket?"

"Alright. Who was that other man."

"Why?"

"His car had Georgia plates."

The fork lowered, then was set down perfectly parallel to her plate. "And?"

"And, the company buying up all the land in Green Bank is from is from Atlanta. And *you* said they went to Green Bank. What for?"

"I—" She wrinkled her nose, and that little line appeared between her brows. "Something about a pipeline? I wasn't really paying attention, but my dad works with US Petrol, and they were talking about securing votes to claim eminent domain." Cricket cocked her head, the words unfamiliar. "Have you heard of a monster killing cattle in Green Bank?"

Her ears flicked up in alarm, and she slapped both hands down, leaning over the table. "Why?"

"Troy mentioned it," she said offhand, then added, "my dad's business associate. He said the locals were afraid of 'some mystery cryptid' but weren't selling."

"Damn right, they're afraid." She straightened and crossed her arms. "Did he say what it was?" Avery shook her head, and Cricket nodded tersely. "Good. First of all, even if someone tells you, *never* say its name, and second of all, depending on who you ask, it fell through when we did, or it's been here for centuries."

"That doesn't make any sense."

"I know." She frowned. Enough of the locals in Green Bank had mentioned a monster, and Cricket had been chased over the ridgelines by one just a few nights prior. But it couldn't be a you-know-what. Could it? "But whenever they got here, they've been haunting these hills long enough for the legends to exist. I've never seen one, but it's supposed to have a skull for a face and massive antlers." The hairs along her arms rose as she weighed what she had just said against the monster she had seen and descriptions of whatever it was stalking the people of Green Bank. "Like a-a zombie faun. It's insatiable. No matter how much it eats, it wants more."

"Do you think that could be what chased you here?"

Cricket shook her head, mouthing, "I don't know," when she really wanted to say, "I sure as hells hope not."

At Avery's frown, she clarified, "I know *something* chased me over the ridgelines, but I never got a good look at it. I guess it could have been a you-know-what, but ..." She pressed her lips together, keeping her next words to herself.

It wasn't that she wanted to lob accusations or scare Avery into taking her side or anything, but her dad was involved with the Georgia company that was forcing Cricket's family out of their homes. And they mentioned a monster at their lunch and had gone to Green Bank to do something with eminent domain, whatever that was. The pieces were lining up too neatly for Cricket to keep quiet.

"The other day, I went for a walk, and I—"

"Cricket!"

She flinched, ears shooting straight up and body freezing at Avery's outburst. Her fingers throbbed, protesting in pain. It was an effort to break her prey-driven stare away from Avery and force it down to her hands, which gripped the edge of the table so hard the tips of her fingers were bent back.

"What?" she managed through clenched teeth.

"You're not supposed to be walking on your foot, I mean, hoof, er, ankle."

"How else am I supposed to get around?" Avery had no answer to that. Instead, she watched as Cricket slowly released the table, flexing her fingers and curling them into a loose fist as she worked blood back into her extremities. "I was in the woods behind the piano room, and something had bedded down there. Something big."

"Do you think it's what chased you?"

"Probably."

At that, Avery reached across the table, brushing Cricket's elbow with her fingers. "Are you okay?"

She stilled at the touch, gaze dropping to Avery's hand, which stayed right where it was on Cricket's arm. She flicked her gaze up to Avery's face and—*oak and ivy, Gods dammit*—she blushed and pulled her hand away. But not *all* the way. It stayed on Cricket's side of the table, fingers outstretched as if the human were reaching for her, and what in the hells Cricket was supposed to do with that, she had no idea.

"It had eaten, too," she said, successfully ruining the moment. Avery pulled away, throat bobbing as she hugged herself. "I don't know if it was human or animal, but there was ... evidence," Cricket kept talking, needing to fill the moment with something other than the thought of Avery's fingers, Avery's tongue, Avery's spring-sky eyes. "Blood and guts on the undergrowth, half-buried bones, and the stench—" She stuck her tongue out, crossed her eyes, and gagged.

"That sounds," Avery swallowed, "monstrous."

"Of course it does. The thing is a monster," Cricket grinned. Avery raised an eyebrow, and it was unfair how endearing sarcasm was on her face. "Okay, *fine*. I'm technically a monster too."

"I didn't say that," Avery demurred. She dropped her eyes, lashes dusting cheeks blushing a delightful pink. A flutter built in Cricket's belly, feeling all too much like hope, and just as quickly as it rose, she stamped it out.

"You didn't have to."

Avery snapped her head up at the change in Cricket's tone, but what did she expect? Her dad was involved with the Georgia men, and no matter how cute she was, Avery couldn't help her. She could barely tolerate being around her, so what was the point of enjoying that blush or admiring those eyelashes?

"Why are you so intent on hating me?" she asked, her eyes shining. "I've been nothing but nice since I found you in the woods. I thought—"

"I'm not some stray you picked up, Avery." She straightened at her name, and Cricket found she liked how the word formed on her tongue. "I'm a faun, my home is being threatened, and your dad has some connection to the people doing it."

"That's a specious claim, Cricket," she retorted, softening the sharp tone on her name. "My dad works with a lot of people on a lot of different projects. Whatever is going on in Green Bank is just one of many—"

"But it's the one that affects *me*," Cricket snapped. "You know what? Nevermind. Why did he bring up the you-know-what?"

"He said one had been attacking the humans in Green Bank."

"It can't be." She shook her head. Even though she herself had been hunted, Cricket couldn't be certain it was the monster Avery suggested. Or maybe, she just didn't want to believe *that* was the creature targeting Green Bank. The you-know-what was a thing of legend, predating their fall through the worlds. Warnings of its presence and appetite had been shared *with* the faun, not by them.

Or maybe she was in denial.

"We would know about any attacks if they were from that specific being," Cricket doubled down. "It's part of our agreement with the humans in town. We protect them from whatever stalks the night; they keep us secret from the rest of the world."

"But you were attacked."

"A ridge away from Green Bank on my way here." *And chased in the woods behind the camp.* "And then I found where whatever it is had bed down. It's not a you-know-what."

"How can you be sure?"

"Because I know what I saw, okay?" She pushed down on the table and rose onto her hooves. "It's large and muscular, and yeah, it had a skull for a head but no antlers." She stepped over the bench, willfully ignoring how Avery rose when she teetered on her injured hoof. The thing in the woods hadn't had antlers, she was sure of it. Those had been branches. And it had been huge and hulking, not emaciated, but Cricket had been terrified, only catching glimpses in flashes of lightning.

And then she'd been hidden in the thornbush, only able to see its claw-tipped paw.

Gods, she was getting to be no better than her family, questioning herself as much as they cast their doubts on her claims. But Cricket knew what she had seen just as well as she knew something sketchy was happening in Green Bank. She just needed more evidence.

"You saw it in a storm," Avery argued, "by your own admission. How can you be so sure?"

"I just...I just *am,* and I'm done having *everyone* question me. Good night, Avery." She grabbed her tray from the table and limped away.

12

AVERY

THERE WAS NOTHING SHE could do but watch Cricket leave. She had duties to attend to, campers to oversee, and reports to file. Her job was supposed to be the most important thing in her life right now, but somehow, befriending the faun and healing whatever had broken in their conversation superseded that.

Why?

What was it about Cricket that had thrown her to the forefront of Avery's every waking thought? When she played piano, she thought of Cricket in the wood, darting from tree to tree with her raspy, playful laugh. When she taught her guitar lesson, she thought of Cricket's fingers and those metal caps, wondering if the F chord would even present a challenge to the faun.

And now, despite the clamor of the cafeteria, all of her attention was on Cricket limping away. Muscles in those lean legs twitched beneath the bike shorts and flexed in her calves. It was an effort to tear her gaze away, but she managed, dropping it down to the half-eaten Sloppy Joe on her plate. Her stomach turned with the realization that eating meat in front of an inhuman that was part *deer* was probably insensitive. That Cricket wasn't eating salads and grains bowls to make a point, but rather because *that was what she ate.*

Gosh. Is that why she was always so terse with Avery? Because she couldn't stand the sight of a human eating—*Don't think it*—flesh?

"Oh, ew." She pushed her plate away.

Although, it's more muscle than flesh. Right? Wouldn't flesh denote eating one's own kind? OH.

Her stomach clenched, bile rising in her throat. Did Cricket think she'd been eating ground *venison?*

Avery rose and grabbed her tray, heading to the trashcans to throw away the rest of her Sloppy Joe. Glancing around the dining hall, she caught Director Murray's eye. She shot Avery a tight smile and stood, gesturing for her to follow into the kitchen.

Cooky glanced over as they entered, jerking their snout up and wiggling their whiskers in greeting. Pots and pans clanged, held aloft and moved around the counters and stovetop by a multitude of tails. Avery schooled her face. She had come to terms with the fact that a rat the size of a WWE wrestler cooked their meals. It was one of a number of ... interesting things she had seen in Elkwater Music Camp, but she still had to fight against the inborn impulse to gag.

"Had an interesting phone call earlier." Director Murray crossed her arms and dropped a hip against the counter. "From a man named Desmond at Lunar out of Atlanta."

Avery startled, unsure if she had heard correctly. "Lunar?"

"The firm your father is working with." Mac nodded, eyes gleaming as a smile spread across her face. "Lunar Asset Management. They want to help the camp find investors. He said something about his colleague being impressed with the grounds and staff."

"Are you sure—"

"I don't know what you said during your lunch, but, *thank you*." Director Murray lurched forward, wrapping Avery in a tight hug. "This is exactly what we need. If they can help us find investors, I can grow the camp, we can welcome more students and—" She cut herself off, releasing Avery to hit her with a misty-eyed smile. "Thank you, Avery. I couldn't do this without you."

"Director Murray, are you sure about this?"

"Please, Avery. It's *Mac*." She squeezed Avery's shoulders and whirled around, mumbling as she strolled out to the dining hall. "Oh, there's so much to do. They want to tour the camp; I'll have to call my dad and get his advice. What kind of wine do you serve investors?"

Avery pressed a hand to her cheek, wincing at the heat flushing her face. She should be excited for Director Murray and the camp—this was what the woman had been working toward. It was what the camp needed, so why did she have this creeping sense of dread?

"If you're gonna take up space in my kitchen, make yourself useful." Cooky snapped her leg with a tail and jerked their face toward the sink. "Ain't gonna do themselves."

"Yes." Avery rushed to the sink. "Of course."

She lost herself to the task, scrubbing through stack after stack of trays, plates, and cups, and ducked out a side door when the last of the campers left for their cabins. Not ready to sit in her cabin with nothing but her thoughts, she paced the length of the dining hall and weighed her options. She could go to the counselor's office, where her co-workers would be chatting and playing video games, but as much as she didn't want to be alone, she didn't have the energy to try and fit in. There was always filing to do, but that would put her in Director Murray's cabin with Cricket. As enticing as that may be, Avery wasn't a glutton for punishment.

That left the practice rooms. Avery needed to lock up anyway, so she might as well clear her head by getting lost in the music before she did. She flexed her fingers, her mood already lifting at the thought of her favorite room, with its upright Steinway and a window with a view of the woods. Eager to get there, she cut along the side of the dining hall and onto one of the deer trails the campers used as shortcuts.

This late in the day, the instructional side of the camp was abandoned in favor of cabins and the shadows beneath the bleachers. Clouds stretched across the sky, blocking the moon, and she paused, letting her eyes adjust to the deeper darkness before pressing on.

Avery relished the quiet; only the sound of her footfalls and the rustling of a breeze through the trees were audible and the world was peaceful in the way only the mountains could be. She grabbed her denim skirt and hitched it up to step over a narrow creek, hesitating with one foot in the air as a loud *snap* echoed through the wood.

Her head swiveled to the trees, her grandmother's words running through her mind at a frantic pace.

If you hear something in the woods, no, you didn't. If you see something in the woods, no, you didn't.

She should look away and keep walking. Keep her head down, make herself small, play dead. But she couldn't look away, she couldn't move, because she saw something in the woods and knew, without a sliver of a doubt, that it saw her as well.

"H-hello?"

The breeze died away, tree tops falling still as clouds drifted away from the moon, casting the backside of the camp in pale blue light. Shadows crawled from the wood, and Avery exhaled.

"You're being stupid," she berated herself. "It was just a twig snapping." Still, her neck prickled, and she peered into the woods, heart juddering to a halt when one of the shadows moved.

A broad figure stepped between the trees, moonlight pouring over a bone-white skull. Avery did not wait to see the rest of whatever the creature was. Hitching her skirt high, she leapt over the creek and ran.

Pounding footsteps followed, shaking the earth. Avery pressed her speed, dropping her skirt to swing her arms and lengthen her stride. The denim tangled in her legs, keeping her from sprinting outright. The trail she followed ran along the length of the orchestra room, and the next gap between the buildings was easily twenty yards away. Even without a skirt on, Avery had never been the fastest runner, but she'd mastered that sixty-foot sprint during her years as a power hitter.

She called on all that muscle memory now, gritting her teeth and aiming for the edge of the building and the breezeway. Sweat poured down her back, half from the hot summer night, half from fear as a dank musk accosted her nose. Musk and something sharp. Minty. She gagged, her eyes burning and a cry strangling in her throat.

There was a rush of hot wind, wet panting in her ear, and the creature snagged her skirt, wrenching Avery back. She landed on her stomach, shrieking and scrabbling at the ground. She kicked her legs, and a shoe connected with something hard and immovable.

"Please," she sobbed, kicking her leg again, grazing what she thought might be a leg. "Let me go." And again, higher and—her shoe connected with something soft. Squishy. The creature let out a noise that was somewhere between a howl and a roar, claws ripping free from her skirt and grazing the inside of her calf. Pain shot up her leg, fueling the adrenaline already coursing through her body. She scrambled away, gaining her feet and sprinting forward. The tear its claws had left in her skirt allowed Avery to open her stride, and she bolted, aiming for the dim lights of the practice rooms and a campfire circle gleaming ahead. There would be people and inhumans. There would be help. There would be—

An arm shot out of the breezeway, snagging Avery's elbow and hauling her between two buildings. Splinters scraped her shoulders, and before she could process what had happened, her face was pressed into a warm body, thin cotton the only thing separating her from a rapidly beating heart.

"Keep quiet," a raspy voice whispered. A hand palmed the back of her head, and an arm snaked around her back, pressing Avery hip-to-hip with her savior. She trembled wildly, burying her face into a slight chest. Something leathery and moist nuzzled her ear, soft lips brushing the shell as they spoke again. "Slow breaths, or not at all, if you can manage."

"Cricket," she whimpered, and the faun held her tighter, shushing in her ear. A shiver joined her tremble, and tears streamed down her cheeks.

A wicked snarl rumbled down the tight breezeway, and she cried out against Cricket's chest. It was close; the creature was so close, and they were barely hidden in the shadows. If it swept its arm, it would snag her skirt. It would drag her away from Cricket and into the woods. It would be her bones the faun found. Her blood staining the earth.

Her arms tightened around the faun, as if she could bind their bones together to keep that thing from dragging her away. To her surprise, Cricket tightened her arms right back, nuzzling her damp nose against Avery's temple and running a velvet-soft thumb along her cheekbone as the creature huffed and scraped claws along the wall.

Her touch was hypnotic. Lulling the sting from the wound on her leg and arousing every one of her senses, drawing every bit of Avery's attention to that gentle sweep and the heart beating under her ear. To the strength in Cricket's arms at such odds with the faun's slight frame.

"I think it's gone," she whispered after a long moment, her thumb never ceasing its tender sweep. Avery tensed, waiting for the inevitable moment Cricket realized what she was doing and who she was holding. But the moment stretched, and still, she kept Avery in her arms.

"What was it?"

"Whatever chased me over the ridge."

Avery raised her head. The motion sent Cricket's hand to cup the base of her neck. Velvet-soft fingertips dusted her throat, and the wide pools of Cricket's eyes were trained on her. "I saw its face," she whispered. "No antlers."

"No antlers." She tilted her head forward, bringing them closer. The erect stand of her ears softened, the tips swiveling toward Avery. "I thought it had you. Are you hurt?"

"My skirt is ruined."

"Oh no," Cricket deadpanned.

"And it nicked my calf."

"Oak and ivy, Avery." Cricket finally blinked, releasing her from that intoxicating stare. She tipped their foreheads together, and blond curls fell forward, tickling Avery's cheekbones and closing them off from the rest of the world. "I heard it in the woods, but it didn't chase me. It seemed like it was waiting for something."

Each word bloomed against her lips, a warmth sent from Cricket to fill her from top to toe. It settled in her belly and crawled up her front, and if Cricket didn't let go, if she didn't step away, Avery feared she'd give the faun a whole new reason to hate her.

But this doesn't exactly feel like hate.

"Waiting for what?" she managed.

"I don't know." Cricket raised her head to again stare at Avery. The soft grip on her throat tightened just so. A possessive touch keeping Avery right where she stood. "It only moved when you came out, coming to the edge of the woods to watch you pace and—" Avery huffed. "What?"

Avery ducked her head, biting her lip and shaking her head. "Nothing."

"No, not nothing, what?"

"You were also watching me pace." She should be embarrassed. She ought to be burning up and horrified that Cricket had witnessed her minor breakdown outside the dining hall, but it was hard to be those things when she was so distracted by how the faun's body leaned into hers, relaxing into Avery's softer curves.

Cricket muttered something under her breath that sounded suspiciously like, "Shut up," then cleared her throat. "I darted ahead when it started chasing you. I thought I could hide, and when it ran by, I'd ... I don't know. Jump on it?"

This time, Avery giggled outright, leaning back to take in all of Cricket's face. "You hid here to save me from that thing?"

"Not all of us are monsters, Avery," Cricket leveled, her expression going serious. "Some of us are—"

Whatever they were, the world would never know because Avery popped up onto her toes and kissed her.

13

— · —

CRICKET

Soft.

Everything about Avery was soft, and Cricket didn't know what to do with her hands. Didn't really know what was happening other than Avery was soft, her lips were warm, and she was in Cricket's arms, kissing her.

Kissing *her*.

Oak and ivy.

She spread her fingers wide, working them into Avery's hair, and she sighed against her mouth, lips parting. Cricket took it for the invitation she thought it might be.

The girl had kissed *her*, after all. How else was she supposed to translate this?

She flicked her tongue against Avery's lips, relishing her tiny gasp before slipping in and fighting against a groan. The salt from her dinner, the subtle strawberry sweetness of her lip balm. Gods, it was too much.

She didn't think; she didn't *want* to because if she thought for even a second, she knew the only coherent takeaway would be how badly she wanted this.

She cupped Avery's cheek instead, marveling at the heat beneath her palm as she slid her other hand up and under her shirt. A low groan rumbled in her throat at the soft, plush feel of Avery's body. Her waist was warm, her back heated, her mouth a blaze as if the human's entire body had flushed as bright as her hair. And her tongue, Gods, her tongue. Slick and strong, narrow and slippery, unlike any of the faun Cricket had tasted before.

Sweet and salt, the feel of Avery's tongue against hers, the tiny whimper that escaped as Cricket's fingers brushed up the smooth skin on her waist and ribs. It was addictive, and she knew with a taste that she would never get enough.

A soft touch on her waist had muscles dancing in Cricket's torso. It was testing, almost wondering, and Cricket leaned into Avery's hand, pressing their hips harder together in a silent plea. *Touch me, feel more, pull me to you. Let me know you want this as badly as I do.*

She dragged fingers down Avery's throat and danced them along the neckline of her shirt. The human arched into that touch, the swell of her breast meeting Cricket's fingers and she pulled away, panting and half mad.

"Avery—"

"Don't read too much into this," she murmured. Her hands slid into Cricket's muscle tank, fingers pressing into the soft down at her waist. Avery licked her lips, eyes darting over Cricket's face, down to her throat, and she fought the urge to cover her pulse. "Thank you"—that pale gaze returned to her face, searching Cricket, but all she saw were Avery's kiss-swollen lips—"for waiting and helping me. And for this, I guess."

"You guess?"

Her eyes dropped to Cricket's mouth, a subtle sadness creeping in. "I wanted to know what it was like."

Cricket tensed, her arousal dwindling from blazing to tepid. "Kissing a girl or kissing a faun?"

A loaded silence followed as Avery dragged her gaze up her face. The grip she held at her waist loosened, Avery's hips pulled away, and she whispered, "Kissing you."

"Oak and ivy," Cricket cursed and swept in. Whatever restraint she'd held before was long gone. A distant mirage, a waft of smoke, a faint memory. She pressed Avery against the wall, sinking into her curves and sweeping into her mouth without hesitation. Her hands had a mind of their own, flying up to Avery's cheeks, curving around her waist, gripping her hips. They were everywhere at once and never where she wanted them to be. There was too much cotton between them; she wanted to feel all of that softness pressed against her every sharp angle. Wanted Avery's hair undone and tumbling down her shoulders, and Avery—*oh, Gods*—it seemed like Avery wanted the same.

She hooked a leg around Cricket's calf. Cricket's hand came down on her hip. She drove her fingers into Cricket's hair. Cricket left a trail of kisses on her jaw and nibbled her ear, adjusting their stance to work a leg between Avery's. A delightful gasp left her as Avery's fingers knotted in her hair, and the flash of pain brought an awareness of their panting breaths and the heady scent of arousal building in the humid air.

She slid her hand down Avery's plush hip, squeezing before trailing fingers along her thick thigh. A quick glance down had Cricket smiling before she kissed her again. The creature had indeed ruined Avery's skirt, ripping a long tear in the denim. She hoisted her leg higher, slipping a hand underneath the fabric to knead Avery's thigh while rocking into her, eyes drifting closed at the ensuing groan.

"Cricket—"

"Avery." She caught her lobe in her teeth, tugging as she applied pressure with her leg. Avery's hips twitched, seeking more friction, more pressure, and she bit off a moan. Her hands danced down Cricket's back to her rear, stopping just shy of groping her outright.

"I don't know what to do." Her admission was breathless, her body begging for more even while she held Cricket at bay with those words.

"You've never done this before?"

"Not with a ... um ..." Avery ducked her head, but her blush of embarrassment blazed against Cricket's hands. She bit her lower lip to keep from grinning outright, rocking into Avery until the hands at her rear gripped tight, keeping Cricket's leg right where it was.

She skated her palm up Avery's side, fingertips skimming the underswell of her breast. Again, Avery arched into her touch, eyes drifting closed as her head dropped back against the wall.

"How do I ... ?" she panted.

"Ears."

Avery hummed, a satisfied, proud sound, like Cricket had just confirmed a suspicion. And then her eyes flew wide. "Oh my gosh, I touched your ears."

"You didn't know."

"But *still*."

"It's fine," Cricket chuckled. Gods, this human was adorable.

"It's not *fine*, I touched your ears, and they're ... they're ..."

"Erogenous?" Cricket pulled her head back, wishing there was more light so she could watch the lovely crawl of a blush over Avery's cheeks. Instead, she cupped her cheek, grinning at the rising warmth. "When you touch my ears like you did the other night ..." She trailed the tips of her fingers along Avery's cheek and her jaw, drawing a feather-light line down her throat. Her chest rose and fell at the touch, her breasts too tempting to ignore. She swept a line across the top of her bra, eyes flicking up to find Avery's stare intent on her. Watching Cricket as she teased and provoked. At the slightest, almost imperceptible nod, Cricket cupped her breast, thumb poised. "... it feels like this."

She brushed her thumb across Avery's nipple, and the girl nearly flew from the wall, pressing into Cricket's hand. Her lips parted on a tiny little whimper, and Cricket drank up the response, leaning in to taste the next sound that escaped. And the next. Avery opened for her, greedily kissing Cricket as her hips rocked against her leg, encouraging the faun to do *more*.

She dropped her hand away, murmuring, "Don't worry," against Avery's mouth before slipping both under her shirt, cupping her breasts, and groaning at the soft heft. She marveled at how they filled her palm, supple flesh spilling from her over-long fingers. Rolling the bud of each nipple between her thumbs and forefingers, Cricket whispered, "Is this alright?"

"Yes, oh ... oh my, yes," Avery gasped. Her voice dropped in tone, an unfamiliar husk entering the words that spurned Cricket on. She ducked her head, taking a nipple—cotton shirt, bra, and all—into her mouth and sucking. Avery cried out, a hand flying to the back of Cricket's head. Fingers tugged at her curls, nails scaled her scalp, and then, finally, she found her ears. "Like that, Cricket, oh my ..."

Her knuckles ran the length of Cricket's ear, ruffling the down in the opposite direction and sending a warble of heat straight down Cricket's spine. She moaned, plunging her tongue into Avery's mouth. Rolling a nipple between her fingers, she relished the soft skin under her palm, traveling her hand lower. She cupped Avery's buttock, gripped her thigh, and teased the expanse of skin revealed by the tear in her skirt.

"And this?" She asked, fingers slipping under her leg.

"Yes." Avery's grip tightened. She raised herself, allowing just enough room between Cricket's thigh and her center. Gods, the initiative on this human.

Cricket bit back a smile, nuzzling into Avery's neck as she teased the seam of her underwear. "And ... this?"

"I thought of you." Her words were breathless, her hands steady as she stroked both ears, sending molten heat into Cricket's loins. "The last time I touched myself."

"Oak and ivy." She licked a bold line up Avery's throat. Gods, she needed more, needed nails scraping the soft down, needed Avery to massage the tips and stroke. Needed her out of the odd skirts and baggy shirts. Needed to see this soft, luscious body laid out in the grass to be explored.

"Fuck it." Cricket wrenched Avery's shirt up and away, still teasing her through her panties. She buried her face in the soft mounds of her breasts and inhaled the scent of her—sweat and salt, floral soap and tropical-sweet sunscreen, and good *Gods* it was maddening. She tugged the cup of her bra away, flicking her tongue over a rock-hard nipple. Avery writhed, panting and whimpering, her hips rocking with voracious need.

"Please," she begged. "Cricket, please."

She switched to the other breast, the human now bared to the moonlight, her skin painted a lovely blue, nipples hard and tempting. "Gods, look at you."

"Cricket." Nails scoured the length of her ears, and she whimpered a bleat, pure desire pooling in her hips. But Avery wasn't done—she kneaded the tips like a Gods-damned pro, sending ripple after ripple of pleasure coursing through Cricket's body. Her good leg began to tremble, the throbbing at her center becoming unbearable. She worked her fingers beneath Avery's panties, eyes rolling back at the heat and the wetness of arousal that met her touch. She parted damp flesh, wetting her finger before circling her clit.

"When you thought of me," she whispered, her voice raspier and lower than she'd ever heard it, "was I doing this?"

"Yes," Avery panted. Another sweep, another circle.

"And what else?"

"I can't—" Her head thudded against the side of the building. "It's not—"

"What else was I doing, Avery." She drew a lazy circle around her clit, and again, just off center. "Tell me what you want."

"I want ..."

"Mmhmm." Cricket hummed into her breastbone, cradling her pussy, the palm of her hand applying gentle pressure. "What do you want?"

"Your fingers," she rushed out, eyes clenched tight.

"Doing what?" She snagged a nipple between her teeth, pinching lightly and flicking the tip with her tongue. "I'll do whatever you want, Avery, whatever you need, but you have to tell me what you—"

"Inside me." Those strong fingers worked Cricket's ears the way they danced over the keyboard, playing a tune that had the faun wound tighter than a guitar string. Her control slipped, and she cursed, burying her face in breasts and her finger in Avery.

Slick heat met her touch. Heat and tight, smooth walls. She was struck momentarily dumb at how similar this all was. For all her bravado, Cricket had never been with a human girl, but Gods, it was all the same: silken heat, smooth walls, and soft, fleshy bits begging to be touched and licked.

One of Avery's hands dropped away from her ears, gripping her shoulder, her arm. She rocked into her hold, whimpers becoming higher and tighter as Cricket crooked her finger, scoring against a place within the human that her tensing and shivering at once. The grip on her arm released, light touches fluttered along Cricket's side, and then Avery cupped her breast, thumb working the nipple through the paper-thin fabric of her bandeau.

A zing of pleasure tingled through Cricket, and the heat in her belly boiled over. She popped off of Avery's breast to catch her breath, and the human surprised her again—catching her mouth in a frantic, hungry kiss. She swept her tongue deep, groaning into Cricket's mouth before snagging her lower lip and tugging.

The throbbing in her pussy bordered on painful. She could barely keep focused, could barely remember to keep working her fingers as Avery rode her hand, body twitching and tightening beneath her. She was close; she had to be close because Cricket was about to combust. She'd be useless to do anything but sleep once she tipped over, Gods, from her ears and a breast alone.

"More," Avery groaned, rolling her hips in a circular motion. "I need more of you."

"Yes, ma'am." She added a second finger, slowing her movements to let Avery adjust to the feel. She exhaled, eyes finally meeting Cricket's, and nodded. At the first crook, Avery sighed, her walls clenching around Cricket's fingers. "Gods, you feel incredible."

"So do you," she murmured. Her hand trailed down Cricket's front, and she caught a devious flash in her expression before Avery splayed her fingers, catching each of Cricket's nipples on the way down. Her pussy clenched, that quick, teasing touch shooting Cricket straight to the edge.

"Avery!"

"You like that?" One hand on her ear, the other plucking, and pinching, rolling nubs between her fingers as she rocked on Cricket's hand.

"Oak and ivy, you're—this is—" She could hardly get the words out, much less form a coherent thought. Her belly flipped, core tightening as her body was played by a fucking master. When had the tables turned? Where had this girl, this *human* learned how to do this?

Cricket dropped her head, no longer able to focus on anything but the sensation riddling her body. Through some miracle, she managed to keep working Avery, her fingers following each twitch and roll of her hips. She was reduced to a pet, following Avery's lead and needing only to bring her pleasure.

That thought, the awareness it brought, had Cricket pressing her palm harder against her clit, scissoring her fingers until those walls clenched tighter and tighter. Until Avery's body tensed, her hands faltering in their movements.

"Let go, sweet girl," Cricket damn near begged, hitching her arm and beckoning with both fingers against that sweet, decadent spot she'd found.

Avery hollered, her body went rigid, and a gush of wetness filled Cricket's palm as she exhaled. She stroked her through her orgasm, reveling in every quake and tremble. Frantic kisses were laid on her throat and shoulders, and two shaking hands grasped her ears, milking the tips until Cricket could no longer hold back the tide.

Stars burst in her eyes, and she slammed a hand against the wall to keep from collapsing on Avery, bleating her pleasure as wave after wave coursed from her ears and her nipples down into her throbbing pussy.

It wasn't enough, Gods, oak, and ivy; it wasn't anywhere near enough. Her strength gave away, and she melted against Avery, pressing her into the wall. She clung to Cricket in turn, panting and gasping until her breathing steadied. She kissed Cricket's cheek, brushed curls away from her ear, and whispered, "That was better than I imagined."

14

—·—

AVERY

"You didn't have to walk me back." Avery tightened her arm around Cricket's waist, the pair leaning on each other to limp to her cabin. Once the adrenaline had left her body, and she'd come down from Cricket's mind-blowing fingers, her leg had begun to sting. Blood from the scratch was sticky against her calf, and her sock squelched with every step.

"Are you kidding?" Cricket shot her a look. "You were just chased by a Gods-know-what. Of course, I'm not letting you walk home alone."

"But then you'll have to walk all the way back to Director Murray's cabin," she argued. "Alone."

"I grew up in these woods, Avery." Though her tone was dry, Avery loved how the faun almost swallowed her name. Her voice dropped low, and a husk entered the rasp as though she savored the taste. The sound of it was sensual and suggestive, bringing heat to Avery's cheeks.

Cricket slowed their walk, glancing at Avery with an indecipherable expression.

"What?"

"It's so easy to make you blush," she answered, smiling so broadly the tiny slit in her upper lip split, her flat teeth on display. Facing Avery, she cupped the back of her neck. "Like a game." Her gaze heated, eyes dropping to Avery's mouth. "I like playing."

"I—" Her skin went from flushed to burning. Thoughts began and frittered away; words wouldn't form. All she could focus on was the soft brush of Cricket's thumb along her jaw. How close they stood. Just as close as they had when she—

This is insane.

It was one thing to touch herself to thoughts of the faun but another thing entirely to act on those whims where anyone could have seen them. She was the assistant director, for goodness' sake. What was she doing messing around with a ... a *monster*.

And just as quickly as that nasty thought formed, her brain and body rejected the idea. *Yes*, Cricket was a monster. She was inhuman. She was real and warm and kind and she challenged Avery, pushing her beliefs and nudging her in the direction she was too afraid to travel on her own.

And she'd made her *feel*.

Anger, frustration, worry, arousal.

She flinched back as all of those thoughts pounded that initial bias to a fast, thorough death.

"It's alright." Cricket's hand fell away. She stepped back, putting space between them.

"No, wait, I—"

"You were scared, I get it." She limped away, hands fisted at her sides. "High emotional state, or whatever. I'm still walking you home."

Avery followed for a few steps, her mind churning through explanation after explanation. The simplest was best, of course, but did anyone ever believe, "It's not you, it's me?" And then she realized she was following the faun to her cabin, not leading, and the horror at her own flinch faded beneath curiosity. "How do you know which cabin is mine?"

"You wake up early." She shrugged. "I saw you leaving the other day."

Oh, thank goodness—an opening.

"So you have been spying on me." She kept her tone light and teasing, wanting to reclaim that soft moment before she flinched for all the wrong reasons. Cricket kept silent, so she tried again. "What were you doing awake?"

"Faun are crepuscular," she answered, gripping the stair rail to Avery's cabin.

"That's the dawn and dusk thing, right?" she asked. Sanoya had mentioned it weeks ago, in one of the rare instances she was in their shared cabin. Avery had been complaining about a student falling asleep in her mid-morning composition class, and the Life Sciences Instructor had rattled off the word.

"You cannot expect a kitsune to stay awake in a class that starts at ten thirty," Sanoya explained. "They are crepuscular, like my companion. You have never seen a hidebehind out and about in full daylight, have you?"

Avery hadn't had the heart to tell Sanoya she'd never seen a hidebehind at all, much less knew what one was. Still, the lesson had stuck: crepuscular animals and inhumans were active in the twilight hours.

"No wonder you're always in a bad mood when I see you," she teased again. Cricket scrunched her nose, ears twitching in annoyance.

"What is that supposed to mean?"

"It means you are cranky and moody, and now I know why," she hummed, striding up the steps and to the door. Floorboards creaked at her back as she sauntered inside, the faun following close behind. The cabin was empty, Sanoya's half neat, tidy, and untouched. Avery sat on her bed, sighing as she took the weight off her injured leg. Cricket came to a standstill before her, settling her weight on one leg, lean arms crossed over her front.

Avery tugged off her shoe and peeled the blood-stained sock from her foot, frowning at it before leaning over the edge of the bed to toss it into the trashcan. Cricket watched her do so, her arms slowly dropping to her sides. She glanced around the room, spotting the white crate with a red cross Avery kept on a table near the door. Without being asked, she limped over, grabbed the first aid kit, and set it on the bed next to Avery.

"Thank you."

"I'm not cranky," Cricket snapped in reply.

"See? That right there. You go from friendly"—Avery's belly flipped at the thought of just *how* friendly—"to off-putting with the flip of a switch. And I only see you at meal times, when you've only just woken up or are about to go to sleep. Cranky."

"You make me sound like a child."

"You said it, I didn't."

Cricket's ears flicked, bouncing the curls that kept them hidden. She exhaled loudly through her nose, rolled her eyes, and dropped to the floor. Though the motion was smooth, it was startling. One moment, the faun was towering over Avery, and then her knees—or were they ankles?—bent backward, and she collapsed to a long-legged sit on the wooden planks. Bending at the waist, she hauled the first aid kit off the bed and flipped the locks.

"I'm not a child," she said. "Haven't been for a long while." The topmost tray was set on the floor, her ears shook her curls, her nose twitched, and she selected a bottle of saline and a bottle of peroxide, talking as she pulled off her muscle tank and held it under Avery's calf. "I've been in the woods since I was five. I think. Time is different here, but my mom always says I was five summers when we fell through."

"That must have been frightening," Avery said. It took every bit of concentration to keep her eyes on Cricket's face and not let them drop to the slight swell of her breasts hidden by a bandeau bra. Or the nipples lining the front of her torso, the nubs just visible through the thin dusting of fur. Cricket frowned, opened the bottle of saline, and poured it over the cut on Avery's calf.

"I'm not scared."

"I didn't say you were." Cricket kept silent, intent on cleaning Avery's wound with the cotton balls. Once done, she glanced around the cabin at a loss. "Under the bed." Avery wiggled her toes in an attempt at a point. "There's a Tupperware of towels."

"Ah." She grabbed the bin and a towel and gently, carefully patted Avery's leg dry. Next, she grabbed the hydrogen peroxide, glancing from her work to warn, "This will sting."

And it did. Avery hissed, gripping the edge of the mattress as white foam bubbled up. Cricket cleaned it away with more saline, patted her leg dry with another towel, and grabbed gauze from the kit, applying it over the wound before wrapping it with a bandage.

Avery watched it all with a sense of awe. The care of the faun, the gentleness of her touch. She bit the corner of her lower lip, wide eyes narrowed in concentration, and when she was done, Cricket set Avery's leg down, resting the heel on her knee. Again, Avery wiggled her toes. "We match, now."

"What?" Cricket glanced up, blinking at Avery as if coming out of a daze. "Oh, right. Sorry. I was … lost in thought."

"About what?"

"The place before." She cupped Avery's heel, fingers resting lightly on the outside of her foot. "I don't even remember it. Not really. It's more like images? Dawn in the woods, a bonfire, sunlight through the trees, my mom and dad dancing. They say we used to have magic."

"Magic?"

Cricket nodded, her expression turning wistful. "Healing magic in our music and our hands, but we lost it when we fell through."

"That's awful."

Another shrug. "I suppose. I mean, we kept some of it." She gestured to her own ankle. "We heal pretty fast, just can't help other people or inhumans. But, like I said, I don't really remember. My cousin probably does. They were fifteen when it happened. Used to say they had just begun to feel the magic, and the closest they've ever come to feeling it here was when they heard this place for the first time. 'The music of the wood.'"

She shrugged it off as if it were nothing, but Avery could hear it in her voice—the loss of something she'd never known and never would. How did you account for that? How did you live day to day with the injustice of knowing something so wonderful, like actual, honest-to-goodness *magic,* was taken from you and *not* sink into the righteous anger that must be frothing just beneath the surface?

So much of Cricket made sense now. The snappish tone, how quick she was to anger, to push people away and assume the worst. And why wouldn't she? She'd had something wonderful stolen from her through no fault of her own, and she had no way of getting it back.

"I never said you were scared," Avery whispered, unable to give strength to the words as she repeated them. "I said that it must have been frightening. I've lived in the same place my whole life. I commuted to college from home. This is the first time I've ever lived apart from my family, and it's *terrifying*."

Cricket's fingers tightened around her heel, the wide gaze slowly rising to meet her eyes. The warm glow of a table lamp reflected in those eyes like a candle flickering in the dark, and Avery couldn't escape the feeling that if she just leaned closer, she would fall right into those deep, dark pools.

"And I'm an adult or something. I can't imagine how hard it was to be ripped from your home and dropped into a strange place as a kid."

"It was," Cricket murmured, blinking in surprise as if she hadn't expected to speak. Her tongue darted out, moistening her lower lip, and she dropped her hand away. The walls came up in an instant, faster than Avery could process. "Why do you care?"

"We're sharing this earth," she tried to explain, but how could she? Her fascination with inhumans was over a decade old. Her desire to be among them, befriend them, *know* them, almost as old as the time they had spent on this earth. Now, she had this chance, this one glorious summer, and no matter what she tried, it was always the wrong choice, the wrong words, the wrong action. "I just want to be a good neighbor."

"Well." Cricket hoisted herself to her feet, standing with her injured hoof hitched. "When I need a cup of sugar, I know where to go."

"Crick—"

"Good night, Avery."

"Cricket, please."

"I said good ni—" A howl shattered the night, tearing through the trees and bouncing off the hills. Cricket's ears shot straight, her head twitching in the direction of the sound, and she froze. Not a flinch, not a shiver, not a blink. The next howl came from further away. Still, it had Avery crossing the cabin, grabbing the faun's arm, and drawing circles on her bicep with her thumb.

"It's alright." She tugged gently, frowning when Cricket didn't budge, her taut figure giving new meaning to the term *statue still*. "Cricket, come away from the door. It's alright. We're inside, see?" She reached across the faun and turned the lock. "Locked in, the windows are latched. Nothing can get in." Cupping her elbow, Avery again tried to guide her to the bed. "Please, stay. I don't want you out there while that thing is anywhere near the camp."

Finally, she cupped the faun's cheek. "Please?"

Cricket's wide-eyed stare twitched down to Avery's face. She blinked, her shoulders relaxing, and then nodded. "Alright."

15

CRICKET

The sky was barely greying toward dawn when Cricket left. It was cowardly, sure, but what the hells else was she supposed to do?

She should have known better. Should have known Avery would backpedal the minute she got what she wanted out of her. *Gods*, she even offered an out, but Cricket was too stupid to take it.

You didn't have to walk me back.

It would have been so easy to say good night and walk away at that, but *no*. Cricket had to go and flirt and touch her face and want *more* when it was so obvious all Avery wanted was distance. It was so Gods-damned unfair. Why couldn't she get infatuated with someone who wanted to be with an inhuman, instead of a human who took what she wanted and shut down the moment Cricket showed interest?

And she'd been so receptive! So pliant under Cricket's hands, her pussy so hot and wet, and, *Gods*, the noises she'd made. Each tiny whimper and needy mewl rang through Cricket's ears as she curled into her nest of blankets on the floor. Because, *yes,* she slept on the floor. There was no way she was going to sleep in Avery's bed, even with the girl pouting at her from the pillows.

Adrenaline.

That's all it was. Adrenaline and fear clouding her judgment. A near-death experience sending Avery running into the arms of the closest being, which happened to be Cricket. She didn't want more. She didn't want Cricket. She was just being kind and taking pity on the poor, limping inhuman.

… so why had she looked so hurt when Cricket refused to sleep in her bed?

And why had Cricket even bothered cleaning and bandaging her wound?

"Ugh!" She threw her hands up, stomp-limping in an angry circle. The lack of answers was more frustrating than the human. She should have known better, should have known Avery was playing with her. She seemed so innocent half the time, asking her weird questions like she'd never been around an inhuman before.

This is the first time I've lived apart from my family.

Alright, so maybe … maybe she hadn't been around inhumans before this. Cricket leaned against the fence in Mac's backyard, thinking back to the guitar lesson she'd witnessed and how abysmally Avery had managed the students, replaying it beneath a different filter. Not one where Avery was prejudiced against inhumans and treated them poorly, but one where Avery simply *did not know* how to manage the situation.

"Huh."

Her ears twitched, a new image of the girl painting itself in her mind. All the questions, the frustrations, the adorable blushes that Cricket could still feel warming her palms. How she'd reached for Cricket's ears that first time and hesitated the second.

"No, she knew." She had to know. It had to be a performance because she'd hummed like she *knew* what touching a faun there would do ... but then again, the girl had ground herself against Cricket's thigh. She had kissed Cricket. *She* had pressed her breast into Cricket's hand. Avery had led every moment of that interlude only to flinch away, and it made no Gods-damned sense. Either she was a damn good liar or was a *really* fast learner because Gods-*damn* she'd given good ear.

She shivered at the memory, running a hand down her front and feeling the hardened nubs of her nipples beneath her cotton shirt. Avery's face floated into view, delightfully flushed and oh-so-pink. The human girl blushed so damn easily, she was probably incapable of lying. Her neck would go bright red if she tried. She'd bite her lower lip and look anywhere but at Cricket. Instead, she'd held her gaze, even after that flinch and again when the howl tore through the woods, those spring-blue eyes silently pleading with her to stay.

"Fuck." She scrubbed her face with her palms and stormed up the steps and into the Director's Cabin, the backdoor slamming closed as she stopped short.

A figure stood beside the coffee pot, their dark, wild curls haloed by the rising sun.

"Ramble?"

The faun spun around, ears stock straight, eyes wide. Their waist was thicker than Cricket remembered, but their face was just the same: warm, oak-bark brown eyes, a smattering of dark fletching across the bridge of their nose that looked like freckles, and a soft, smiling mouth.

"Where," they gasped out, blinking from their stupor. "Where have you *been?*"

Before Cricket could reply, Ramble rushed across the kitchen, gathering her in soft, plush arms. They'd always had thicker haunches and more curves than Cricket, but a decade of living among humans had left its mark on her cousin. Ramble was sturdier than other faun, softer around the edges but no less strong. Cricket sank into the hug, wrapping her arms around Ramble so tight she thought she might never let go.

"Oh my Gods, Crick, we thought you were gone."

"I left." Ramble's hair muffled her words. She nuzzled their neck, seeking comfort in the cousin who had left and found a new home. A *safe* home away from Green Bank.

"I know." They loosened their arms, gripping Cricket's shoulders and leaning back to see her face. "I went to Green

Bank for a visit when the camp road stayed closed. They said you'd left, and with the reports of a monster in the wood ..." Cricket's stomach sank. How had Ramble known? They hadn't been back to Green Bank in ages, not since before the monster began stalking the human homes. And for the last few days, it had been stalking the camp, bedding down in the woods, and—and Cricket slept during the day, and that howl last night had come from a distance. Who knew what the creature got up to during daylight hours? "One of the border patrol came back with your jean jacket. We thought that *thing* had gotten you. There was so much blood, and you—" their voice hitched, and Ramble blinked rapidly. "You love that jacket."

"You gave it to me," she said dumbly.

Ramble tightened their arms around Cricket, giving her a big squeeze before releasing her. "I heard it last night when I got in. Do you know what it is?"

All Cricket could do was shake her head. "I was hoping you'd know or that someone back home had seen it." Ramble's ears drooped, and their lower lip thrust out. "I only caught glimpses the night I got here. It's big, bigger than any faun or wolven I've seen, and it bedded down behind the camp. There was so much blood. But now that you—"

"It *what?*"

"Now that you're here," Cricket pressed, "we can go together and convince the family to move. I saw an assessor near my family's den, which means the land sold, and the Georgia men are *here*."

"There is an actual monster in the woods," Ramble snapped, eyes narrowing. "A monster *hunted* you here, and the Georgia men are what you're worried about?"

"I—"

"Crick." They sighed, sweeping a hand through their curls. "The family isn't going to move; you've got to drop this."

"No, I don't!" she hollered. Ramble's shoulders shot up, along with their ears. They cocked their head toward the ceiling, raising a finger to their lips in warning. "We're getting pushed out," Cricket argued, this time in a whisper. "They keep buying up the land around us, forcing us to live in smaller and smaller glades, and they won't leave!"

"It is not so easy, Crick."

"You did it."

"I got lucky and met someone who understands us," Ramble countered. "And even then, half of my wife's family refused to come to our wedding. The only place we can live without being bothered is at this camp."

"You have a home." Cricket's eyes burned, her throat tightening around her voice like a noose. "And no one is trying to kick you out."

Ramble pressed their lips together, gaze darting over Cricket's face before gathering her into another hug. "I know this has been hard for you. It's been hard for all of us. We lost our home and got dropped in a new one, and you were so young."

The burn in her eyes heightened, tears threatening to fall. She held onto her cousin, fingers gripping tight. If anyone would understand, it was Ramble. Regardless of their belief that the family wouldn't move, they understood the fear Cricket carried over losing Green Bank. The fear of being displaced yet again. Those same fears had her cousin registering for the border patrol at sixteen and moving into Elkwater at twenty.

"Stay as long as you like," Ramble whispered, holding Cricket tighter. "We have enough room, and we can find work for you in the camp. It's not glamorous, but it's steady. Consistent."

"It's your home." Her voice cracked, the tears she'd held at bay for days finally falling as she clung to her cousin. Her family.

"It's my home," Ramble agreed, "and you're my family. You are always welcome here."

⁕ ⁕

Acorn whiskey sloshed against the sides of the bottle, burning down Cricket's throat to warm her belly. That, at least, it could do, as it was utterly useless at erasing Avery's face from her mind.

She'd spent the day in the cabin and, after a quiet breakfast with Mac and Ramble, had escaped to the guest bedroom to read, sleep, and sleep some more until sunset when her body clock demanded she wake and move.

But where could she go? The monster was still in the woods, and Avery was in the camp. Cricket was no coward, but, damn, a faun was allowed to have a day of brooding to themselves, weren't they?

Ramble was no help. They left after breakfast to drive to Green Bank and let the family know that Cricket was alright.

"I won't make you come if you don't want to, but they need to know."

All Cricket could do was nod and poke her granola with a spoon. Topped with berries and walnuts and sprinkled with brown sugar, it was leagues better than anything the dining hall served. One glance at Mac, shoveling spoonfuls into her mouth while gazing adoringly at her spouse, told Cricket she thought so as well.

"I'll take Aksel with me to check out the bedded-down area," Mac said around a mouthful of granola. At Cricket's raised eyebrows, she clarified, "The marching band coach." She swallowed her bite and chased it with orange juice, wiping the remnants away with the back of her hand. "He's wolven, keen eyes and a good sniffer."

"Gods, he found me in, what, two days?" Ramble laughed. "I thought we were being so clever."

"Wait." Cricket jerked upright. "They don't know you're here?"

"The older counselors and teachers know since they've been coming here for years," said Mac. "Sanoya, Aksel, Cooky, but for the most part, Ramble is a bit of a secret."

"Some of the campers have seen me." Ramble hunched into their shoulders, ears and nose twitching with embarrassment. "I just don't … like being seen."

"Took me an entire summer to get them to talk to me." Mac reached across the table and squeezed Ramble's forearm. "Not that we did much talking."

"Oh, my Gods." Ramble's spoon clattered to the table, and they covered their face in their hands. "I was gone for less than a week!"

"And you're leaving again." Mac's smile fell. A muscle in her jaw twitched. "I don't want you driving back at night. Not with that *thing* out there."

"I will stay the night. Cricket's parents will have questions about us." They waved a long-fingered hand at the kitchen, the door, the camp beyond. "About all of this. It is best if I give them the chance to ask questions as they think of them, rather than try to catch everything and answer letters as they come."

Cricket couldn't argue that. It was how the faun worked, especially the older generations. Sounds or scents or a flash in the corner of their eye would draw their attention, sending their brains on a rapid jaunt from one topic to another. They could be singing a song in idle leisure, and the snap of a twig would have them regaling whoever would listen about the white oak they were married beneath. Or dozing in a glade during daylight hours when the errant scent of wildflower would have them asking another faun where they had sourced a specific oil for their leathers.

Ramble's generation wasn't as bad, though they still tended to lose focus and chime in at the weirdest moments with a random thought, but Cricket had definitely benefited from growing up on this earth with its cars and radios. Her focus had been honed against humans and their technology, teaching her how to recognize the crunch of gravel beneath a Honda versus a Ford.

"I will be back tomorrow," Ramble assured their wife. They left after breakfast, knuckling Cricket's head and kissing Mac goodbye. She'd looked away at that. They made it look so easy to have everything Cricket wanted: a job, a partner, a home. So it was little surprise that she'd grabbed a bottle of acorn whiskey from the sideboard and carried it up to her room.

The front door opened sometime after sunset. The guest bedroom had no clock, so Cricket had no idea of what time it actually was. She assumed it was after dinner and before lights out. Campers dawdled along the main path, and campfires burned from scattered pits across the grounds. Light music filtered through her open window: strings, brass, and a lone oboe.

It was lovely, she supposed, but nowhere near as lovely as the assistant director standing in her open door.

Wait.

She blinked, rubbed an eye with her fist, and blinked again. "Yep, still there."

Avery set a container down on the dresser and crossed her arms. A lovely little furrow formed between her brows, and Cricket immediately wanted to smooth it away. "Are you drunk?"

"Maybe." She kicked her legs up and rolled off the side of the bed, landing on her injured leg. Her knee buckled, and she hit the mattress with a *whumpf*. Leaning to the side, she propped an elbow on the bedside table and grinned at Avery. "Why d'you ask?"

"Because you look and sound drunk."

"Welp." She shrugged. A long, tense moment stretched between them, pulling the air in the room as taut as a rubber band before it snapped. "One more thing for you to hate about me."

The snap of her words had Avery visibly recoiling. Cricket dropped her elbow and rolled onto her back, staring at the window to keep from seeing the look of disgust that was surely crawling across Avery's face.

A floorboard creaked, and the door quietly snicked closed. "I didn't know faun drank."

Cricket rolled her head to the side, hitting Avery with a flat look. "A week ago, you didn't know what faun were." She raised an arm, waggled her fingers, and let it fall across her middle. "See how far you've come."

"You don't have to be so mean," Avery snapped. "I've been nothing but nice to you since I found you in the woods."

"You've done nothing but pity me."

"Is that what you think this is?" She smacked the container on the dresser. "You think this is *pity?* Last night, when we—"

"You were scared."

"Of course I was scared!" Her voice slammed against the ceiling and shot right back down, pommeling Cricket's chest. "A monster was chasing me, I thought I was about to die, and then you grabbed me, and all I could think was 'this is my last chance'. How can you possibly think any of this is pity?"

"Fine, not pity, then." She closed her eyes, straightening her head on the pillow. "Fear."

"It's not fear!" Her voice rose even higher, an edge of desperation entering the words. Cricket curled her hands into fists, fighting the urge to bolt across the room, take Avery into her arms, and console her. Anything to stop the tears she could practically smell. Anything to stop this shouting and make her smile and look at her like she had in that breezeway. "It's twenty-two years of Evangelical upbringing, and I'm having a hard time!"

The floorboards creaked, and the edge of the mattress dipped under Avery's weight. The warmth of her body, so close to Cricket, bled into her calf.

"My whole life," she sniffled, "I've been brought up to think and act a certain way. I hate these stupid skirts, I hate having my hair this long, and I hate how everyone stares at me when I pray before a meal. I hate that I'm always on the outside looking in, and I'm stuck there no matter how hard I try to break through. It's never the right word or the right action, and if I don't get into Carnegie my dad is going to pressure me to get married and start popping out babies, and I don't want that." She took a stuttering breath, stifling a sob. "I don't want any of that; I want—"

Cricket opened her eyes, biting her lip at the sight of tears shining on Avery's cheeks. Her face was blotchy and pink in a way that made Cricket's heart feel like it was being squeezed in a fist. She adored that blush, relished the pink crawl over Avery's creamy skin … but not like this.

What was it with this human? How had she gotten so deep beneath Cricket's coat that she was impossible to brush out? She'd come here to get help from Ramble, not get hung up on a human girl who didn't know what she wanted. A human girl who barely knew how to function around inhumans. Who wouldn't let her eat a meal in peace, followed her into the woods, and brought her dinner when she didn't show up in the dining hall. A human girl who—

"And right when I think I'm making progress," she blubbered, "right when I think I've finally figured out how to be a part of this new world instead of watching from the sidelines, I say, or I do something, and I don't know what you *want*."

Cricket's ears shot straight at that admission. She propped herself up on an elbow, frozen in place by the force of Avery's burning blue eyes.

"I don't know what I ever said or did to make you hate me, but I don't hate you, and it's *maddening*." She turned her hands palm up, fingers curled into claws. "I'm sorry I'm not good with inhumans, alright? I'm sorry this is all new to me, and I'm–I'm fu…" She screwed her face into a scowl, pressed fists against her eyes, her entire body tight and trembling as if she were gathering the strength to force out the word. "I'm *fucking* it all up because I don't know what I'm doing or what you want. All I know is that I want *you*, but nothing I do is ever going to convince you that I—"

Cricket bolted upright before she could think better of it. Swinging her knees beneath her as she reached for Avery, cupping her cheek and drawing her forward. Their mouths met in a tight-lipped kiss. Hard and demanding for all its lack of sweetness.

Avery's eyes flew open, red-rimmed and glassy blue, meeting Cricket's steady, determined gaze. Her mouth softened, her brow relaxed, and then her hand clasped Cricket's hip, squeezing and tugging the faun closer, harder against her. And in that squeeze were a thousand little details. A flinch borne from realization and not rejection. A kiss driven by longing rather than fear. A smile in the wood and a whimpered sigh of relief.

All of it compressed into one tiny gesture where Avery tugged Cricket closer. Where Avery flicked her tongue against Cricket's lips, and *Avery* slid her hand up Cricket's ribcage to cup her breast. Avery, who said she had no idea what she was doing when she was doing everything right.

Gods, how had she ever thought this human girl didn't know what she wanted?

Cricket pulled away, cupping Avery's cheeks and sweeping tears away with her thumbs. She leaned into the touch, eyes drifting closed as a soft smile curled her lips. Her thumb drifted idly across Cricket's nipple, and a shiver of delight fluttered into her belly and up to her ears, drawing an admission before she could stop the words.

"You're so brave."

Avery's eyes flew open, her lips parting. Now that the words were out, now that she'd spoken her true opinion of Avery to the room, Cricket didn't want to put them away. Let her hear them; let her know what others thought of her. She needed to hear the truth. *Deserved* to hear it. So she stole a kiss for courage and spoke.

"You came here despite where and how you grew up. You took that chance, and you came here. When we first fell through, Gods, everyone was so afraid. We hid from people and scavenged in the middle of the night. We tried to pass ourselves off as deer and elk to avoid notice. It drove my cousin insane. I was so little when we fell through, but they were old enough to join the border patrol. Old enough to remember what we lost. They couldn't sit still."

"What did they do?" Her words teased across Cricket's mouth, warm and sweet. If she just nudged forward, those lips would be on hers. She would tip over into the desire kindling in her belly with every sweep of Avery's thumb. Back and forth. Back and forth, teasing the hardened nub until Cricket's breathing became heavy. But she needed to get the words out. Needed Avery to *know* how brave she was.

"They came here—" She slid her other hand into Cricket's hair, fingers brushing the base of an ear. Cricket closed her eyes, swallowing a tiny moan. "They met someone and never ... never came back. Gods, Avery."

Nails tickled the curve of her ear, and the maddening human urged her with a whisper. "Keep going."

"I, ooh, oak and ivy." She fisted her hand and lightly punched the bedspread. Heat shot low into her core, a dull throbbing growing as Avery swept her finger over soft, sensitive down. "I always wanted to leave," she panted. Her core tensed. She was aware of her body making tiny movements, rocking and twitching, needing to be closer to Avery. To feel the girl's weight over her. To feel her warmth. What in the hells had this human done to her? "Wanted to come here with them, but I was too–too afraid. I couldn't do it until the Georgia—Gods—the Georgia men."

"The company buying up land?" Avery pinched her nipple and leaned closer, her breath a brand on Cricket's throat.

"Yeah," she gasped. "They want us out. It was the push I needed, but you—you just *did* it."

There. The words were out, and Cricket was about to combust. She gripped Avery's arm, stilling those fingers teasing her ear. Needing the human to hear her, to understand how brave she was. "You left all on your own. You made a plan, you executed the plan, and you're *here* having a full-on conversation with a monster."

16

AVERY

AVERY STRAIGHTENED AND SKIMMED Cricket's face, taking in the wild, crazed look in her eyes. The erect ears and the uneven breaths. The trembling in her fingers as she gripped her arm.

Something like power thrummed in her veins—power and pride that she'd been able to do this to the bold faun. That she'd been able to wring such a confession out of her with touch alone. The realization had her inching closer, bringing her lips to Cricket's throat. The faun tensed as if she feared any further movement would have Avery retreating. The thought made her smile, and she breathed her next words against her throat, right where soft down faded to warm skin.

"You're not a monster."

"Gods." Cricket's hand shot up, cradling the back of her head, those long fingers working into her braid and tugging. Avery grinned outright, twisting and bringing her knee up onto the bed. Her skirt tangled in her legs, pinching her waist. She begrudgingly pulled away, tugging at her skirt and pinning the fabric to the mattress with her knee.

"Take it off," Cricket demanded in that husky, raspy voice. "You hate it so much; take it off."

"I'm not supposed to."

"Fuck 'supposed to'." She reached forward and tugged the skirt low, revealing the black lycra bike shorts Avery wore beneath. A slow smile stretched across Cricket's face. The sweet little split in her upper lip widened as her eyes drank in Avery's thighs. She gripped one, squeezing soft thickness, and licked her lips. "So much better."

A flurry set off in her belly at the hungry way Cricket looked at her. She had forgone the bandeau bra, and her nipples were peaked beneath her shirt—another modified muscle tank in heather gray with a screen-printed image of a naked woman adorned in flowers beneath the words *Lilith Fair*. The urge to take one in her mouth and suck until Cricket cried out was overwhelming.

So she gave in.

Kicking her skirt off the rest of the way, she cupped Cricket's cheeks, hauling her into a kiss. She straddled her lean legs with all the freedom of movement the shorts allowed and eased Cricket onto her back. She went all too willingly, pliant and submissive in Avery's hands. It was exhilarating and dizzying being given this much *control* over someone, and the heady rush of power lent her a confidence she would normally lack.

She'd been with girls, she'd had hook-ups and a secret girl-friend in college, but she'd never had anyone like Cricket. The girls at Messiah had all been raised like Avery. There was a comfort in knowing her partner struggled with the same guilty hang-ups as her: that she was a disappointment. That some-thing was wrong with her, or that this was only a passing phase. But the comfort always turned to apprehension and frustration. She wanted to be with someone who would hold her hand in public. Someone who was confident in themselves and their desires.

Someone like Cricket with her wild curls and wide, deep eyes like wells that Avery felt she could fall into and never hit bottom.

She tasted of vanilla and honey, faint spice, and a slight nut-tiness that had Avery plunging her tongue deeper, sweeping along Cricket's broad, flat tongue as if she could drink the taste. Her hands traveled from her cheeks to her shoulders, down the length of Cricket's lean waist, and up again. She wanted to gather the faun to herself, wanted to hold her entirely, and never let go.

It was impossible to kiss her deep enough, impossible to for-get the sensation of her tongue. It wasn't slick like a human's, but textured, the slight scrape and subtle grip on Avery's tongue setting alight nerve endings she didn't know she had.

Cricket kneaded her thighs as they kissed, her hips rocking, seeking out pressure and friction. Tiny whimpers lodged in her throat, the hardened tips of her nipples teasing Avery through her shirt. She broke their kiss and straightened, ripping her t-shirt over her head and tossing it across the room. Cricket went still, her gaze caught on Avery's chest. Her own nipples were hard, poking the thin cotton of her un-lined bra, and though she wasn't wholly on display, she felt vulnerable beneath the faun's intent stare. She started to cross her arms, and Cricket's hands shot up, seizing her wrists and guiding Avery's hands back to her.

"Don't." She shook her head, blond curls bouncing against the pillows. "Don't hide from me."

"I'm sorry I'm not—"

"You're perfect." She released Avery's wrists and cupped her breasts, sighing happily. "So pink and soft and *Gods*, these breasts."

Cricket arced forward, capturing Avery's nipple in her mouth. Even through the cotton, the feel of her sucking sent a jolt of pleasure through her bones. One hand flew to the back of Cricket's head, while the other drove between them. She yanked the muscle tank aside, baring Cricket's breast and pinching the nipple. The faun gave a muffled shout and snagged Avery with her teeth. The flash of pain and soothing stroke of Cricket's tongue had her head dropping back. She gasped, writhing and panting as Cricket tugged her bra cup down and laved her nipple.

"Oh, Cricket." Heat like melted chocolate puddled in her groin. Her pussy clenched, seeking to satiate the dull, demanding throbbing.

"I've got you," the faun whispered into her flesh, sucking and rolling Avery's nipple between her lips. Soft fingers stroked the swell of her breasts, teasing the band of her bra. A pinch and a pull, and the garment fell away, the heft of her breasts caught in those same hands. Cricket moved to Avery's other nipple, wringing gasp after gasp from her lips until she was panting and rolling her hips, seeking something, *anything*, that would soothe the rising ache.

Cricket crooked her leg, and Avery's gasp became a strangled moan as delicious, delicious friction met her throbbing pussy.

"Oh, oh gosh."

"That's it, sweet girl," Cricket murmured. She circled one soft thumb against a nipple, speaking directly into the other. Her words vibrated through sensitive flesh, clenching Avery's belly. She clung to the faun, nails digging into the soft, tightly grown fur at her shoulders. It was too much, all of this attention, this worship of her breasts too much. She was going to combust, and Cricket gave *too much*.

With a tiny snarl, she pushed the faun away, shoving her hands under the hem of her shirt and dragging it up. Small, pert breasts waited for her, their nipples a dusky brown and tightened to enticing buds. She spread her fingers wide, her pianist's reach allowing thumb and little finger to tease both nubs.

Cricket shivered at that first brush, and a tiny bleat escaped as Avery trailed her fingers further.

Four more nipples lined her torso, two on either side, tight against her toned body but no less sensitive. She'd felt them the night before, a quiet wondering she'd had answered by the little ridges her fingers had explored in the dark. But now, seeing the faun stretched out beneath her in a lighted room, Avery could barely breathe.

She was stunning and wild, other and so achingly familiar. Each tweak and pinch, each gentle circle, had Cricket writhing in pleasure, her chest rising and falling in deep, panting heaves. Narrow hips rose, seeking more touch, more of Avery, and she was all too happy to comply.

Bending low, she snagged the tip of one of an ear in her teeth, a pinch and nibble. Nothing more.

Cricket cried out, hands clasping Avery's rear as though she needed to hold onto something steady to keep from flying off the bed. "Oh, Gods," she panted, her breath hot against Avery's shoulder. "Oak and fucking *ivy*, Aves."

"Aves," she murmured into the sensitive down, running her lips down the length of an ear as she pinched, plucked, and teased those nipples. Cricket's body trembled beneath her, and her hands were everywhere. On Avery's rear, her waist, skimming her soft sides and tugging on the end of her braid.

There was a harder tug, followed by softer ones, and Cricket hummed in a way that sounded victorious. Avery glanced down to ask what she was so proud of when her hair came cascading free from its braid. Cricket sighed, running her fingers through the mass and smiling at Avery.

"Like fox-fur," she whispered, her tone full of awe. She closed her hand into a light fist, wound Avery's hair around her wrist, and pulled. Another flash of pain was subsumed by a hot rush of pleasure as Cricket took her breast into her mouth, resuming the laving and sucking that had driven Avery to the brink before.

The throbbing in her pussy went from almost forgotten to all-consuming, and the only thought in her head was to make Cricket feel as good as *this*. To feel as worshipped and wanted and so full of desire that all else left that pretty, complicated mind of hers.

She drove her hand between them, cupping Cricket and smiling at the damp warmth that met her hand. The faun gasped, her punishing licks stopping long enough to tell Avery she was on the right path to what she desired: Cricket writhing with pleasure from her touch.

She curled her fingers, circling the apex of Cricket's thighs and smiling when the faun let out a needy whine. "May I?"

"Gods, yes." She pressed against Avery's hand, a desperate note entering her breathy voice. "Please, Aves."

"Aves." She dragged her fingernails up the front of the bike shorts and along the hem. "I like that."

"Good, great," Cricket panted. "Aves. Aves, Aves, Aves, sweet girl, baby girl, *please*."

"Need something?" Cocking her head, Avery bit her lower lip and played the coquette. She could get used to this submissive, needy version of Cricket begging for her touch. Slipping her index finger between the band and Cricket's hipbones, she drew a light line and let the elastic snap against her down. Cricket hissed, eyes flashing, but she didn't complain. Instead, she raised her hips to lift her rear off the bed and cocked her head in question.

Avery was no fool. She hooked her fingers in the waistband of the bike shorts and tugged them low, revealing a lightly furred torso, the tawny down darkening to a dusty brown at the juncture of slim, elegant thighs. Cricket kept still, and it was only when the silence stretched between them that Avery glanced up to find the faun watching her closely. Her breaths were tiny and tight, her eyes hooded but intent on Avery, and her hair was a wild, wanton mess spread across the pillows. She looked—

"Beautiful," Avery whispered. "You're so beautiful."

"I—" She silenced whatever Cricket had been about to say with the sweep of a finger through damp fur. A nub met her touch, and Cricket cried out when she circled it. Whatever tension the faun had held, whatever apprehension had had her looking at Avery in such a way, vanished. She melted into the bedspread, tight, tiny mewls forcing their way from her throat. And she looked so painfully lovely.

Avery bent low, taking one pert breast into her mouth as she split Cricket's lips, mind reeling at the heat of the faun. The slick damp that seemed to suck her finger in.

"Like that," Cricket panted, rocking into Avery's finger. "Oak and ivy, like that, Aves."

Crooking her finger, she angled her wrist, seeking and finding that soft, spongy place so similar to her own. She cupped Cricket's ear, stroking the tip as she stroked her pussy. Winding the faun tighter and tighter, suckling, licking, nibbling, stroking.

That lean body trembled beneath her, breathless cries squeezing from her throat. Her thighs clamped around Avery's hand, delicate muscles in that hot, slick channel tightening. There was a wonder in seeing her brought to the very edge. In seeing Cricket coming undone before her very eyes. Gone was the cranky, bossy faun, replaced by the most beautiful creature Avery had ever seen, made powerless by *her* touch. It was addicting, and already, as Cricket gasped and panted her name, muscles twitching, nostrils flaring, Avery wanted *more*.

She slid a second finger in, bringing her palm flush with Cricket's clit, and with the nails of her other hand, she lightly scraped them down the rim of her ear.

The faun jolted, tensed, and came with a bleating cry. She grabbed Avery's arms, half holding her hand where it was, half pushing her away, crying, "Gods, Gods, oak and fucking ivy."

Quiet whimpers followed. Her legs fell away, and her body went utterly liquid, seeping into the mattress as Cricket gazed at the ceiling with unseeing eyes.

"Oak and Ivy, Aves."

"You said that already." She grinned and slid her fingers away, wiping them on her discarded skirt.

Cricket stroked one of Avery's thighs, squirming against the pillows to better address Avery. "Where in the hells did you learn to do that?"

"I played softball." She winked and flipped her hair over her shoulder. "You do the math."

"I literally have no idea what you're talking about." She grabbed Avery's other thigh and squeezed both, gaze dropping to her breasts still on display. In an instant, the languid, sated Cricket was gone. Mischief glinted in her eyes, and the corner of her mouth kicked up. "My turn."

She slipped her hands around and under Avery's legs. Before she could react, Cricket flipped her onto her back and hooked her legs over her shoulders. The ease with which she hoisted Avery and tossed her onto her back sent her mind reeling. For all the submissiveness, for all the power Avery had felt in making Cricket melt beneath her hands, at any moment, she could have turned the tables. Could have pinned Avery to the mattress and taken the lead. But she didn't, giving that space to Avery, who had taken it and run headlong into a borrowed confidence.

The realization was glorious. It was freeing, unfettering the bonds Avery had fought against from the day she realized she wasn't watching *Xena: Warrior Princess* for the fun mythology. She could have this; she could do this. She was with someone like her—no, not just someone.

Cricket.

Cricket, who let Avery lead when she could easily take the reins. Cricket, who melted beneath her fingers just as easily as she tossed Avery onto the bed. Cricket, with Avery's legs on her shoulders, Avery's rear against her chest, and Avery's pussy …

"Oh, Aves," Cricket sighed, closing her eyes and inhaling. "You smell so dang good."

She inhaled again, chest rising beneath Avery's backside, and exhaled with a warm sigh that fizzed straight from cunt to crown.

"Oh, oh my …" Fire blazed in her core as Cricket nuzzled and nipped the lycra, teasing Avery's clit through her shorts.

"Strawberries, cream, and salt, fuck." Cricket tugged the waistband of her shorts. Cool air kissed Avery's backside, raising goosebumps on her arms and belly. "I have to taste you Aves, please." One leg was bent, and Cricket's dextrous fingers slid the shorts and her panties away, leaving them dangling from a calf. "Please, sweet girl, say I can taste you." She hoisted Avery's knee back to her shoulder, kissing her calf, the inside of her thigh. "I need you on my tongue, you smell so fucking good."

"Yes," Avery breathed, arching her back and bringing her pussy closer to Cricket's mouth. She reached for the faun, wanting to tease those lovely ears, play with her breasts, touch her, hold her, weld their bones together. "Yes, Cricket."

"I love when you say my name like that." Teeth nipped her inner thigh, the ticklish pain mixing with the ache in her core. Avery squealed, shivering in pleasure as that broad flat tongue swept her center.

Cricket rumbled, tightening her grip on Avery's thighs and driving her tongue deep. It was unlike anything she had ever felt. Deep and penetrating, warm and writhing.

"Oh, gosh." The moist tip of Cricket's nose rubbed her clit; lips teased her folds and that *tongue*. Avery's belly flipped, and heat shot through her extremities, building as a pressure in her chest and her throat, finally escaping as a deep moan. The sound urged Cricket on. Her pace quickened, and tingles built in Avery's fingers and toes. Her breaths came in quick, tiny pants she couldn't control, and her hips had a mind of their own. Rocking and thrusting as if she could bury Cricket deeper in her pussy.

Distantly, she was aware of the call for lights out echoing through the camp. Distantly, a howl broke from deep in the woods. But there was only this room, only this bed. Only this faun.

Only Cricket.

She withdrew her tongue to suck on Avery's clit, wringing a tight mewl from her lips before driving deep once more. Licking and rolling, sucking and nibbling and humming. The buzz shot into her core, white spots danced in the corners of her eyes, and Avery was beyond words. Mindless in a sea of sensations too big for her body.

She couldn't think. Couldn't breathe. She was nothing but pure pleasure riding along the edge of a towering peak. Her hands shot into Cricket's hair, fumbling at her ears as the faun rocked against her. A hand cupped Avery's breast, the other disappearing between her legs and—

"Oh!" Avery's eyes flew wide as a finger joined Cricket's tongue. And another. Two of those gloriously long fingers crooked and stroked, masterfully scoring a place she could barely reach. "Oh my ..."

Her vision blurred, whiting out at the edges. Her bones felt like they were ready to shatter, her body wound so tight, so tight that there would be no surviving the mounting pressure if she didn't release. She couldn't breathe, couldn't think, couldn't—

Cricket hummed again, her fingers crooking just so, and Avery shattered. Her back bowed, eyes flying wide as she screamed, "Oh, my God!"

Wave after wave of utterly divine pleasure lapped at her body, her pussy clenching and releasing around Cricket's fingers and tongue as the faun lapped through her release. A low growl rumbled in Cricket's throat, her ears shooting straight, and when Avery finally relaxed, liquid and sated with her legs wrapped around Cricket's face, the faun hummed.

"Gods." Her praise was a warm, humid exhale. She circled Avery's ankle, easing one leg down and stretching her hands across her soft belly. "Oak and ivy, Aves, you're amazing."

"Me?" She huffed, unable to fully catch her breath. "That was incredible."

"Yeah, well." Cricket shrugged, catching Avery's ankle as it slipped from her shoulder. She pulled the bike shorts and panties the rest of the way off, separating the pieces and faltering on the waistband of her pink, flower-dotted underwear. "Who is 'Elizabeth'?"

"Huh?" Avery's head was a cotton ball of fluff, thoughts forming and slipping away on the gentlest breeze. Cricket cocked her head and twisted the panties around, showing her the label sewn into the waistband. Her cheeks heated, then burned as Cricket's eyes gleamed at the slow crawl of pink down her throat and onto her chest. "Oh, that's, um, my name."

"Your name isn't Avery?"

"It is." She pressed her elbows onto the mattress, starting to sit up. Cricket set her hand between her breasts, keeping her in place. "Elizabeth Avery Payne. Avery was my grandmother's maiden name, my mom's mom."

"Ah." She tossed the panties aside and crawled forward, setting her head between Avery's breasts and nuzzling into her. "Well, it's nice to eat you, Elizabeth Avery Payne."

"Oh, my *gosh*."

17

CRICKET

A DOOR SLAMMED SOMEWHERE in the cabin, rousing Cricket from a deep, delightful sleep. She stretched her arms and legs, groaning lightly, and a weight shifted beside her. Memories of the previous night flooded into her mind. Rolling onto her side, her back to the door, she propped on an elbow and gazed at Avery, unable to stop the broad, goofy grin spreading across her face.

The girl was dead asleep, her breathing heavy and slow, plush lips parted, and, oak and ivy, she was drooling.

No one had ever been more adorable.

Another door slammed, followed by a muffled, angry voice. Avery snorted, fists curling in the blanket and pulling it tighter around her shoulders as she snuggled into the bed. Cricket glanced out the window to gauge the time—graying sky, a few stars, and a planet just visible above the ridgeline. Dawn. She entertained ignoring every inborn instinct and staying right where she was.

Or maybe she could wake Avery up the same way she'd put her to sleep. Her ears flicked at the thought, heat curling in her belly. She'd probably taste as sweet as she had last night. Hells, she'd probably taste even *better* after a night beneath blankets. Sweat and sweetness on her skin, between her thighs. Her breasts warm and inviting, soft belly more welcoming than any pillow.

Cricket pressed her knees together to ease the dull throbbing and swallowed a mouthful of anticipatory drool. Gods, how could she be so hungry for one human and her sweet, sweet whimpers? Idly, she circled her nipple, pressing her lips together as the throbbing between her legs sharpened to outright need.

I'll wake her with a kiss.

She snuggled closer, spooning Avery and propping her chin on the girl's shoulder.

Right behind the ear, my hand on her waist.

She did just that, fingertips brushing the slight swell of Avery's lower belly. Her breathing changed, rising out of the deep of sleep, and she wriggled against Cricket's thighs, fitting that grabbable ass perfectly against her as if the Gods had built Avery for that purpose alone.

Cricket slid her hand higher, cupping a handful of breast and teasing her nipple. Another happy hum was her reward, this one paired with a tiny smile. Without opening her eyes, Avery grabbed Cricket's wrist, guiding her hand down her front, over that lovely little swell, and toward the nest of curls. Heat and damp met her touch, thick thighs widening to welcome her fingers.

"Yes, ma'am," she whispered against Avery's neck, earning a delighted little wriggle. She parted her lips with a finger, circling Avery's clit before sweeping through the gathering slick. She gasped, turning her head and seeking Cricket's mouth.

Footsteps thundered in the hall, and the door slammed open, both faun and human freezing as Mac hollered, "Cricket, thank God. Have you seen Avery?"

Fighting every prey instinct in her body, Cricket craned her face around. Mac was a mess. Her cropped hair was tangled and wild, eyes shadowed, and her clothes were muddied and rumpled as if she'd spent the night in the woods.

"She said she was bringing you dinner, but no one has seen her since then, and that *thing* in the woods—oh, God. Have you seen her?"

Cricket swallowed, glancing at Avery, bright pink in her bed, then back over her shoulder at Mac. "Yes?"

"You have?" Mac sagged against the doorframe, dragging her shoulder down. "Oh, thank God. When?"

"Um..."

Avery clamped her thighs together, forcing Cricket's hand away, and hugged the blanket to her front as she sat up. "Hey, Director Murray."

Mac blinked, the color fading from her cheeks. She gaped at Cricket, then Avery, then Cricket again as she backed out of the room and yelled, "RAMBLE."

"Yes?" Cricket's cousin answered from downstairs, their voice as ragged and weary as Mac looked.

"I need you for this." Mac shook her head at Cricket and Avery, wiped a hand down her face, and walked out of sight. "And coffee. Lots and lots of coffee."

⁂

Avery hunched over her coffee, grasping it with both hands as if the speckled mug were the only thing keeping her in her seat. Across from her, Mac chewed her thumbnail, bouncing her knee beneath the table hard enough to jostle the bowl of fruit at the center while Ramble circled a spoon in their tea, studying Avery with a closed expression.

Cricket hated it. She hated that anyone could make Avery feel bad for what they had done. Hated that anyone, even her cousin, could take away the joy and confidence she had seen blossoming in the girl and replace it with this cowering, frightened thing beside her. If there were any two persons Avery ought to have been comfortable around right now, it was Mac and Ramble, and yet they'd given them the silent treatment and sat them at the table as if they were children in need of scolding.

Cricket scowled at her cousin, opening her mouth to tell them exactly what she thought of this treatment when Ramble crossed their arms and scowled right back at her.

"I cannot believe this," they stated. Cricket arched her neck, raising her chin. "Crick, your parents are beside themselves. The entire family was freaking out! They thought you were dead, and you have been here fucking Mac's employee?"

"Whoa, Ramble." Mac threw her hands out, frantically glancing between Ramble and Cricket. Avery stiffened, her knuckles blanching from her grip on the coffee cup. Her cheeks paled further, and Cricket saw red.

"Like you're one to talk," she lobbed across the table. "You wandered here to finger Mac a decade ago and never came home."

"Okay, you two, that's enough." Mac rose and set her hands on the table, frowning when her wife shot her a mean glare.

"How can you be so calm?" They jerked their head at Avery, curls bouncing. "That cabin is destroyed; there was blood on the floor! You have been up all night looking for ... for ..." Ramble squinted at her. "I do not know your name."

"Avery," she whispered, eyes trained on the coffee. Her answer went unheard.

"All night," Ramble repeated, lost in their tirade. "You called me in tears thinking some monster had eaten her, and she has been here with my cousin, who everyone at home thought was dead."

"Ramble, sweetpea, I know you're upset—"

"I am not upset; I am furious!" They slapped the table. Avery flinched, coffee sloshing over the sides of her cup. "Cricket, you put my wife in danger. Why did you not tell her that … that …" She glared at Avery and snorted. "I am sorry. Who *are* you?"

"Avery," she whispered again. "Avery Payne."

"Avery Payne." Ramble blinked and straightened. Their ears perked, fixed on the human girl cowering in her chair. "As in Payne Strategies? The lobbying firm?" Avery nodded, her eyes tight and downcast. "Run by Nathan Payne, the rabid anti-inhumanist?" Ramble gaped at her, shock warring with fury. Avery's cheeks paled even further, every freckle standing out like crumbs on parchment. "What are you doing here? How did you even get a job in this camp?"

"Babe," Mac warned. Ramble shook their head in disbelief, turning all of their anger on Mac.

"What is she doing here?" Their voice pitched high and frantic. "Mac, what were you thinking?"

"She's a good kid."

"I'm only six years younger than you," Avery muttered.

"And she's great with the campers," Mac argued, then reconsidered. "Well, she's getting better, even if she did take my advice a little too literally." This was paired with a glance at Cricket.

"Oh, my god." Avery buried her face in her hands.

"Mac," Ramble warned.

"It was my dad, alright?" Mac flushed and threw up her hands in defeat. Avery jerked her face up, mouth hanging slack. "He said he owed someone a favor in DC, and asked me to consider her application."

"*Mac.*"

"You hired me because your *dad* told you to?" Avery glared across the table, her lower lip trembling and eyes shining bright.

"No!" Mac pressed her hands in the air. "I mean, I interviewed you as a favor, but I hired you because—"

"I threw away a fellowship with the Boston Symphony for this!"

"I'm so confused," Cricket muttered.

"So am I." Her cousin flopped into their chair, rubbing their temples. "Mainly as to why my loving *wife* hired an Anti-in-human Specist to work in her integrated camp." They dropped their hands and glared at Avery.

"Excuse me, I am *not* my father," she fumed. Bright red splotches grew on her cheeks, and those pale blue eyes blazed.

"Avery—" Mac held up one hand, halting Avery, and gripped her wife's arm with the other. "Let me."

"This had better be good," Ramble grumbled, angrier than Cricket had ever seen them. Their mouth was a tight line, eyes narrowed, and ears pressed flat against their head.

"It is," Mac assured. "I promise." And then she made them wait, refilling coffees, making Ramble a new cup of tea, and setting out a basket of breakfast bars and packaged muffins.

Cricket and Ramble both reached for a granola bar, their eyes meeting. She sent a question across the table with a look, silently begging her cousin to relent. To be nice.

Ramble's expression remained hard, and one ear flicked in annoyance.

Avery remained still while they waited for Mac to explain, hunched in her chair with her arms crossed and gaze vacant, completely disassociated from the conversation and the persons in the room. Seeing this shut-down version of Avery, when she had been so *alive* just hours before, made Cricket uneasy. She set her palm against the flat of her back, wanting to comfort the human, and Avery straightened, leaning out of her reach.

"Like I said," Mac finally started, "my dad owed a favor to a colleague and asked me to look at your application."

"Why your dad?" asked Cricket.

"He's a congressman," she answered. "Congressman Murray, 3rd District, Ohio. I guess he owed Payne a favor from years back."

"I can't believe this." Avery bent forward, her forehead thunking against the table.

Cricket thought back over their conversation surrounding the camp, recalling that Avery took this job to be a better version of herself. Her fears that she was failing, that she wouldn't be able to break free from years of biased nurturing. She recalled that ill-fated guitar lesson she'd stumbled upon and the guilt that had so clearly ravaged Avery at her behavior and paired it with every exchange, both sweet and sour, where the human girl asked questions, learned, and adapted—never making the same small-minded mistake twice in a row.

"But not to hire her?" she blurted.

"Come again?" Mac asked.

"He asked you to interview Avery but not to hire her?"

"That's what I said," the camp director squinted, tilting her head in question.

"Then why did you?" asked Ramble.

"Because she was the best for the job."

"Liar." Ramble shoved back in their chair and crossed their arms.

"I'm not lying!" Mac put her hands up. "Avery is a poly-instrumentalist. She marched at Messiah for three years and served as drum major for the fourth. Her resume is stellar."

"And?" Ramble prompted.

"And?"

"Mac," they sighed, shaking their head. "Babes, I have known you for a decade. You cannot lie to me. Why did you really hire her?"

Mac stared at her wife. A long, hard stare that was more a conversation than a look. When Ramble did not relent, Mac sighed and dropped heavily into her chair.

"I thought ... I thought that maybe if I could change Nathan Payne's daughter's mind about inhumans, we could get to him."

"WHAT?" Avery shrieked.

"And his clients," Mac added as a mumble.

"Mackenzie!" Ramble hollered. "You are using her to prove a point?"

"Yes, alright?" Mac again threw her hands. "I need to raise funds for the camp. I need investors if we're going to expand, and I miss my family, Ramble. I hate that only my parents and a cousin came to our wedding. I hate that we can't go visit Columbus without people hissing slurs at us." Cricket's jaw fell open, her heart sinking low in her chest. She'd had no idea her cousin and their wife faced such prejudices in the world, had no idea Mac came from a family that might disapprove of their union. "I hate that they hate *you*."

"Oh, Mac." Ramble jolted from their chair and gathered Mac in their arms, murmuring quiet words even Cricket's ears could not catch. A heavy, weighted silence followed her admission, a silence full of meaning. Cricket had never once considered that her cousin's wife struggled with being married to an inhuman or that her family was as bigoted as the city humans tended to be.

She'd met Mac and gotten to know her at Spring and Harvest festivals over the years. Had stood behind Ramble at their wedding, but she'd forgotten how empty Mac's side of the bower was.

All the faun were in attendance. A naga family and their children, a few wolven, gnomes, and moon-eyed. Former students, friends, and colleagues who had celebrated Mac and Ramble so joyously that the lack of humans in attendance was hardly felt. But now ... now it was all Cricket could see.

She glanced at Avery, glaring at the table, and grabbed her hand, refusing to let the girl pull away.

"Why are you here, Avery?"

Ramble pulled their head from the crook of Mac's neck, watching the pair from across the table with wide, liquid eyes.

"I want to be better than him," Avery said, her voice flat and hollow. "It never felt right how my dad talks about inhumans and how our church treats you." She blinked, and a tear squeezed free, curving over the apple of her cheek. "They're so angry all the time, and when I started to realize that I—" She pressed her lips together, nostrils flaring. "I want to be better than that. Than him."

"You are."

"Am I?" She turned her head, reddened eyes boring into Cricket's. "You saw me in that class, I could barely treat the students equally."

"Because they aren't equal," Cricket stated. "That Spearfinger is always going to have better fingering on a guitar. It's how she was born, and she's always going to have that advantage. Those advantages are *always* going to exist, whether it's cross-species or within your own. And yeah, you got frustrated, but they were all talking over you and complaining. Anyone would get frustrated. You did the best you could, you apologized, and you learned. You gave your time and patience as best you were able, and you tried again. Just like you did with me."

Avery sent her a watery smile and, miracle of miracles, squeezed Cricket's hand.

"I still don't trust it," said Ramble. "She—"

"Ramble, come on." Mac straightened and grabbed her wife's arm.

"Think about it, though. If her dad hates inhumans so much, which he does, and I have the newspaper clippings to prove it, why would he ask your father for that favor? Why would he want her here?"

Mac pressed her lips together and shook her head, eyes drifting to Avery.

"He doesn't," she answered. "I fought with him for weeks to even apply. I had to build a business case for why working at Elkwater would be the best step for my career."

"And then he just changes his mind one day?" Ramble countered. "Calls in a favor from a prominent congressman to get his daughter a job at a summer camp?" They frowned at Mac. "I love it here as much as you do, but we both know this place isn't worth a congressional favor."

"It could be," Mac whispered.

"I know." Ramble softened and cupped their wife's cheek. "But still, I do not believe it."

"You're not being fair."

"I am being *more* than fair, considering her family"—they nodded at Avery—"is buying up every piece of property in Green Bank that they can."

"What?" Avery and Cricket shouted as one.

"They're forcing my family out of their home, and then suddenly her dad pulls a favor to get his daughter a job at an integrated camp? Come on, Mac, you are smarter than this."

"What do you mean we're buying up property?" Avery cut in, glaring at Cricket. "I thought you said it was a Georgia company."

"It is," she said.

Ramble scoffed. "Oh, sure. Your daddy pulls a favor, and now you want us to believe you did not know?"

"I didn't!" Avery argued. The red was back in her cheeks, the fire blazing in her eyes. Cricket took it in, marveling at the fact she recognized that reaction as Avery telling the truth. Not a hint of deception masked those lovely features, and she was struck anew by the human.

"How do you?" she asked her cousin.

"I was stuck in Elkins until the road cleared," Ramble explained. They nodded at Cricket. "A few of the family were there. They mentioned Nathan Payne had been in town, and another suggested he was looking at more property." They shrugged and, at Mac's hand falling to their forearm, continued. "I was curious, so I went to the assessor's office yesterday before seeing the family."

Mac groaned and palmed her face. "You have *got* to stop watching so many police procedurals."

"What? Jerry Orbach is a compelling actor." They shrugged and shook their head as if this were an old argument that would never be resolved. "Anyway, I was curious. It is not a character fault." Ramble pursed their lips and leaned conspiratorially across the table. "Spoken like somebody who's never owned a Jag." At the blank stare Cricket sent them, Ramble frowned and straightened, glancing around the table. "Seriously, does no one watch *Law and Order*?"

"No," Avery whispered.

"You watch the reruns at dawn," Mac muttered.

"Bad reception in Green Bank," Cricket supplied.

Ramble rolled their eyes and flumped back in their chair. They fluttered a hand at Avery. "The Georgia Men only broker the sale of the property if I am reading the filed paperwork properly. But the taxes are being paid by Payne Properties."

"That doesn't mean it's my dad." Avery stubbed her finger against the table. "There are a lot of Paynes in this country, and I have a large family. It could be an uncle, or a cousin, or my—"

"True. Fair. It could be any of them, but the name on the signature line is Elizabeth Avery Payne," Ramble stated. Avery froze. "That's you, isn't it?"

18

—·—

AVERY

"WHAT?" SHE JOLTED BACK in the chair, head spinning. "That's insane. I don't own any property. I'm a *musician*. I've never even been to Green Bank."

"Would not have to have been," Ramble sniffed and picked at the corner of a cereal bar. "Not if the Georgia Men were brokering the sale. All you would have to do is sign."

"But I didn't sign anything!"

"Of course you didn't." Cricket squeezed her hand. "Ramble, explain."

"What is there to explain? The personal representative is listed as Elizabeth Avery Payne, and it is that name on the signature line. That is you, is it not?"

"I—yes, but ..." This made no sense. How could she have signed any paperwork, much less been paying property taxes? Elkwater paid above minimum wage, but even in this part of Appalachia, that was nowhere near enough to own property. And when was the last time she'd signed anything? The only things she ever signed were college applications and the job letter for the camp. Sure, there was the odd check or credit card receipt, but even then, she meticulously filed her documents and sent them home for her dad to ... to ... "Oh, my God."

"She said 'God', oh shit." Cricket bolted to her side, kneeling beside her chair. "Aves?"

"I—he wouldn't." Her lips felt numb. Her fingers tingled. Why was the room so large? "I'm his daughter. He wouldn't ... who would ..."

"Care to share?" asked Ramble.

"I send home my receipts and carbon paper checks so my dad can balance his accounts. And the other day, he had me use my emergency credit card for lunch, but he kept the receipt and I-I ... I'm going to be sick." She pushed away from the table and staggered out the door, barely making it down the steps before she emptied her stomach in the yard.

Her father wouldn't do that; he wouldn't be so *cruel*. Who would defraud their own daughter?

But if what Ramble and Cricket said was true, the Georgia Men had been buying up land in Green Bank for years. Payne Strategies buying the land outright, the land their client, US Petroleum, wanted for a pipeline, would be a gross conflict of interest ... and she'd been sending him paperwork with her signature for years.

What was it he had said in Elkins?

That's my good girl.

Another roll of nausea surged up her throat. She spat into the bushes, coughing and sobbing and falling to her knees. The grass crunched, and a long-fingered, tawny hand appeared gripping a glass of water.

"Are you okay?" Cricket's raspy voice enveloped her like a slightly scratchy wool blanket. An unwanted comfort.

"No," she spat. "I'm far from okay, thank you."

"You're welcome?"

Avery angled her head, taking in the faun through bleary eyes. "I was being sarcastic." She pushed to her feet, wiping the back of her hand under her nose. "You don't believe her, do you? That I would—that I bought—"

"Oh, hells no." Cricket shoved the glass into Avery's hand, forcing her to take it. "Do you know how boring it is in this cabin during the day? I've been snooping through Mac's papers to keep from going insane; you're barely paid enough to buy groceries for a week, much less half of Green Bank."

"My dad," she hiccuped. Cricket nodded at the glass of water. "I think he's—"

"Signing paperwork in your name?" She tapped the bottom of the glass and glared pointedly at Avery. "I figured. Overheard him talking with Mac the other day; he seems like a real skeezeball."

The Valley Girl slang coming from Cricket earned a tiny laugh from Avery. She raised her head and found the faun standing nearby. Close enough for comfort but far enough away not to crowd her. She fluttered a smile at Avery and held her arms out, fingers bending just enough to beckon her forward.

She gripped the water glass, took a tiny sip, and collapsed into Cricket, sighing when she held her tight and close.

"You want to know my guess?" she asked. Avery nodded into her shoulder. "I think your dad saw an opportunity to get you out of the way for the summer and a reason to be in Green Bank."

"By letting me work here," Avery intoned. It made sense. Her dad was conniving and opportunistic. He was always looking for the next connection or means to get ahead of everybody else. She'd witnessed him bribing members of their church to get a better pew and had heard him imply knowledge of teachers' private lives to bump up her brother's grades. He was a successful lobbyist, and Avery had been all too willing to believe he was a good father, a good *man*. All too willing to forgive the bribery and the lies, but she had never considered fraud. Or that he would use his conniving, opportunistic nature against his own daughter.

"Come on." Cricket guided her across the garden. "Let's get you showered and back to your cabin."

"Not so fast," Ramble filled the top step, hands on their hips. "You are coming with me, Crick."

Cricket stiffened, the easy roll to their step faltering and ceasing altogether. "Where?"

"Home."

"What?" Her arm tightened around Avery's shoulders, ears shooting upright. "No way, I'm staying here with Avery."

"Not a chance," the other faun shook her head. "Mac has investors coming, and we need to stop the family from freaking out."

"What do those two things have to do with one another?"

"That thing is still out there." Mac joined her wife on the porch, looping an arm around their waist. She raked her free hand through her hair, and Avery finally clocked how tired she looked. Still in her filthy clothes, she leaned against her wife as though Ramble were the only thing keeping her upright. "I've got the local inhumans watching the perimeter. That thing showed up with you—"

"It *chased* me. It's not my fault!"

"And I have to make sure everything is running at peak performance before these investors show up," Mac returned with a glare at Cricket. "Tonight."

"Wait, what?" Avery jolted. "The Lunar Asset dinner is tonight?"

"Your father's associate called yesterday to set it up," Mac explained. "Which is why I was looking for you in the first place. We need to assure the campers that everything is fine, and then I need you focused. This might be my last chance to secure any reasonable funding in time to schedule construction before next summer."

"And you need to go home and put the family's mind at ease," Ramble added. Cricket's grip tightened even more on her shoulder. Avery winced, grunting lightly, and Ramble's attention zeroed in on their cousin's hand on her shoulder. The possessive hold. Their expression softened as they descended a stair. "You can come back; whenever this thing goes away, you can come back. I will come to talk to your parents about letting you stay here for the rest of the summer, but right now, it is best that you go home."

"She's right, Cricket," Avery whispered. Cricket's face jerked toward her, pain and betrayal pulling her mouth into a frown. "You've been here for a while; maybe they need to hear you say this place is safe. That the people of Elkwater and Elkins are open to integration." She twisted to face her, gripping Cricket's elbow. "Tell them about the sasquatch working at Meander's, and the Mothman bartender. The gnomish mechanic at the gas station."

"They need to hear it from more than me, Crick," said Ramble. "Say your goodbyes, and we will go."

<hr>

The goodbye was terrible. Cricket was sullen and avoiding eye contact, pulling away when Avery needed her most. She needed Cricket's pragmatism to help her process her guilt. She'd heard those howls, heard them and ignored them for the sake of pleasure, sleeping peacefully beside Cricket while a monster ravaged the camp. She needed Cricket's strength to help her process everything she had learned—that Director Murray was married to a faun, to Cricket's *cousin*. That her dad was conceivably, probably, almost certainly defrauding his own daughter to buy up land in Green Bank.

But most of all, she just needed *Cricket*, and all she got was a quick press of lips against her temple. A gesture of defeat when Avery wanted passion.

"I don't want you to leave," she whispered into one of those lovely ears, leaning into Cricket's body as if she could keep her there by will alone.

"I don't want to go," she replied. Her arms tightened around Avery for a heartbeat, and then the faun stepped away. "I'll—" She pressed her lips together, a determined expression hardening her features. "I'll come back. I'm just a few ridges away. Once this all blows over, I'll come back."

And then she left, following her cousin out the door without so much as a glance over her shoulder.

"Come on, Avery," Director Murray said after a long moment. "There's work to be done."

She followed her boss through the camp, trying hard to avoid the curious stares and heavy silence. Mac, showered and changed into clean clothes, nodded and waved at the campers, quietly assuring everyone that Avery was fine, the camp was safe, and nothing was being canceled or postponed. It struck her as odd until they rounded the counselor's office, and she saw her cabin at the very end of the row.

The door hung on one hinge, scored with claw marks, the frame was less than splintered wood, and the tattered remains of curtains lay crumpled in the grass. Avery halted, hands flying to her face as she took in the damage. A stair was shredded to splinters, and churned earth surrounded the cabin as though a herd of beasts had attempted to dig their way in.

"Aksel identified your blood on the floor," Mac said in a low voice, pressing her hand between Avery's shoulder blades. The earth stopped tilting to the side, and only then did she realize she'd been about to fall over. "We saw the destruction and assumed the worst. Didn't you hear … ?"

"No," she mouthed, shaking her head. "It chased me the other night. Caught my leg." Her hand fell to her side, lightly gesturing to the gauze wrapped around her calf. She'd worn her bike shorts for the brief walk, relishing the warmth of the summer sun on her legs. Now, guilt poisoned the fleeting joy as she recognized the weight behind Director Murray's reassuring words to the campers, the curious looks and relieved smiles from her counselors.

They had been up all night searching for Avery. Howls had sounded in the woods, her blood on the floor. It was all too easy to understand how Mac had jumped to the conclusion that she had.

"It scratched me," Avery said in a flat tone. "It tore my skirt and scratched my leg. Cricket, she … she patched me up." Mac sighed, rubbing soothing circles into Avery's back. "I didn't realize I'd bled on the floor."

"It wasn't a lot, a few soiled rags"—Avery flinched. She had left the towels and cotton balls Cricket had used in the trash. Was that what attracted the monster? The scent of her blood?—"some drops on the throw rug, but you know Aksel. He's got a good nose."

To say Aksel "had a good nose" was selling the wolven marching band instructor short. He was singularly responsible for their middle-grade campers showering on a regular schedule, claiming the first waft of their stink was an affront to his senses.

Avery nodded dumbly, following her up the broken stairs. The interior of the cabin was worse than the outside: her mattress was flipped and torn, and her clothes ripped to shreds. Claw marks scraped down the walls, and glass from a picture frame lay in shards on the floor, the photograph of her mother and siblings crumpled and slashed.

The destruction was staggering and only on her half of the cabin. Sanoya's side lay as untouched and pristine as the day she moved in. It was unsettling to see such an obvious line drawn between Avery and her roommate, between her and the inhumans in this camp.

She pinched the corner of a torn blanket and raised it from the ground, frowning at the waft of lavender and a bright, fresh note she couldn't quite place. She scrunched her nose, stifling a gag. It was the same overpowering scent she'd smelled on the monster before, lavender and musk, and that sharp, minty scent, albeit absent the heat of its body. *No, not mint.* She sniffed the blanket again. *Wintergreen.* A cold lick of fear ran down her spine at the familiarity because she'd smelled this exact scent before. Not on the monster that chased her, but somewhere else … on someone else …

"There you are," a soft, breathy voice spoke in Avery's ear. She jolted and spun around, a scream lodged in her throat. Sanoya stood behind her, white-blonde hair drifting to her waist on a non-existent breeze, haloing the Life Sciences Instructor in moonlight pale strands a shade lighter than her skin. Her wide eyes were hidden behind a pair of large, round sunglasses, and her dusty purple lips were pressed together in a sympathetic moue. "We were out all night looking for you."

"I heard." Avery gathered the blanket in her hands, casting a sad glance around her side of the cabin. "I'm sorry about the mess. I should have it cleaned up shortly."

"Don't worry," Sanoya said. "The Hidebehind and I will handle it."

"The Hidebehind." Avery glanced around the cabin, failing to spot anyone other than Sanoya. On the porch, just out of sight, Mac's voice rose and fell, assuring someone that Avery was alright. A tightness cinched her throat, her eyes burning as a chorus of children and teens replied, all of them expressing concern and fear. For her.

She rubbed a knuckle under her eye and faced Sanoya. It wasn't the first time she had mentioned a hidebehind, and Avery was seriously beginning to wonder about her errant roommate's sanity when, out of the corner of her eye, the mattress heaved upright.

"Please don't scream," Sanoya rushed out. "He is a little shy, but mostly he is afraid you will blame him for this."

"What is he?"

"A very old friend," she sang with a smile. "We packed what was left of your clothes, and he helped me set up an extra bed in the piano room you favor—the one at the end of the hall with the window, yes?"

"Yeah." Avery wavered where she stood. "You did that for me?"

"Of course we did; you're part of the Elkwater Family." She smiled as if that should have been obvious. Which it wasn't. This was only the third time she and Sanoya had spoken since meeting at the start of the summer, and their last conversation had consisted of a terse "hello" in the cafeteria followed by a "no room, sorry" when she'd tried to join the rest of the counselors at their table for dinner.

"I am sorry about that." Sanoya cocked her head, frowning in time with Avery's thoughts. "The Hidebehind is intolerably shy, and there was only enough room for him that day. I should have asked you to sit with us the following night."

"Can you ... never mind." She shook her head, unable to rid herself of the feeling that Sanoya was reading her mind. Considering she had only recently figured out her roommate was inhuman, Avery had no idea what sorts of abilities she had. It was possible she *could* read minds.

Maybe that's why she doesn't sleep in here; my head is too loud.

"It's more that I keep different hours," she said. Avery jumped back and immediately began playing the *1812 Overture* in her mind. "And you know how the Hidebehind is; too much noise in the camp. The quiet of the woods is so peaceful, don't you think?"

"Right, I ... yes." Whatever it was holding her mattress up snuffled in agreement. "And, um, why is he afraid I'll blame him for this?"

"Whispers in the night," Sanoya shrugged. "A creature in the wood. The one that chased you that the faun can barely describe. The loggers have said very many mean things about the Hidebehind, but he is a sweetheart, truly. He would only hurt someone he intended to eat, and even then, he would do so politely." She smiled in the direction of the mattress, a blueish tint filling her cheeks.

Avery followed her gaze, catching the twitch of a rounded, furry ear before the Hidebehind ducked behind her mattress. "Right ... so if it wasn't him—and I'm not saying I think it was!"

The Hidebehind snuffled. "If it wasn't him, does he know what it is?"

"We do not speak his name," a voice rasped in her ear, hardly more than a breeze in the trees. Avery spun around, every muscle in her body twitching, her arm pulled back and ready to swing.

There was nothing there.

Nothing but the broken door and the camp beyond. Her mattress flumped to the floor and she whirled back around, seeking out the Hidebehind.

"Oh, he's so *fast,* isn't he?" Sanoya giggled lightly. Then she tutted in the direction of the shared closet set into the rear wall. "I do hope you're wrong, and it is not a He Himself. They make such a mess."

Avery's scalp prickled at Sanoya's words, spoken as though she not only had heard of a *whatever-it-was* but knew exactly what they were. "Have you ever seen one?"

"Oh, yes." She nodded and pinched the arm of her sunglasses, sliding the frames onto the top of her head. Wide, alien eyes gleamed back at her, round and dark as a cavern pool. "They have been in these hills as long as I can remember, the poor things. Always so hungry. If you're ever out for a hike and feel an unnatural chill or catch decay on the wind, you are in the presence of one." Sanoya pursed her lips and shook her head sadly. "Terribly shy, worse than my Hidebehind, and such awful table manners."

She drifted past Avery to the mattress, grappling it from the ground. A waft of lavender and wintergreen rose from the destroyed bedding, making them both sneeze.

Again, Avery racked her brain, trying to place where she had caught this same scent before. Not in the camp, they were all advised against perfume and cologne to keep from attracting bugs. So where?

"Do they have antlers?" she asked.

"Oh yes," Sanoya grunted, propped the mattress against the bedframe, and glared at the closet door. "A little help?" Avery headed for the mattress and halted as the door creaked open. Footsteps padded across the floor, the boards groaning under a new weight, and the mattress shifted upright. She gaped at it, catching only the corner of a furred elbow and the glistening triangle of a snout as it disappeared. "Thank you," Sanoya sniffed. "And yes, great, broad, lovely things. Numerous points dangling with delicate strips of ... leather."

"Leather?"

The inhuman twisted her face around to stare blankly at Avery. "Would you like me to tell you what they actually are?"

"Um..." Avery could imagine, even if she didn't want to. "No, thank you." The Hidebehind snorted in what was unmistakably a laugh. "Only," she continued, "the monster that chased me and Cricket—it didn't have any antlers."

"Fascinating." Sanoya and the Hidebehind wrestled the mattress onto the bed, the bear-like, or so Avery assumed, inhuman dropping under the bed to avoid notice. Boxes and shoes were shoved out from under the frame, and Sanoya gathered them all, setting items near the door and frowning at Avery when she tried to help.

"Go on." She shooed her out of the cabin, grabbing an old broom from the porch and waving it at Avery. "You're part of the family now," Sanoya said. She popped onto her tiptoes and set the broom back onto its hooks above the door. "We look out for one another."

19

CRICKET

"IF YOU HAD LET her leave, she probably would not have felt the need to run away!" Ramble shouted from the other room, their voice carrying through the thin woven wall. They had been arguing for hours now, ever since Cricket mentioned going back to the camp in a few days when Ramble left. Her mother, Thistle, had cried out, and her father, Bosk, burst to his hooves, antlers scraping the thatched roof as he bellowed.

It hadn't taken long for Cricket to throw up her hands and storm away, but what was the point? She'd been making the same arguments her entire life—that they should integrate, if not with the entire world, then at least with Green Bank. That they didn't have to live in huts, that they could get jobs, buy clothes, and go to school.

She tried to tell them about the wolven and the sasquatch marching in a band together. Tried to get them to imagine a naga and a gnome sitting at a table, eating side by side instead of tearing through the woods as predator and prey. She had even told them about the assessor hiking through their woods with his surveyor's maps, but they didn't listen. They *wouldn't* listen, not even when Ramble confirmed everything she said.

In their minds, Cricket was still their youngest daughter, the only child who had fallen with them into this new world. They refused to see that she was grown and that she wanted a life beyond the woods of Green Bank. They were going to keep her here and Avery was going to leave in a few weeks, and that would be it. The end of her adventure and attempts to escape the tiny life her parents had planned for her.

So she stormed to her room, flopped down in the nest of blanket-covered pine straw, and that's when she saw it—the parcels and bundles stacked against the door. Her belongings. Her *life* packed and ready to go.

And *that* was when the real yelling began.

"So you're just giving up and moving? *Again?*" She stormed into the main room, not caring if she startled her parents and Ramble.

"Only deeper in the woods, honeybee," Thistle said. "Near the hollow, at Deer Creek."

"Only deeper." She scoffed and stomped in an angry, limping circle. "Only deeper? They're pushing us out, why can't you see it? They're going to keep buying up land; they're going to keep bribing or bullying the people of Green Bank until we have *nowhere left to go*. Is that what you want? To force all of us to live the way *you* want?"

"Crick ..." Bosk warned.

"Don't *Crick* me, dad. I don't want this! I want to go back to the camp; I want to be part of this world we live in."

"We have a responsibility to—"

"To who, dad? To what?" She stormed up to her father, craning her neck to glare him in the eye. "Are you going to tell me? Or claim I'm too young? Too rash? Too *emotional?*"

"Uncle Bosk," Ramble condemned, "you did not."

"I would not expect you to understand, Bramblethorn," he replied. They stiffened at their full name, nostrils flaring, but before they could retort, Bosk continued, "And yes, Cricket, you are too rash to be brought into the family's reasons for staying where we do."

"But we aren't staying, are we?" she sniffed, her eyes stinging. "We're moving—again and again and again, deeper into the woods—and you won't *do* anything about it!"

"Cricket, dear, this cannot continue forever," Thistle cut in, approaching Cricket the way a mouse approaches a seeping lynx. "There is only so much privately owned land the Georgia Men can purchase; after that, they will have to buy it from the government, which, I am told, is a far more difficult process."

"It's not the Georgia Men." Cricket swiped the back of her hand across her nose. Ramble twitched their gaze her way, eyes widening as Cricket's words landed. "It's not the Georgia Men at all."

She limped from the dwelling, trying not to cry when no one followed her. There were more important things than crying—like getting to Marlinton and the County Assessor's Office. Getting copies of the records bearing Avery's name, if they even existed, and getting someone, *anyone* in the family, to listen to her. Ramble would help. That's why they hadn't followed her out the door, because in that look, she knew Ramble had understood what Cricket did—once the government got involved, there would be no stopping the purchase of land. Because the Georgia Men represented Payne Properties, which was run by Nathan Payne, a man with enough political clout and connections to get *Mackenzie Murray* to interview his daughter.

There couldn't be two more diametrically opposed people than Nathan Payne, the anti-inhuman trashbag, and Mackenize Murray, the wife of a faun and director of the first fully integrated camp in the nation.

The sun was high in the sky by the time she reached Marlinton. One upside of living in Green Bank—there was always someone looking to escape the pressure that clamped around their skulls if they spent too much time near the telescopes at the heart of the NRQZ. Always someone willing to give you a ride out of the National Radio Quiet Zone and enjoy amenities like a microwave. Today, it came in the form of a trio of teens headed to Lewisburg for a movie. Normally, Cricket would have covered the distance on hoof, grateful for the chance to stretch her legs at full speed. But her ankle still pinched, her hoof ached, and a car would be faster than she was now.

The teens dropped her in the heart of Marlinton, waving out the window as she limped into the assessor's office. To her surprise, the county assessor, a sallow-faced older man named Charlie, was all too willing to help out a curious inhuman taking an interest in his job.

He set her up at a small table tucked in a narrow hallway, the chair facing the door and front desk, adding file after file to her pile. "The bulk of 'em are from this last year," he explained. "Oldest dates about four years back. You one of them faun out of Green Bank?"

Cricket nodded, her tongue fat and heavy in her mouth. She'd known a lot of the land had been sold. She'd known the problem was only growing, but seeing it all laid out before her, each folder representing the piecemeal destruction of her home … it was almost too much to bear.

"Aint't seen one of y'all in a few years. Good you're still around, thought I might stumble upon ya when I was up that way."

"I saw you," she mumbled.

He smiled softly and nodded. "Suppose that's why you're here. Say hello next time. You know what you're lookin' for?"

"Um," she swallowed. "Not really. Signatures?"

Charlie nodded and grabbed the topmost folder from the stack, setting it on the table and flipping it open.

"Registered agent's signatures are here." He pointed to a scrawled name she didn't recognize and flipped the page. "Looks like they signed on behalf of Lunar Asset Management, and the buyer's signatures are here, here, and here." In quick succession, he tapped Avery's signature down the page. One-two-three. "Looks like they signed as the personal representative of an estate. It'll be the same in most of these; not many lawyers round here to manage the contracts, so 'less that city boy took them down to Charleston to be notarized, the paperwork's all the same."

"Thank you." She smiled at him, and Charlie nodded back, patting the stack.

"Shame what's happenin' up there," he said, wandering back behind his desk. "The whole place is goin' to the dogs."

That said, Charlie tucked into his book, and Cricket got to work. Digging through the files, she began to notice discrepancies in the signature. Not those of the registered agent but Avery's. There was a stilted, careful quality to the handwriting even in the cursive humans were so fond of. The letters in Elizabeth and Avery didn't connect in the seamless manner they should, whereas Payne was always scrawled with an easy stroke. Cricket pulled aside the most obvious ones, creating a stack of what, in her mind, was evidence.

The signatures became smoother over time, almost as if the signer had gotten more comfortable with the name and the flow. But it never changed. Always the same curve to the A and looped tail on the Y. For four years, the signature remained the same, and something about that stood out as odd. If someone were signing *this many* contracts, wouldn't their hand get lazy? The signature less legible? But these never did. Each was as crisp and clear as the very first Elizabeth Avery, and then that sloppy Payne.

The front door slammed shut. Cricket jumped in her seat, hooves slipping on the sage and tan vinyl flooring. She shifted in the plastic chair, ears twitching at the sound of shoes slapping across the floor. A muscle in her back pinched, and she winced. How long had she been sitting here?

"Charlie, my man!" A broad-shouldered figure entered, leaning against the front counter with their back to her tiny table. A leather briefcase slapped on the formica, and the man shifted, his profile coming into view. Cricket straightened, bringing a hand up to smooth down her ears, which had perked in interest at the sight of the Georgia Man.

The one from Mac's office.

"Got a few more for you," he drawled, pulling a manila folder from his brief.

"The Johnsons sold?" Charlie sidled over, hands flying up the catch the folder as the man tossed it across the counter.

"That they did!" He flicked the front lapel of his coat aside to slide his hand into a pocket. The move sent a waft of cologne across the room, tickling Cricket's nose with lavender and wintergreen. She clapped a hand over her nose and mouth, stifling a sneeze. The man glanced her way at the sound, eyes flicking over Cricket and her stack of folders. His brows rose, nostrils flaring, and he sent her the same wolfish grin he had from the parking lot at the camp. "Don't suppose you've heard the rumors out of Green Bank, Chucko?" He faced Charlie, releasing Cricket to sag in her seat. "About that—"

"We don't spread rumors 'round these parts, Mr. Wilkolak," Charlie interrupted. "Best not to call attention to the things you don't see in the woods."

"Aw, c'mon, Chuck. You've never seen anything lurking in the pine?"

"No sir, I have not." He shook his head and ducked beneath the counter, returning with a large self-inking stamp and punching it down far harder than necessary. Collecting the paperwork, Charlie wandered out of sight. The hum of a copy machine filled the silence, and the Georgia Man, Wilkolak, again looked in Cricket's direction.

She jerked her face down, eyes burning from the stench of his cologne, strong enough to make her want to gag but not enough to hide the musk flowing from the man. His gaze was heavy, burning into the top of her head and making it hard to concentrate. She idly turned pages, her fingers beginning to tremble when Charlie returned.

"Here're your copies, Mr. Wilkolak. We'll have these filed in seven to ten days."

Wilkolak faced Charlie, releasing Cricket from the weight of his direct gaze. She kept her head down as far as she could while still being able to watch him. "Pocahontas County is at the forefront of industry thanks to your hard work, Chuck." He tore a check free from a leather folio, sliding it across the counter. "I expect you'll see me again in a few days."

"You so sure?" Charlie pressed back from the counter, eyes twitching to Cricket. She jerked up the folder in her hands, hiding her face. "The folks up in Green Bank don't seem to be playin' ball the way you'd like."

"Oh, they will, Chuckles." Wilkolak let out a barking, breathy sound that reminded Cricket of wolven laughter. "Give it a day, and they'll come around. Keep that stamp of yours warmed up."

"Will do, Mr. Wilkolak."

"Always a pleasure." Wilkolak snapped the clasps on his briefcase closed. "Say, how long does it take to drive to Elkwater from here? I've got a dinner to get to, and I don't want to be late."

"Less than an hour."

"Excellent, excellent." The soles of his shoes slapped against the vinyl flooring; he opened the door and—

Cricket peered over the folder when the slam never came. Wilkolak stood in the doorway, staring directly at her. Papers trembled in her grip, and his attention dropped to her hands before he closed his eyes and inhaled deeply.

A slow, tight-lipped smile stretched his mouth, taunting Cricket as it crinkled his cheeks. He opened his eyes, pinning her to the chair with an amber-hued gleam. "Found you."

❧ ❧

"Pick up, Aves. Come on, come onnnnn." Cricket danced hoof to hoof, wincing whenever the weight came down on her still sore injury. It had healed enough to not need a crutch, but oak and ivy, if it didn't ache like a son of a gun. The line rang and rang, the sun hovered over the hills, and Cricket was about to truly start freaking out. The moment Wilkolak drove away, she had sprinted from the Assessor's Office in search of a payphone, wanting to warn Avery before the investor's dinner, but what good was a warning when she wouldn't pick up? "Pick up, pick up, *please.*"

"To continue your call, please deposit twenty-five cents."

"Shit." She dug in her beltbag, pulling out a handful of coins and dropping a few on the ground. Earpiece pinched between her cheek and shoulder, she crouched, fumbling at the ground to pick them up. Her nail-less fingers slipped against the thin edges. She cursed again, this time at herself, for leaving the remainder of her caps on the small birch table in her bedroom. Finally, she managed to pluck dimes and a nickel from the ground, slamming them into the payphone as the automated voice started up again.

The robotic woman stopped, the ringing began again, and Cricket thought she was well and truly going to lose it in a phone booth in the middle of Marlinton, West Virginia. She needed to warn Avery and Mac, tell them what she found, and warn them about the Georgia Man. About Wilkolak.

"Please, please, please." She pounded a fist against the pay-phone, praying to the Gods that they pick up. Avery, Mac, a camper, *anyone*, but the phone rang and rang and—

"Elkwater Music Camp, Assistant Director Payne speaking."

"Aves!" Relief flooded her veins with adrenaline. Oh, Gods, she could warn her, tell her everything, but she needed to speak quickly. How long would twenty-five cents last? How much time did she have before the robotic voice cut her off? "Avery, I found him. He found me, it's the man from the camp, the Georgia Man. He was here, and he had these papers at the assessor's office, and he was filing more with Charlie. *Avery*, your signature is on everything going back four years. You've got to call the cops, or, or, the tax man or *something*; I don't—"

"Cricket, geez, take a breath."

"I am breathing!"

"No, you're freaking out," said Avery. "Slow down and tell me what happened."

"I was at the County Assessor's Office," she panted, "looking over the property tax filings."

"Okay."

"Your name is on everything."

Avery sighed, and Cricket could easily envision the human girl pinching the bridge of her nose. "Isn't that what your cousin said?"

"Yes, but I got copies and your signature—there's something weird about it. Like, it stays the same."

"Signatures tend to do that."

"No, but you have to see it, okay? It's like whoever did this was careful at first, then got better at your hand, but it never got sloppy. You have to see it; I got copies."

"Oh," she said. "Okay, so that's something, right?"

"It's more than something!" Cricket hollered. "And *then* the Georgia Man walked in—"

"While you were there?"

"No, while I was taking a nap. *Of course,* while I was there, and he saw me, I think he recognized me from the camp."

"When did he see you at the camp?"

"The day you went to lunch with your dad, they had a meeting with Mac. It was something about funding or investments, I don't know, but he saw me."

"In the meeting?" Avery asked, her voice muffled. "Hang on a second."

Cricket wanted to scream. How was this so hard to follow? The Georgia Man, Wilkolak, had the paperwork with her signature. He was at the camp; he worked with her dad. Why couldn't she just pay attention?

"Avery."

"One sec," she answered. A shuffling static muted her end of the line. "It's Cricket." A pause. "No, I know, I'll make this quick." The static again, and then Avery's voice came clearly over the line. "Crick, I've got to go. The investors from Lunar are due any minute, and Mac needs to me to—"

"He *saw* me, Avery. He smelled the air and got all weird and said he found me."

"I thought you said you weren't in the meeting. Are you sure he saw you?"

"No, I wasn't in the meeting, and *yes*, I'm sure!"

"Okay, fine, calm down."

"Avery ..." Cricket clenched her eyes, seething through her teeth. "He saw me through the upstairs window when they left to go to lunch with you. He smiled at me."

"Smiled at you."

"You wouldn't understand." She dropped her head back, rubbing her temples with two fingers. "It was a creepy smile ... a predator's smile."

The silence on the other end of the line stretched a little too long before Avery sighed in a way that Cricket could see her shudder. "No, I think I understand. It felt like that whenever he looked at me during lunch."

That anyone would ever make Avery feel less than the amazing person she was, that anyone could make her feel as small and vulnerable as a faun did when sighted by prey ... if Cricket hadn't already been panicked and angry, that alone would have made her furious.

"The guy is a major douchebag."

"Yeah, no kidding." Avery sighed again.

"There's something else," Cricket added. "A scent on the papers."

"We're back on the paperwork?"

"It's super faint; I don't know if a human could smell it, but when he walked in, the smell smacked me in the face, like it was *his* scent."

"It makes sense if he's the one that's been filing the papers."

"Aves," she lowered her voice to a whisper. Why? No idea. Marlinton was abandoned this close to dinnertime, all the humans and inhumans safely in their homes. Still, she whispered. Who knew what was listening from the trees? "It was the same scent I caught on the monster. Musk and lavender and—"

"Wintergreen," she finished. It wasn't a question, more a confirmation. Like Avery had already known. "Crick, are you suggesting that Troy, the Georgia Man, is the monster? The one that chased you over the ridge and has been stalking the camp?"

"I know it sounds crazy, but scents are unique to the inhuman. It was the exact same scent from the papers and the monster, I swear."

"It doesn't sound crazy," Avery stated in a flat voice. "My cabin was destroyed. All my clothes, my mattress ... that's why Mac was such a mess. I forgot to clean up the rags and cotton balls you used on my leg, and I must have bled on the floor. The monster smelled me, and, ugh, Crick, the whole cabin stunk of Obsession for Men. If Sanoya were in the cabin, he would have—"

"Please insert twenty-five cents to continue your call," the robotic voice chirped.

"Shit." Cricket dug in her pocket and scanned the ground for coins. "Avery, I don't have any more coins."

"—it doesn't come back tonight. The last thing Mac needs is a monster running around while the investors are here. It took us all day to—"

"Aves, I don't have much time. The man, Troy, he said Green Bank wouldn't be a problem in another day. That everyone would fall in line. Like he had a plan and—"

"Please insert twenty-five cents to continue your call."

"Cricket, you're cutting out."

"You need to leave," she rushed out. Her pulse was pounding so hard she could feel it in her fingers, worry and fear warring for dominance as little dots connected.

"I can't leave; the dinner."

"I know!" she shouted, slamming her hand against the pay-phone. The dinner. The Georgia Man, the way he had smiled at Cricket, making sure she heard him ask about the drive to Elk-water. "I know, Avery; you need to leave or hide or something. Don't go to that dinner."

"What! Why not?"

"Lunar Asset Management! It's the Georgia Men, whatever is happening, it's happening—"

"Your call has been disconnected."

"Tonight." Cricket slammed the receiver down, again and again, until the plastic cracked, and she was panting heavily, caught somewhere between wanting to cry and needing to scream. So she did both. "*Fuck*."

20

— · —

Avery

For as much as she dreaded the dinner, it was no worse than any of the other political elbow-rubbing social engagements she'd been forced to attend as a kid. Cooky had made fettuccine Alfredo with a medley of grilled vegetables, and while the men of Lunar Asset Management launched into a discussion of the camp's future prospects, Avery put her effort into keeping her mouth full instead of saying something she would regret. Just like she had for countless business dinners hosted by her father. The main difference now, of course, was Mac.

Nathan Payne demanded his children behave, smile, and stay silent, no matter what was said at the table. Over the years, Avery had become skilled at half-listening to his guests' posturing and pride. Whether lobbyists, politicians, CEOs, or local commerce leaders, they were all aligned with her father, and their opinions were just as crude and backward.

When she was fourteen, she won the privilege of speaking at dinner, so long as her words were demure and docile and spoken only to agree with whatever fell out of the men's mouths at the table. She lost the privilege when she was nineteen and dared to express what her father called an "inappropriate" opinion regarding the funding of Planned Parenthood.

Mac, unlike her father, wanted to involve her in the conversation. Not in any way that felt like she was parading Nathan Payne's daughter around for everyone to see, but she couldn't quite escape the feeling that that was precisely what she was doing.

The director had all but admitted to it, regardless of how well she knew Avery's resume or could recite her qualifications for the job—which she had done at least three times since Cricket left with Ramble. It felt like Mac was trying to convince herself that Avery was the best choice when they both knew full well that she wasn't, and in that effort, kept dragging her into the conversation around future plans for the camp, what funding they would need, and the organizations she had targeted for fundraising.

Avery had to admit, as upset as she was to learn she'd been a tool used by both her father and her boss, Mac's plans for the camp and her desire to involve Avery and hear her thoughts were chipping away at the wall that had been thrust between them, even if she would never get the chance to come back after this summer and see those plans enacted.

Still, no matter how many times Mac attempted to drag Avery into this conversation, she was being carted out and placed on display, sandwiched between two suited men and being leered at by a third.

And not just any third.

Troy Wilkolak. The Georgia Man.

He sat across from her at the small dining room table, his attention as heavy and aggressive as his cologne. She'd caught a whiff of it the moment he entered the cabin, the lavender and wintergreen tickling her nose when he handed off his coat. Now, enclosed in the tight dining room, the scent was overpowering and undeniably the same one she'd caught in her cabin and on the monster in the wood.

Troy Wilkolak was inhuman, but what was he?

"Of course, we'll have to adjust your proposal to reflect the leanings of our target audience," one of the asset managers, a lean, rangy man who had introduced himself as Camden, said.

Mac froze, and a sauce-drenched chunk of zucchini fell off of her fork. "What sort of adjustments?"

"The ratio," another of the Georgia Men said. Avery thought his name was Josh, but they all wore identical suits and identical haircuts; it was hard to tell them apart. Except for Troy. "A fifty-fifty human-inhuman will never fly with some of the people we would be targeting. If you alter the acceptance rate to the camp to, say, seventy-five twenty-five, we could capture the interest of more conservatively aligned parties."

"Good thinking, Thad," another of the men said. "Involve the wives, you know how they get. They want to be seen as socially progressive, but not *too* socially aggressive, as it were."

The old anger rose. That banked fury Avery felt at every one of these dinners. Men arguing what was best for women and children. For the country they were becoming increasingly out of touch with. Who were they to decide how Mac ran the camp? Elkwater was privately funded through donations and Mac's tireless work. There were no shareholders to please, no palms to grease. Why was she even entertaining this dinner?

"That would go against everything this camp stands for." Mac threw her fork down, splashing Alfredo sauce on the sleeve of the asset manager beside her. He frowned and brushed it off with a napkin. "Some of these kids have nowhere to go. They have no opportunities in the world thanks to the"—she crooked her fingers in air quotes—"'more conservatively aligned parties' you want to target for money. Elkwater fosters their talent. This place nurtures those kids by giving them direction, a heading, a *chance* outside of these hills."

"Well, little lady," Thad started. Mac visibly bristled, curling her hand into a fist on the table. "Be that as it may, this is the reality of the world. Inhumans are still new—"

"They've been here for over a decade," Mac argued. Red crawled up from the collar of her button-down and into her cheeks, barely hidden by the light layer of foundation she'd worn for dinner. "Hardly new."

"And the world is hardly ready to fully accept them," Thad finished. He glared at Avery, tipping his head slightly. It was a gesture of acknowledgment, lending credence to his next words, but his tone was derogatory enough that Avery slunk down in her chair on Mac's behalf. "You've done great work here with the integration, but imagine what you could do with excess funding."

"It's a minor adjustment." Troy pointed his fork at Mac, the tines gleaming in the lamplight. "In the grand scheme of things."

Avery blinked, startled by the clean utensil, and peered at his plate—untouched. She glanced around the table as he spoke, noting the same of each of the asset managers' plates. Their meals were untouched, and the utensils held in their hands unused.

What?

"We ran the numbers, and at seventy-five twenty-five, with full funding from our target donors, you'd be able to secure enough ROI after the fifth fiscal to adjust the acceptance rate without any real detriment to your donations," said Camden. "I could have the boys put together a projection at, say, seventy-thirty and see where we land, but there is our broker's fee to consider."

"I—" Mac worked her jaw, voice creaking in her throat. "Five fiscal *years?*"

"For the audience we're targeting?" Camden chuckled. "Five is optimistic unless Gore wins, which, c'mon."

A torrent of laughter broke out around the table. Mac clenched her jaw, lips pressed together so hard they turned white.

Avery jumped to her feet. "More wine?"

Half a dozen men leveled their attention her way, sizing her up. Troy raised his glass, white wine sloshing within, and brought it to his mouth, downing the alcohol in one long swallow.

"Now *there's* a young lady who knows how to negotiate." Thad lightly pounded the table to a chorus of agreement from the rest of the men. Troy's gaze never left Avery, and his lower lip bulged as he ran his tongue over his teeth. "I don't suppose there's a bottle of Screaming Eagle Reserve back there, eh?"

"I'll go check."

She all but ran into the kitchen, gripping the counter with her head hanging between her shoulders. The door swung closed behind her, muffling masculine voices as they continued to tell Mac how to run their camp.

Their camp.

When had this become *their* camp?

"It's good to see you again, Miss Payne." Troy filled the space behind her, the heat of his body blanketing her back. She hadn't heard the door re-open, which meant he had slipped in silently behind her.

She raised her head, staring at their reflections in the window over the sink. He loomed close, filling the frame and cutting Avery off from the rest of the cabin. A sharp grin stretched across his face, hungry and predatory. A wolfish grin that was completely wiped clean by the time she whirled around.

"Mr. Wilkolak."

"Thought I'd come and help you with the wine." He didn't move, keeping a distance that was firmly in that uncomfortable space of too close yet still respectful. "A good girl like you shouldn't be expected to know her way around alcohol."

The stink of his cologne tickled her nose. Avery licked her lips, throat tightening with the urge to vomit. Every cell in her body screamed at her to run, flee, hide, but if Troy were the monster, he would catch her, and God only knew what he would do then. "I think I can manage it."

"Nonsense." He eased away, sidling across the kitchen to the rolling island against the wall. Manicured fingers danced over bottles, circling the neck of one and lifting his chosen vintage. He held it out, examining the label. "The law of being a Southern gentleman, I'm afraid. What would your father think?"

"I'm not sure I can speak to my father's thoughts."

"Hm." He set the bottle down and chose a second one. Though his attention was on the label, he cocked his head in a way that made Avery feel like a rabbit being watched out of the corner of a wolf's eye. "Don't take what they're saying in there to heart." The bottle clinked as he slid it back into place and chose a third. Avery edged across the kitchen, reaching for the doorknob. "It's all business. The numbers, the bullying, talking your boss into a corner. All just business, you understand."

"I do." She spun and twisted the knob, easing the door open.

Troy's hand slapped against the particle board, pressing the door closed. Her entire body flinched, breath catching in her chest as that broad, powerful figure again stepped too close. He'd moved so fast, and she hadn't even heard him. He'd been across the kitchen; how had he moved so *fast?* She closed her eyes, willing her voice not to tremble. "Please let me leave."

"In a moment," Troy rumbled. "Need a little refresher." His body was too warm, his musk and that scent too overpowering. Overwhelming. It snuck into her senses, wrapping around Avery's mind until all she knew was terror. Her arm shook, hand still gripping the knob, and she bit her lips to keep a rising sob from escaping.

Troy leaned in close, ducking his head until it hovered above the crook of her neck.

And then he *inhaled.*

"What are you—"

"Only business, Elizabeth Avery Payne," he exhaled, breath hot against her ear. "All of this is just business."

21

—·—

CRICKET

"WE NEED TO GO." The woven reed door crashed against the wattle-and-daub wall. Three sets of eyes landed on Cricket, all ears intent on her. Ramble's father, Iver, was the first to recover, lurching to his feet. Though shorter than Bosk, his antlers were no less impressive, the tips falling a hair's breadth short of scraping the ceiling.

"Cricket, where have you been?"

"No time." She slashed a hand through the air and held it out toward Ramble. "I need the keys."

"The keys?" Her cousin blinked and shook their head. Iver cast them a wary look while their mother, Coni, frowned. "For what?"

"The truck. Charlie won't drive me all the way to Elkwater." She swept her hand in the air, gesturing for Ramble to hurry up. "We've got to go. The Georgia Men are there and they—"

"Oh, Gods." Iver rolled his eyes and dropped to the ground, settling heavily on his knees. Pine straw and dust whoofed up in a cloud around him. "Coni, go tell Bosk his crazy daughter is at it again."

"Dad!" Ramble glared at their father and stood.

"What?" he asked, taking a fork and attacking the sprouts and grains on his trencher. "Fool of a faun has been spouting nonsense about these Georgia Men for years."

"Because it's true!" she hollered. "And I have proof, which I can show you, but *first,* we have to get to Elkwater. Avery, she's—"

"Hosting a fundraising dinner at the camp," Ramble finished. "She is fine; I spoke with Mac earlier." They crossed the room, catching Cricket by the arm and guiding her out into a pale purple twilight. "Cricket, what is this about?"

"I went to Marlinton."

"Oh, Gods." Ramble smacked their forehead. "Is that where you've been? Bosk has been losing his antlers over you all day."

"I saw the papers, the signatures." She paced in a tight circle, trying to get out everything she had learned—about the properties, the Georgia Man, and the dinner. The pressure was building within her, the need to go, go now, *fast.* "And it's hers, but it's not. And that man was there, Ramble. He was there, he saw me, and—"

"Cricket."

"I need the keys; we have to go." She grabbed her cousin's arm, all but pulling them in the direction of the trailhead where they had parked the truck.

Ramble planted their hooves. "No."

"What?"

"I said no." They jerked their arm out of her grasp and pointed at Cricket. "You need to go home. Get some sleep and get your head on straight."

"We have to *go*. The camp is in trouble."

"I *know*," Ramble said, raising their voice to match. "Why do you think I am here? Mac is trying to raise enough money to expand and bring in more teachers and students. We are barely keeping the camp open as it is. She needs investors, but the people with access to that sort of money have a hard enough time accepting Mac, much less that she is married to me."

"No, no, it's not that," Cricket shook her head. "I mean, it is that. Like, wow, that's a lot to unpack. But the men at the dinner. They're from Lunar Asset Management."

"Okay?"

"It's not okay!" Gods, why wasn't anyone else capable of seeing what a problem this was? Ramble said they had seen the property tax filings; they *said* so, so why couldn't they put this together? "That man works for them!"

"What man?"

"The one at the assessor's office!" She threw her arms wide, panting in panic. "I saw him at the camp with Avery's father. They went to lunch, and the signatures matched, but they didn't, and he was there. Today. Filing more paperwork, and he saw me and he asked how long the drive was to get to Elkwater.

Don't you understand? He works for Lunar Asset. He smelled like lavender and wintergreen, and he's in the camp with Avery and Mac!" Ramble chewed their lower lip, watching Cricket pace. "The scent was the same. It was on the papers and on him. I smelled it that night. Ramble. Please, we need to go."

"What ni—" Ramble stopped themself, shaking the thought away. Their ears twitched, only the tips visible under their hair. "I'm sorry."

"Ramble..."

"Crick, I want to believe you. I want to help you, but I have to put Mac and the camp over whatever you think is going on."

"Ramble, please."

"It's my home, Crick. We have worked too hard for this. One day, you might understand, but what we are trying to build, what Mac is achieving, is setting the tone for broader integration. I cannot put my wife's goals at risk because some businessman with bad cologne smiled at you."

"Right." Cricket straightened, rolling her shoulders back. A cold calm washed over her as she raised her face to the setting sun, little more than a sliver of gold crowning Bald Knob to the west. Ramble wouldn't help. Her family wouldn't help. No matter how many times she begged and pleaded, no matter how much evidence she presented, she would always be the faun who cried wolf. Never the faun who was trying to save them, which meant she was on her own. The steadiness of her realization was better than any bandage or balm and without a further word, she walked into the woods.

"Cricket," Ramble called after her. "Where are you going?"

She didn't answer. What good would words do? Her cousin had seen the papers, had seen the signatures with their own eyes, and was resigned to stay away. They were resigned to … they were resigned. And why shouldn't they be? Ramble had found a home outside of Green Bank. They had found a partner who would save them if the worst happened, and what did Cricket have?

Nothing. No one. Her home was being taken from her, the thinnest sliver of hope was in trouble, and no one was coming to save her. No one was coming to save Avery.

So Cricket would save them herself.

"Cricket!" Ramble's voice was thin through the trees, a faint echo that barely reached her ears. She balanced against a boulder to stretch out her uninjured leg, then rolled the ankle on her injured leg, wincing at the lingering tightness. Though she wasn't fully healed, whatever latent magic the faun had kept in their fall had healed the wound enough, and Avery needed help.

The Georgia Man had been so confident, so sure that Green Bank wouldn't be a problem. So certain the holdouts would fall in line. Cricket wasn't smart enough to puzzle through the what, exactly, but she was clever enough to have ideas.

Rumors of a monster in the woods. The monster that had chased Cricket lingering at the camp, chasing Avery and destroying her cabin. Her signatures on the papers and that lavender and wintergreen scent clinging to the Georgia Man. Whatever he was going to do, it was happening tonight.

"Cricket, for the Gods' sake," Ramble cursed, their voice closer. Cricket glanced back, spotting their silhouette through the darkened trees, and she shouldered into a run. The first hoof-fall on her injured leg warbled up her thigh, her ankle protesting and hoof pinching. On a good day, on two good hooves, it would only take her an hour and a half to run the ridges between Green Bank and Elkwater. Two, if she kept to the well-trod deer trail; three, if she attempted the run in poor weather.

But injured, exhausted, and wound tighter than a banjo string? The weather might be clear, but the best Cricket could hope for was three.

The dinner would have just started and the Georgia Man wouldn't attempt anything in daylight. All of the attacks had occurred at night when the camp was quiet, and the moon high overhead.

That's not true.

She tripped over a root at the thought, hissing and spitting.

Because it wasn't true. The monster had chased her at night during a storm and then again a few hours after dawn. She vividly recalled the pale orb of the moon, just visible in the sky as she cowered in a thorn bush.

She gritted her teeth and clenched her fists, fear driving her up a small hill and over a creek. All she had was the hope that the monster, the Georgia Man, would wait until full dark—until after dinner. But what if he didn't?

What if she was already too late?

Fear pushed her on, adrenaline the only barrier between Cricket and the ache in her hoof as she chased the sunset over a lesser ridge, down into a ravine, and up again. Summiting Bald Knob and heading north along the ridge as the last of the day was swallowed by the trees and rolling hills.

The descent to Shavers Fork was harder than the climb. Full dark swallowed the Monongahela the moment the sun was out of sight, and she stumbled, her eyes unused to the deep, impenetrable black. Her ankle throbbed with every step, and her hoof felt as though someone had driven an iron spike into the pads, but she pressed on, following the creek at a pace no human could match.

The moon rose at her back, casting the woods in sultry blue light. As if on cue, an eager howl shattered the night.

Cricket grabbed the narrow trunk of a tree, jerking to a halt, her ears pricked, and every hair along her neck raised. She knew that howl, and she knew the terror of hearing it close at her back. She knew it over the sound of wild thunder and over ridgelines, and to hear it now meant only one thing: the monster had begun his hunt, and Cricket was too late.

22

AVERY

The blood-red pinpricks of tail lights vanished behind a bend in the road, and Mac wilted against the porch, letting out a long, sustained sigh.

"What a sanctimonious bunch of—"

"Assholes," Avery stated, earning a wry grin from Mac. "You're not really thinking of working with them to find investors, are you?"

"No?" She cocked her head, brows screwed together. "Maybe?" She heaved off the porch rail and collapsed into a rocking chair, legs stretched out, her heels driving into the planks. "I want to expand, bring in a choir program, performing arts, the works, but we're barely operating in the black as it is. The pianos need tuning, the concert hall needs new lights, the field is full of holes, half the bleachers collapsed in that storm, we only have two functional bullhorns," she counted off on her fingers, frowned at all five, and dropped her hand with a slap against her thigh. "Cooky says we need a new walk-in, and the nurse's office needs a new roof. We need the money."

Avery propped her elbows on the railing, scanning the woods at the edge of the parking lot. A narrow gap in the trees, barely visible from their singular streetlamp, marked the start of a trail that serpentined behind the camp, connecting to the broader trail systems she and the campers frequently used and, eventually, to the Monongahela National Forest system.

"How much land does the camp own?" She tipped her head at the trees. "Could we sell any to fund repairs?"

"Nope." The rocking chair creaked as Mac pushed her feet against the porch. "Elkwater owns the land outright. I tried to portion some of it off a few years ago to open an RV campground, but the National Park Service requires us to keep a perimeter of undeveloped woodland. Something about noise control."

A howl rippled over the ridgelines, punctuating Mac's words. Avery frowned in the direction of the sound. It came from far beyond the camp, but the mournful, haunting note was as clear as if it had been sung directly in her ear. Floorboards creaked at her back, and Mac stepped beside her.

"I'll go check the field," she said, eyes trained on the trees. "You good to do a cabin sweep?" Avery nodded and started down the stairs, halting as Mac brushed her shoulder. "Cabins, and then straight to the practice room. Lock the doors behind you, alright? And if you hear or see *anything*, you run straight back here."

"I will."

"I mean it, Avery. If you hear any sound or see any hint of anything suspicious, you'll come back here. There's a rifle in the closet in my room; the locker code is the last four digits of the camp phone. Shells are on the top shelf. Do you know how to fire a gun?"

Her stomach dropped, her tongue going dry at the implication of what Mac thought might be in the woods. She hadn't told her about that moment in the kitchen with Troy; she hadn't been able to find the words. How did you explain to your boss that a businessman trapped you in a kitchen and *smelled* you?

Still, she managed one tight dip of her chin. "I do."

"Be quick." Mac nodded, mouth a tight line. She squeezed Avery's shoulder and released. Avery rushed down the stairs and was halfway to the main trail leading through the camp when Mac called out, "Hey, Avery?" The director descended the stairs, the tight strain to her expression softening. "About you and Cricket ..."

"I'm sorry," said Avery. A flush heated her neck and cheeks, and she ducked her head. "I know it's probably inapprop—"

"No!" Mac blurted. "No sorries. I just—I know I said you should give the inhumans a chance, get to know them a little, and while I didn't quite mean that in the biblical sense, I'm proud of you." Avery raised her head, struck dumb by the admission and the praise. "I know a lot of this is new to you, the camp and … and Cricket, but if it ever feels overwhelming, or you have questions about the faun or need an ear, I'm here. Alright?"

"Alright." She toed the dirt, barely able to bring her voice above a whisper. Something new fluttered in her chest at Mac's offer. At her acceptance. Something new and lovely and fragile that she was too afraid to share, so she held it close and safe and said, "Thank you."

"The faun are special," Mac continued—her voice light and wistful. "Ramble is very protective of their family, but they'll come around. Once they see how good you and Cricket are for each other, they'll come around."

Avery opened her mouth to respond, but only the tiniest little squeak came out.

"It's pretty obvious." Mac waved her hand, dismissing the sound. "I've met that cranky little deer a few times but never seen her smile the way she smiles at you." Avery's cheeks flushed hotter, and Mac took pity, jerking her chin at the camp, a smile in her voice. "Go on, make sure all the campers are in their bunks and get to yours."

"Yes, Director Murray."

"Avery," she warned, and at that, Avery could only smile.

"You got it, Mac."

The howls continued, puncturing the night from a distance in a baleful melody. It was enough to have the campers rushing into their bunks. The memory of Avery and Sanoya's cabin, of the terrible destruction, was fresh enough in the collective camp mind that not even the full moon could entice campers to wander unchaperoned.

Avery hustled along the meandering center trail, forgoing the shortcuts behind the buildings to stick to the dimly lit path. A handful of campfires burned, the logs and stumps surrounding them abandoned. Aksel wove between the cabins, his broad-shouldered figure lending a sense of security to the campers, and counselors observed the flames from the front porches of their cabins, whispering among themselves and waving at Avery as she walked by. In the distance, hair glowing in the moonlight, Sanoya swept the perimeter of the marching band field, followed closely by a large shadow darting from bleachers to trees to trashcans.

All was well, the campgrounds secure, the campers safe.

Still, she couldn't shake the memory of Troy's leering smile and the cloying musk of his cologne. The sticky heat of his breath when he'd exhaled against her neck, almost as if he savored the scent of her. What had he said?

Need a little refresher.

A gag and a full body shiver had her hustling to the practice rooms, hand shaking as she fitted the key into the lock, shouldering the humidity-swollen door open and shoving it closed. She slammed the deadbolt into place, jiggling the knob to be absolutely certain the door was locked, the building secure, and only then did she exhale and drop her forehead against the window in the door.

Sleep was going to be a long time in coming, that was for sure. At least she had her favorite practice room and the only properly tuned piano in the camp to keep her mind occupied. Already, she could feel the music surging into her hands. Something in four-four time. A driving composition. Rossini? No, Khachaturian. *Sabre Dance.* The frenetic chords and arpeggios would burn through her energy, leaving Avery panting and sweating at the end of the movement, clearing her mind so she could think.

She was fairly certain Troy was behind the attack on her cabin, and she believed Cricket when she said the papers had smelled like him; she just couldn't figure out *how*.

There were a few shifters at the camp—Aksel, for one. He was wolven, and he could have caused the destruction they saw in her cabin, so it was possible they were dealing with another of his kind. But when he shifted, he shifted into a wolf. Not a bipedal monster that smelled of stale cologne.

So whatever Troy *was*, he wasn't any sort of shifter Avery had met before. Granted, that list was very small and entirely made up of the shifters in the camp, but when she took Sanoya's comments about the *whatsitcalled* into account, Avery knew in her gut that Troy was something else.

But *what*.

With her head full of thoughts, she walked the length of the hall, idly checking the doors to the practice rooms and finding each one locked. Moonlight filtered in through the window in the door, illuminating the hall just enough for Avery to peer through darkened windows, each room empty, as they should be.

All the campers and counselors were safe in their cabins and bunks; the howls had only grown distant as the night deepened, and soon, Avery would be too tired to think. She would play until her fingers ached and fall into her makeshift bunk to sleep off this endless day. Tomorrow, Ramble would come home, and maybe they would bring Cricket, and they could—

Avery stopped in front of the door to her favorite practice room, the only one without a window facing the hall. A faint light glowed through the crack at the base, which wasn't unusual. She hated entering a dark room and had gotten in the habit of leaving a lamp on years before. But her lamp glowed a soft yellow, not the cold blue of moonlight.

She stepped back, a hand pressed to her mouth, as she assessed the door. The only sound in the hall was her tight, panicked breathing, and the only light came from the window at the entrance and under her door. The practice rooms were empty and locked. Everything was fine; she was fine.

Been a long day, is all—a long day after a series of long days.

She just needed to go to bed. Needed to play out her nerves and her thoughts and get some sleep.

"Stop being a paranoid dummy," she muttered, "and go to bed." Rolling her shoulders and lifting her chin, she grabbed the knob, twisted it, and shoved the door open.

Moonlight streamed through the window set into the rear wall, casting her room in a ghostly pallor. Her makeshift bed, a twin mattress on a cot Sanoya had wrangled from storage, filled the far wall. An overturned crate beneath the window acted as a bedside table, and at the foot of the bed was the upright piano she favored. Curtains wafted in a slight breeze coming in through the window, tickling Avery's nose with the faint scent of lavender and wintergreen. She pressed her mouth into her shoulder, stifling a gag, only to have her stomach turn at the lingering stench of Troy's cologne on her shirt.

"You're being stupid," she said to the room. "You forgot to turn on the lamp, that's all."

Avery shook out her hands and strode into the room. Glass crunched beneath her sneaker. She froze, squinting in the low light, and just barely able to make out the shape of her lamp on the floor in front of the crate. She crouched and picked it up, examining the broken bulb. Her gaze tracked upwards, snagging on the window and the wafting curtains. Every hair on her arms rose, unease breathing warm and sticky across the back of her neck.

"You left the window open," Avery told herself, praying silently that it was true, that she was right, that she'd only left the window open. "You left it open, and a breeze knocked over the lamp. E-easy peasy."

"Too easy," Troy rumbled.

Avery lurched to her feet, spinning around and swinging the lamp. Glass tinkled as the broken bulb collided with an overly muscled shoulder. She wrenched it free, using her momentum to swing again, this time higher. He caught the body, wrestling it out of Avery's grip. Her shoulder screamed in pain, *she* screamed in pain, and Troy laughed. He tossed the lamp aside, moving his bulk between Avery and the door.

"I thought you'd give me another chase, Elizabeth." His voice was still slick and smooth, but there was a snarl to the words, a bestial roughness as though he'd been shouting for hours and was now trying to speak. "This is much better. They'll find your corpse, bloody and mangled, in the one place Mac Murray promises human children will be safe from *us*."

He advanced, crowding Avery into the tiny space. Moonlight danced over swells of muscle, allowing her glimpses of his hulking form: a bulging thigh, knobby, hairy fingers that sharpened to claws, and scraps of cloth hanging from his shoulders and torso.

"What are you?" she breathed, unable to make sense of what she was seeing. A tremble built in her limbs, and bile rose in her throat.

"What do you think, little girl?" He stepped fully into the moonlight, giving Avery just a second to take in the long snout, with lips curled back to reveal terrifying fangs. Bone stretched over the length of his snout and brow, his face a wretched skull with keen yellow eyes burning in the low light. "Inhuman."

Troy lunged, teeth snapping. She jumped back onto the camping cot, arms thrown out, and pressed her back against the wall. Fangs closed over empty air where she'd been standing, and Troy straightened. His nose twitched as he breathed deeply, exhaling with a lusty sigh. "Your fear smells delicious, little girl."

"Stay back!" She swept an arm through the air.

"Or what?" Troy laughed, advancing. "Where's your little faun, Elizabeth? Where is your pet inhuman to keep you safe?" He cocked his head, feigning listening. "That's right, she isn't here. It's just you"—he set one paw-like foot on the edge of the cot. The frame groaned beneath his weight, and Avery whimpered—"and me and the moonlight."

Metal creaked, Troy launched himself at Avery, and she jumped to the side. The wall gave way to nothing, and she barely had the time to process Troy's pained *yip* as she collided with the ground outside. The window rattled in its frame, wood cracked. Avery scrabbled onto her hands and knees, feet catching in her skirt as she tried to stand. Cursing under her breath, she gripped the fabric in both hands and lurched to her feet.

Howls shattered the night, pushing Avery's frantic pace. She followed the trail for a few yards, darting into the woods and onto another trail and another, leading Troy as far from the camp as she could. Branches scraped her arms, thorns shredded her skirt, but she ran. Ignoring the shouts rising from the camp, barely audible through her own heartbeat pounding in her ears. Another howl rent the night, this one closer—far too close. She slapped a hand over her mouth to keep from screaming and pressed her speed.

On the trail ahead, a fallen tree blocked the path. Vaguely, Avery was aware of where she was—that this was the tree that had fallen in the storm. The tree on the trail where she'd first met Cricket, who had been chased to the camp by a monster.

By Troy.

But the only clear thought in her mind was the memory of a splintered hollow cloaked in shadow and shrouded in the scent of decaying oak. She scrambled over the trunk, slipping down the other side. Splinters and bark flayed her palms, and another howl had her scuttling into the hollowed trunk, hugging her knees and biting her arm. Listening for any footstep, any hint of where Troy was, how far away he was.

Where is he? She rocked in place, too afraid to close her eyes. *Where is he where is he where is he?*

23

CRICKET

Lavender and wintergreen hung heavy in the humid air, choking Cricket with each rasping, sawing breath. She pulled the neck of her shirt up, attempting to filter the perfumed musk through the fabric, and followed the scent along Elkwater Run.

It had grown stronger as she descended the last ridge, and once she hit the creek feeding into the larger stream running through the camp, the stench became unbearable.

A chorus of howls rose over her harsh breathing, bleeding through the thick night and pushing Cricket onward. Fury drove her every step, powering her through the ache in her legs and the blinding pain in her ankle.

She dropped into a creek and waded through calf-deep waters cold enough to help her forget the pain, but all too soon, she was clamoring out the other side, hands slipping on mossy roots and dislodging loose stones.

She was never going to run after this. Hells, she would be lucky even to be able to, and if she could, she would never run again for pleasure, that was damn sure. Easing into a jog, she clenched her jaw so hard she thought her teeth might crack. The ache in her legs she could deal with. The sharp twang and pinch of strained muscle and tendon she could ignore. But her hoof ...

Gods, she wanted to ignore it, but it was all she could think about. If she thought about Avery and what those howls meant, she would start panicking, and then she'd start crying, and then she'd be *useless*. But if she thought about the pain—about the wicked snap she'd felt after falling on the western face of Barton Knob, the sound of it like dry twigs snapping in half; if she thought about the feel of splinters driving into the pad of her hoof, she could keep going.

Her hoof was going to slough off, that much she knew. An injury like that? No way it hadn't damaged the tissue underneath. Until it regrew, she'd be stuck with that damn crutch again, hobbling around the camp or Green Bank or wherever she ended up. But until it sloughed off, she could press through the pain, let it stoke her anger, and fuel her body enough to get to Avery.

She leapt over a gully. Her good hoof landed in an unseen divot on the other side and, arms flailing, she tumbled and hit the ground, tucking somewhat into a roll. Her shoulder hit a rock, ivy tangled around her legs, and she crashed against a tree stump. Bark and leaves tumbled around her. She lay in a daze, blinking away the sting in her eyes.

Get up.

Gods, she was so close, and the scent was so strong.

Get the hells up.

Lavender and wintergreen, the musk of male. Close enough, heady enough, that when she rolled onto her side and pressed her hand to the forest floor she could *taste* the Georgia Man on her tongue.

You're so damned close. Get. Up.

Lavender and wintergreen. What had Avery called it? Obsession? Whatever it was, it clogged the woods, the scent no longer a trail but a web. She pushed to her knees, biting her tongue to stifle the scream as a new ribbon of pain wound up her leg.

"Fuck," she panted, dropping her weight against the tree stump. Her hair snagged in the bark, eyes going unfocused as she fought off the tears, the pain. A slight breeze wove through the glade, wafting away the shopping mall miasma. Not entirely, but enough to clear Cricket's head. She stretched out her uninjured leg, massaging the calf and inspecting her ankle and hoof.

No breaks, no splinters.

Thank the Gods.

Settling against the stump, Cricket dropped her head back and closed her eyes, just for a moment. Just long enough to catch her breath, to let the worst of the pain fade. Enough to breathe the cleaner air, inhaling grass and moss instead of lavender and wintergreen. Grass and moss, wet earth, and ... salt.

She lifted her head, ears pricking as she scanned the glade. High overhead, the moon peered through the pine, painting the world in shadows and clean blue light. Low branches and shrubs filled eye level, densely packed, and impassable unless you knew the deer trails behind the camp. She tripped her gaze from branch to branch to bush, picking out the details: broken twigs and trampled undergrowth. Pine needles bent at an angle, and a lone scrap of cloth caught in thorns.

Nostrils flaring, she inhaled again, dropping onto her hands to crawl forward and catching the scent of salt once again. Salt and fear.

She knew the scent and stink of that fright, as well as she knew her own. And that salt was a sweat she had tasted.

"No." Staggering to her hooves, Cricket rushed to the thorn-bush and grabbed the cloth, pressing it to her nose and breathing deep. Her tongue was fat and thirsty in her mouth, dry as bark, and barely able to form the word. "No, no, no."

Flowers dotted the fabric, a light, summery linen torn from a skirt she knew—a skirt she had seen tangled around soft, sturdy legs.

Her knee buckled. She stumbled to the side, grunting at the throb of pain and barely catching herself on a boulder. Gods, she was so close—close enough to smell Avery's sweat and her fear. Where had she gone? Which way had she run?

Cricket wobbled in a circle, her back to the deer trail, searching the darkened wood as her ears swiveled, straining to catch any sound: the camp, a frantic heartbeat, panicked breathing. Anything to tell her where Avery might be. To tell her she was safe—

"Found you," a deeply masculine and predatory voice snarled from behind her. Cricket whirled around, tweaking her ankle and swallowing the cry as she scanned the shadows. Still. Everything was so still ... too still. The sort of still that set her hairs on end and sparked the urge to flee.

The shadows shifted just to the left of the deer trail, a mass forming among the trees. Too tall to be human, too broad to be faun. Too muscular to be any of the inhumans she had seen in the camp, even in their shifted form.

Fright held her in place. That wretched instinct every faun had to freeze at the sight of bright lights, though instead of the momentary blindness that came with human machines, this was pure, unadulterated *fear*.

Moonlight poured over a bone-white face, swallowed by a fold of impenetrable black splitting the skull's brow in two. The creature heaved through the wood, the ground shuddering as a massive paw stepped into the glade. Cricket took in all of him and pieces of him at once: that skull, bilious yellow eyes, bulging muscle in thick thighs, the claws at the tips of his toes and fingers, the teeth ...

"Your human's given me quite a chase," he snarled, lips curling back over vicious fangs. A sick, shuddering sigh hissed from his throat, and he prowled closer. "Leading me through the woods in circles. Back and back again, twisting her trail with scraps of cloth." He tossed a handful of fabric in her direction. Ribbons of cloth fluttered and fell to the ground, identical to the scrap in her hand.

Cricket's heart sputtered, tripping over beats as adrenaline spiked in her veins. Her fingers quaked, her legs trembled. She gripped the cloth as she gasped, trying to fill her lungs enough to scream for help.

"Why don't you run, little deer?" the creature taunted.

A whimper was all she could muster, the pathetic sound burbling past her lips and dying just as quickly. He advanced, the moonlight revealing the true terror of the creature ... the *monster*. Twigs snapped beneath every step, the earth protesting against his weight and size as he paced in a slow, predatory circle. Even if she *could* run, she could never outrun this.

"Your human ran," he taunted. A hand swept his browbone, fingers tracing the fold in his skull that swallowed the moonlight. No, not a fold, a crack. A snide laugh escaped as a tight bark. "Jumped right out the window. Damn near broke the wall when I hit it. Who knew a girl that soft could be so fast?"

The breeze kicked up again, bringing the scent of the beast to Cricket's nose: musk and sweat, the sharp tang of exertion. Lavender, and wintergreen. She gagged, eyes watering as she took in the monster with new understanding. "Georgia Man."

He tipped his head back, arms hanging loose at his sides. An unearthly howl tore from his throat, rattling the leaves and needles overhead. In the distance, a chorus of identical howls sang in reply. Cricket cowered down, her body battling the warring urges to run, cry, vomit, and piss herself.

"You faun are so stupid." He lurched forward, spittle flying from his muzzle. "So easy to manipulate. How long have you been here, a decade? Longer? And you've remained just as back-assward as you were back home."

"What are you—"

"But you ..." He wagged a clawed finger at Cricket, pacing in a tighter circle. "You're a little cleverer than the rest, aren't you? Wanting to integrate, raising a red flag about the 'Georgia Men.' Crying *wolf*."

He snapped his teeth a hair's breadth from her nose. Cricket flinched back, her hoof catching on a root. The sob forcing its way out of her throat became a cry of pain and she fell against a tree, trembling as those threatened tears finally slipped free.

"Pathetic," he snarled. "How the faun were entrusted to maintain the wood is beyond me. You're all so soft." He held out a clawed hand, fingers furling as if crushing something in his leather-padded palm. Snuffing out a light or a life. "So weak."

A cry, deep in the wood, jerked him around. His body tensed for just a moment, and then he angled that terrible skull face back to Cricket. "They're coming, little deer."

She pressed harder against the tree, blinking to clear the tears from her eyes. Distant lights bobbed and wove through the trees, flashlights and lanterns dancing to the cadence of faint voices.

The campers, she realized. *Mac and the counselors, oh, Gods, no.*

"Be here any minute now." A vicious grin spread beneath the skull, sharp fangs white in the moonlight, a drooling tongue lolling to the side. "Do you know what I'm going to do when they get here?"

"K-kill me."

"Kill you?" If that monstrous skull had eyebrows, they would have raised. "Oh, no, no, no, I'm going to defend you"—he flicked his fingers in the direction of the lights—"and kill them. Well, some of them, at least."

"Why?"

The monster did not answer. He raised a hand to his face, gripped his skull, and pulled. Bone came away with the gesture, and only when the moonlight revealed a wolven face and sharp, predatory eyes did Cricket realize what she'd been looking at.

A mask. A deer skull mask. He fingered the fold running up the brow, lip curling into a snarl. "Bitch of yours broke it," he muttered and faced Cricket, leaning close and cocking his head to the side. Claws scraped over bone, and he replaced the mask. "I suppose this will do. What do you think?"

She whimpered, muscles twitching and ready to run. But there would be no running, not for Cricket. She doubted she would make it half a foot before those powerful jaws clamped around her leg, and those claws tore into her body. So she pressed back against the tree as if to will the bark to absorb her and shield her from this monster. "Why?"

"To make them fear you," he said. "You faun are so simple, so kind. You are so *stupid*, and you always have been. Keeping to the trees and befriending backwoods hillbillies. Even in our home world, you were loved and lauded, while werewolves were cast aside as less than. As cursed, nothing *beasts*. But here, in this world?" He crowded into her space, looming over Cricket. The heat and musk of him choked her nose and mouth with dank lavender and decaying pine. "The naga have no power over water, the wolven have lost their speed, and you have no magic to heal. All you can do is lure the deviant with your big eyes and bucolic song."

"We never—"

"I've seen that faun with the camp's director," he said, foam frothing on his lips and tongue. "I've witnessed those idiots in Green Bank look away from a monster in the woods, I have *smelled* you on Elizabeth—I'm sorry, *Avery* Payne."

"You keep her name out of your mouth!" Cricket hollered, her voice far stronger than she felt.

"No problem-o." He grinned again and raised his hand, waggling furry, clawed fingers in her face. "I'll keep it in my hand instead."

"You—" She lunged for him, only to be thrown against the tree, the wind knocked out of her as a clawed hand drove into her chest. Bone and cartilage protested, the last air compressed from her lungs as he slid his palm up her sternum to her throat. Claws pinched her neck, his grip tightening.

Cricket scrabbled at his wrist, his hand. Soft velvet slipped against his dense fur, her nail-less fingers unable to grab hold, unable to injure or tear. She kicked her hooves against the bark, and the pain had her gasping for air. He pressed harder. White stars burst at the corners of her eyes, and she felt her hide popping beneath the press of his claws. Felt warmth dribbling down her throat.

"They're close, little deer. Do you hear them?" He leaned in, dank breath and spittle crashing against her cheek. "Poor, stupid humans. They will see a deer-like monster in the woods killing their children. And when I find Avery Payne, I will eviscerate her where they all can see. Maybe I'll add antlers, really dial in on the faun effect; what do you think?"

Cricket wheezed, the stars in her eyes dimming.

"No more rumors of a monster." He raised his arm, the heel of his hand pressing harder into her throat as she was lifted into the air. Bark scraped against Cricket's back, her hooves flailing, kicks slowing. "No more dances in a moonlight glade or whatever the fuck it is you tragic deer do to bedevil the humans. No more looking away. They will fear you and take whatever shitty deal my firm offers them for their land, and there will be nowhere left for the faun to go."

"Why ..." she wheezed. The strength in her arms sapped away, her grip on his wrist weakening.

"What was that?" He turned his head slightly, angling a pointed ear at her. "Sorry, you're a little breathy."

"Why—*urk*." Cricket's eyes bugged as he gripped her throat tighter. "Why Avery?"

The Georgia Man threw his head back, barking out a laugh before glaring her in the eye. "Can't have a dyke daughter be-smirching Nathan Payne's good name, now can we?"

"Does ... does he know?"

"Of course, he does, dumbass." He straightened his arm, leaning away from Cricket to leer at her. "Whose idea do you think this was?"

"Wha—" The Georgia Man shoved all of his weight into his arm, entirely cutting off what little air Cricket could sip. Her hooves kicked weakly, her hands grabbing, patting, falling away as the world grayed out, her vision tunneled, and—

"Hey, douchebag."

He turned his head into the fierce swing of a tree branch. One moment Cricket was pinned to the tree, strangling, and the next, she was crumpling to the ground. Pain howled up her leg, and she barely registered the sickening crack of bone against bark and the shudder of the woods as that massive figure thudded to the ground.

She hacked and coughed, wheezing as her stomach heaved, her entire body working to fill her lungs and clear her vision, and then a familiar warmth slipped around her back, strong fingers grabbing her wrist and hauling her arm over a soft, sturdy shoulder.

"What are you doing here?" Avery grunted.

"Where is your skirt?" she asked in return, unable to take her eyes away from moon-pale, freckled legs in filthy sneakers and bike shorts. Her voice was a sandpaper rasp, and the effort of speaking made her throat ache.

"If you're going to lecture me about proper attire for a young lady, save it," Avery grunted. Her arm tightened around Cricket, and she hefted them both to their feet. Well, her feet and Cricket's one hoof. "And seriously, what are you doing here?"

"I came to—" she wheezed, then coughed, then hacked and panted. "Came to wa—"

"Oh, my gosh, don't talk, you *disaster*." Her tone was dry and so exasperated that Cricket couldn't help but huff a hoarse laugh. "We need to get back to camp. There's a trail right—" Avery dropped from beneath Cricket's arm, her words transformed into a scream as she was yanked away.

24

—◆—

CRICKET

For the second time in minutes, Cricket crumpled to the ground, her injured ankle and hoof barking in pain. She gritted her teeth, pressing against pine straw with one hand and reaching for Avery with the other.

She shrieked, kicking wildly with one leg and clawing at the earth as she was dragged across the glade and lifted into the air. Blood runneled down her pale calf in black, twisting lines. The plaited tail of her hair whipped around as she kicked and hissed, unable to reach the monster.

Half the deer skull mask had shattered from the impact of Avery's tree branch, and one bilious eye squinted at them in fury. The beast curled his lip, revealing blood-stained gums and a cracked canine. "This is even better. Those idiots will see two faun tearing Elizabeth Payne limb from limb."

"No!" Cricket rasped.

"Troy, you dick!" Avery wriggled and kicked out, landing her heel in his ribs. The beast winced but held tight. "Put me down!"

"Okay." He released his claws, and Avery grunted as she hit the ground. She was quick to roll over, far quicker than Cricket would have thought—faster than Cricket could even react. Avery flipped onto her stomach, the toes of her sneakers digging into the ground, launching herself away from Troy.

He was faster, though, and snagged her by the ankle. Avery shrieked as she was dragged backward and again raised by the leg, blood now running in a liquid sheet up her shin. She slipped in his grip—*No*.

Bile surged up Cricket's throat as she realized Avery hadn't slipped. His *claws* had sliced deep, shredding flesh and muscle.

All sound cut out. The woods fell unearthly still as the scene played out before her. Avery's mouth opened in a silent scream, tears leaking from her eyes, across her temples, and into her hair. The beast, the Georgia Man, *Troy,* pressed out his chest and threw his head back, howling to the moon. His free hand wrenched twigs from a tree and shoved them into the remains of the bone mask like antlers.

"No." Cricket pushed her to hooves, stumbled, and caught herself on a knee. Sound crept back in. Avery's whimpers and cries, Troy's sharp and manic laughter. "No!" She lurched upright, limping across the glade. Her ears swiveled forward, intent on the threat, as her eyes scanned the ground for any weapon, any tool. Avery's tree branch lay snapped in half, too far to reach. No rocks, no jagged stones. Nothing but pine straw and dirt. "Let her go!"

"Or what, little deer?" He leveled the full force of his mad gaze at her, yellow eyes bright and feverish. Hungry. He tightened his grip, the muscles in his arm bulging beneath sleek fur. Avery, Gods, Avery. Her face had gone pale when it ought to be flushed from being held upside down. Pale and soft, her eyes glazing over and rolling back into her skull.

Beams of light cut through the trees, closer now. Shouts and hollers echoed and drew near. Troy glanced at the approaching counselors and campers, his grin spreading with lupine ferocity.

"Showtime."

He swung his arm, releasing his grip on Avery as he did. Cricket lurched for her, too slow on her injuries, too dizzy from being strangled. Avery hit the ground with a terrible thump, rolling onto her side, and Cricket was there a heartbeat later, gathering her into her arms.

Troy prowled the edge of the glade, a low growl rumbling in his chest, primal and terrifying. Instincts warred within Cricket. The inborn faunish desire to *run! Predator! Run, flee, hide!* at odds with her desire to gather Avery to herself. To keep her safe, to soothe her pain and fear away. It took every nerve, every last bit of will for Cricket to keep moving. She crawled across the glade on hands and knees, reaching for Avery as a Gods-be-damned *werewolf* watched her every move.

The moment she had her hands on Avery, Troy snapped his jaws and dropped onto his palms, his twisted body gruesome in its shifted shape—humanoid and monstrous. Caught between wolf and man. A froth built at his mouth, those yellow eyes burning behind the deerskull. He looked rabid, bordering on insane with his desire to ruin the faun and for *what?*

Troy gnashed his teeth, his growl building in volume. The stink of decay washed over the glade, and a beyond-cold lick of fear dribbled down Cricket's spine. Terror filled the woods, replacing the hot, humid night with a cave-like chill.

"Time's running out," Troy jeered. His voice roused Avery from her stupor, and she flopped onto her back, eyes going wide and round at the sight of the werewolf pacing nearer. She screamed, digging the heel of her uninjured leg into the ground, pushing herself away from Troy and into Cricket's arms.

She hauled Avery close. Pressed chest to back, their frantic heartbeats matched in a terrified cadence. Gods, they were both too injured to run. This was it, there was no escape, no shadowed breezeway to hide in.

"Over there!" A voice shouted in the wood, deep and masculine.

"Oh, my God. Is that ... an elk?" Another hollered.

Troy glanced in the direction of the shouts, head cocked as he listened, before returning that vile gaze to Avery and Cricket. He bunched onto his haunches, lips curled back, teeth ready to rend and tear as he prepared to leap across the glade. "Out of time, little deer."

Avery sobbed, trembling as her attempts to escape gave over to unadulterated fright. Cricket held her tight, brushing hair away from her temple and kissing the tears away. If this was it, if this was how it ended, she wanted her to know—

"You're so brave, Aves."

Troy's growl rose, revving like the motor of a car. Fur bristled along his arms and neck.

Avery twisted into Cricket. She wrapped her arms around her back and buried her face in Cricket's chest as she whispered the soothing words Avery should have heard every damn day of her life. "So gods damned brave and beautiful."

Troy snarled. Avery's nails dug into Cricket's back. He launched across the glade and—

An arm the size of a tree trunk swept him out of the air. He let out a high-pitched yelp as his back hit an actual tree, bones snapping like twigs. Pine needles rained down on Cricket and Avery, shook loose from the impact.

His body fell, lifeless, and landed like a sack of potatoes on the ground. A cloud of dust and leaves rose, fluttering back to the earth without fanfare as a terrible stench filled the air.

Avery gagged. She turned her face, and Cricket palmed the back of her head. "No." Pressing just the tips of her fingers against her skull, she urged Avery to look away. "You don't want to see this."

"Is he—?"

Before Cricket could answer, the temperature in the glade plummeted, turning their trembles of fright into outright shivers. A wave of decay and rot followed. Cricket gagged and pressed her nose to Avery's hair, inhaling the sweet florals and salt that was *her* as she witnessed a true terror stalk into view.

Taller than Troy, taller than the topmost points of her father's antlers, the beast that stepped from the shadows was massive and monstrous. A nightmare brought to life.

Shreds of withered velvet peeled from twelve, no, fourteen? Cricket squinted, fighting a roll of nausea as she tried to make sense of what she was seeing. Fourteen-point antlers warped to sixteen, to ten, to twelve again, as if her brain were trying to make space for this creature in all that it knew of the world, seeking relations to the faun, to earthly elk and deer, and unable to make any singular image stick.

It hurt her eyes, so she stopped trying to count, dropping her gaze away to view the bald skull of its face and blazing, eldritch eyes stacked over a gaunt, massive frame.

Exposed ribs enclosed a hollow chest. Every muscle was sinewy and root-like, the veins of its arms withered in the moonlight.

Without sparing a glance at Cricket and Avery, the terror loped for Troy's body, grabbing the lifeless douchebag and dropping him over one bony shoulder like a sack of wheat.

Only then did it turn toward Cricket. The blaze in those horrible eyes did not flicker. It did not falter, and she felt, rather than saw, its attention drift to Avery, taking in how she clung to Cricket. How Cricket held her close and dear.

That horrid attention again rose to Cricket, and the creature nodded once before turning to the wood and disappearing into the shadows of the trees.

A frigid, rancid breeze followed, pricking her ears with the barest rasp of a whisper:

"Take care, little sister."

It was a very, *very* long beat before Cricket was able to speak again.

"What the *fuck* was that?"

"An old friend," a soft, breathy voice answered. Another inhuman appeared from the wood, thin and wispy enough that Cricket half thought she'd drift away on the next breeze. Moon-pale hair rose around a face gleaming ivory white, and though a long bathrobe obscured her feet, Cricket was fairly certain the inhuman was floating. "One of the first to fall through, long, long ago. This world has not been kind to him, but he survives on the stories that are told."

"I don't—"

"I will not dishonor him by speaking his name," the new-comer said. "He does not care for defamation." She glanced around the glade, large, dark eyes taking in the shards of deer skull, broken twigs, and blood. "Honestly, I am surprised he did not shred that impostor to bits right here." She cocked her head at Cricket. "He must like you. Avery certainly does."

At the sound of her name, Avery pressed against Cricket's hand, still cupping the back of her head. "Sanoya?"

"And my Hidebehind." Sanoya gestured to the trees. "We heard everything; how terrible for you." The shadows at her back nodded. Cricket closed her eyes, shook her head, and squinted past Sanoya.

The shadows waved.

"I will happily speak with the authorities," Sanoya continued. "The humans in these hills have long trusted the word of the moon-eyed."

"What," Cricket croaked.

Sanoya drifted closer, bending at the waist and peering at the pair. Her delicate features blurred to nothing, drawing all of Cricket's attention to the large round orbs of her eyes like a moth to the flame. Deep as the caves riddling the hills, black as night save for the gleaming crescent of a moon serving as a pupil. Eyes she could stare at for hours. Days. Weeks. A lifetime.

"About Avery's father and that nasty werewolf." Sanoya straightened, snapping whatever spell had been cast between them. Cricket's arms tightened around Avery, and she cast a glance around the glade, half expecting to have been caught by those eyes long enough for the sun to rise. "Come along, let us get you back to camp. The students are in an uproar, and Director Murray is about to fall to bits."

"I don't think we can walk," said Cricket.

"That is alright." Sanoya gently pried Avery away from her, lifting her into a bridal carry with ease. "I am stronger than I look."

The shadows detached from the trees, melting into the shape of what Cricket could only describe as a black bear crossed with a labrador. It loped up close, nostrils flaring as it inhaled Cricket's scent. She froze, damned prey instincts kicking in once again, and the Hidebehind sneezed in her face.

"He will not hurt you," Sanoya said. The Hidebehind grinned as dogs do, soft pink tongue lolling free. "But that tongue has a mind of its own, and you are both so ... sweaty."

25

AVERY

Magic wasn't real. Avery knew this; science proved it repeatedly, but through some art of luck or *magic*, the injuries Troy had caused only required stitches.

A *lot* of stitches, there was no denying that, but only stitches.

She stared at her leg, stretched before her in the bed, cleaned and wrapped in bandages, then glanced at the faun lying in a similar position beside her.

Cricket's head rested on the pillows, her eyes closed, and long fingers interlocked over her stomach. A band of raw skin and worn down wrapped around the front of her throat. Avery blinked and looked away, unable to bear looking at the lingering proof of what they had gone through.

What they had survived.

Nurse Almaden had been quick, cleaning the wounds and staunching the blood flow enough to work whatever magic it was nurses were taught in medical school. Then she'd handed

Avery a paper cup full of pink liquid and Cricket a handful of what looked like horse tranquilizers.

"To give you some time," the hawkish inhuman had whispered, squeezing Avery's arm and nodding at the cup. "The cops will be here soon. Sanoya and Mac will make a report, but I thought you'd like a few moments to ..." She glanced at Cricket, who had her palm pressed against her mouth. She grimaced as she swallowed, then stared bleakly at Avery and the nurse.

"What?"

"I brought water for you." Nurse Almaden gestured at the side table. Cricket shrugged and nestled against the pillows, lacing her long fingers together as she closed her eyes.

She hadn't moved since.

After a few minutes, her breathing deepened, and the tightness in her features eased as the tranquilizers worked.

The pink concoction had eased Avery's pain, letting her drift along, vaguely aware of flashing lights outside the window. Of voices in the main cabin, doors closing, stairs creaking, but she couldn't grasp the passage of time. Couldn't discern words from the hushed tones. So she drifted, glancing at Cricket every so often to keep rooted to the earth. To this room. She didn't know how much time she had left at Elkwater. The summer, if she was lucky, but Avery had never been lucky. She had been driven and determined, and that behavior had led to a werewolf attack and identity theft.

But it had also led to Elkwater and Cricket sleeping beside her in this room, and she decided that was where she wanted to be.

The door creaked open, and Mac poked her head in, glancing at Cricket's slumbering form and then Avery.

"Come on in." She waved the director closer with a heavy limb.

Mac stepped inside, easing the door closed, and whispered, "I don't want to wake her."

"She's so zonked; I doubt an earthquake *and* a stampede of elepanths could wake her."

"Elepanths?"

"'Kay, so I might be zonked too," Avery said.

Mac smiled, though it was tight around her mouth and did little to relieve the weariness dragging at her eyes. She walked quietly across the room, skirting the creaky floorboard and perching on the bedside table. "How are you?"

"Tired," she admitted. Mac nodded, sweeping a hand through her hair and staring into the empty air. "Sore. Mad." Avery looked at her hand, scrubbed pink and clean. Curling her fingers to glare at the broken nails. A band tightened around her rib cage, squeezing out everything she'd been keeping safely inside like a Flintstones Push-Pop. Her eyes stung, and she clenched them tight, willing the tears not to fall when she couldn't stop the words. "I'm so ... so *mad*."

Her shoulders shook. Once, twice, and the damn broke.

"I don't know what I ever did to him," she cried, her cheeks hot and wet with rage. "I'm a straight-A student, I got a scholarship to Messiah for music, I played varsity softball. Why would he *do* this?"

Mac was seated on the bed in an instant, wrapping her arms around Avery and letting her cry. All the anger and rage, the terror that she had felt in that glade, that she still felt with every tiny, unexpected sound, but mostly the anger at her father, Nathan Payne. She'd heard what Troy said in the glade, heard him tell Cricket that defrauding her, forging her signature, setting Avery up, and then *hunting* her had been her father's plan.

The anger she had felt at the realization had fueled her swing, lending her more strength than she'd ever felt with a softball bat in hand.

How? How could a father do that to his daughter? His own flesh and blood?

She held onto Mac, wailing into the camp director's shirtsleeve. Shaking and trembling against her until the worst of it was out. Her throat ached, snot ran from her nose, and through it all, Mac held her, rocking Avery gently while whispering, "Shh, shh."

When the worst of it subsided, she leaned away. Mac let her go easily, waiting for Avery to speak with a gentle, open expression.

She sniffed, rubbed the back of her wrist under her nose, and said to the ceiling, "I don't understand how someone can hate their own daughter so much."

"It's not you, Avery." Mac patted the comforter between them, leaving her hand accessible should Avery need someone to hold onto. "It's what you—what *we* represent."

"Sin," she spat, her eyes fixed on the bed.

"No. Strength." Mac slapped the comforter. "Strength and kindness. Openmindedness. *Love.* People like your dad are afraid because the world is changing. The balance of power is shifting out of their hands, and they are too small to possess the ability to adapt and evolve. People like us?" She ducked low to meet Avery's eyes. "We represent the future. The way the world could be, the way it should be, and that is something to be proud of."

Avery sniffled, nodding weakly. Mac's words, though, resonated within her, spiraling deep into a vital place where they would plant as a seed and grow roots, forming the new foundation of Avery's world. But at this moment? They were too large to comprehend. Too heavy of a burden to bear.

Cricket shifted in the bed, snorting in her sleep. Both Avery and Mac watched her for a moment, and then the director took Avery's hand and squeezed.

"I'm not saying you need to shave your head, pierce your nipples, and carry a sign that says *Tacos 24/7.* I mean, if you want to, sure. Fine. I've got clippers in my bathroom, but you're on your own for the piercings." Avery couldn't help but chuckle, and Mac's mouth curled to the side, driving a tiny dimple into her cheek. "What I'm saying is, you've got family around you."

"Thanks, Direc—"

"Oh for… can you just call me Mac?" She threw her hands up, and her exasperation pulled a full laugh out of Avery.

Cricket jolted awake, sitting upright, hands pressed into the mattress. She jerked her head to the left, the right, then flopped against the pillows, dropping an arm across her face. "Gods, what's happened now?"

Avery curled her fingers under Cricket's. "Just Mac telling me I've got family that won't, you know, try to forge my signature for financial and political gain and then feed me to a werewolf."

"Oh, right." One round, coppery eye peered at Avery. "Obviously."

"Well, that," Mac said, "and also, downstairs."

Avery twisted around, wincing as the move jostled her leg. "What?"

"They just got in. Drove straight from Harrisburg." Mac glanced at the door and dropped her voice to whisper conspiratorially, "Your mom refused to post bail."

Avery gaped at her, the implication circling in her head until even the words didn't make sense. She dragged her gaze to the door, clutching the comforter in one hand and grasping Cricket's fingers with the other. "My mom?"

"And siblings," Mac confirmed. "There are so many redheads down there, it's like a wildfire." She shook her head, gaze going distant. "Your dad's an asshole, but he must be great in the sack because that is a LOT of kids."

"A whole football team," Avery murmured, easing her hand away from Cricket's and gripping the bedpost to stand. Mac hopped up, fetching a crutch from against the wall and helping Avery gain her balance.

"You don't have to do this right now."

"I know." She sent her boss a tight smile, then glanced at the bed. Cricket had managed to right herself, but her eyes were glassy, her limbs loose. Avery's chest warmed at the sight. Even drugged with goodness knew what tranquilizers and injured—*again* —Cricket wanted to stand beside her; wanted to be there for her.

"Stay," Avery whispered. "Please, get some rest."

"Are you sure?" Cricket asked, her head already dropping.

Avery nodded and jerked her chin to the empty half of the mattress. "Keep it warm for me. I'll be right back." And with a nod to Mac, she hobbled out of the room.

❧❧❧ ❦❦❦

She moved slowly down the stairs, hesitating at the first glimpse of ash blonde hair in a braid. Her mother stood in Mac's office, one arm wrapped around her front, fingers pressed to her lips.

Her eyes were pinned on something out the window, her back straight and proud. Avery's heart clenched at the collision of worlds. In a few short weeks, Elkwater had become a sort of home, and she hadn't recognized how precious she held the camp until this moment—when her mother stood in Mac's office. The representation of the life Avery had been running from, the life she could never escape. The life she would be forced to return to, either now, or at the end of the summer, but forced to return either way.

Pressed and proper. Clean and tidy. Her mother was the culmination of every cultivated image Nathan Payne presented to the world. Everything Avery was not.

She glanced at her borrowed clothes—bike shorts and an OSU hoodie. Her hair hung loose, spilling over her shoulders in a wave of frizzy red. One sock. She could not have looked any further from the Payne ideal, and the thought had her backing up a step, heat crawling up her neck as embarrassment set in.

A floorboard creaked beneath her crutch, and Avery's mom whirled around. Her poise shattered, tears filled her sky-blue eyes, and in a blink, she was rushing from the office and launching to the base of the stairs, wrapping her arms around Avery.

"My baby girl," her mom wept into her hair. "Oh, my Avery."

At those words, at the sound of her name, the image Avery had crafted of her mother, of Nathan Payne's wife, was swept away in a deluge of tears. She dropped her crutch, wrapping her arms around her mother. They were jostled by a weight colliding into them. And another and another. Arm after arm, body after body, crashing into Avery and her mom and hugging them as best they could.

"They came after midnight," her mom explained. Avery only caught snippets of her siblings' voices, but they were the pieces that mattered. "Warrants for his arrest ... multiple counties ... corroborated witness accounts ... forged signatures ... trial ... jail ... no bail."

⁕⁕⁕

Sanoya's narrow frame drifted down the main trail, the Hidebehind hopping from shadow to shadow behind her. One by one, lights in the cabins winked out, and the warm, flickering glow of campfires illuminated the grounds. Counselors' voices echoed in the dark, and lithe figures darted from the shadows, running hand-in-paw and hand-in-hand.

The screen door swung closed, clacking against the frame, and Cricket's uneven hoofbeats tocked against the wood. She dropped a picnic basket on the topmost step and propped her crutch on the porch rail to settle beside Avery.

Avery glanced at the basket and raised her eyebrows.

"Mac's idea," Cricket replied. Her ears twitched, and the bare skin on her throat flushed. "Something she and Ramble used to do, I guess."

"Sit on the stairs?"

"Picnics, smartass." Cricket opened the basket and pulled out two camping mugs and a bag of peach rings. She blinked at the candy, nostrils flaring. The tawny down on her cheeks deepened in hue where it softened to fuzz. "Okay, so *these* were definitely Ramble's idea."

"How is that going?" Avery tipped her head toward the door, not wanting to pry but needing to check in with the faun. After everything, when her mother and siblings had left for Elkins and the drugs had worn off, Cricket filled her in on the Assessor's Office and Green Bank, this time with far less freak-out rushing her words. There was anger there, and hurt, and it was impossible to miss that the direction had changed. She'd been resigned when admitting her family had not believed her, but when it came to Ramble ...

"They're embarrassed." She stretched out her injured leg, rubbing her thigh and staring across the front yard. "Won't stop apologizing whenever we're in the same room, which I guess is fair." Her long fingers toyed with the top of the bandage wrapped around her calf, plucking the pink bow Avery had tied under the influence of Nurse Almaden's painkillers. "This wouldn't have happened if they'd just driven me."

"They did what they thought was right for Mac and the camp," said Avery. "Just like you were doing what you thought was right for your family. You can't fault Ramble that."

"Yeah, that's my point," Cricket grumbled. "Everyone should have listened to me from the start."

Avery chuckled, warmed by the return of Cricket's cranki-ness. She took it as a sign that the faun was feeling better. Or, at least, well enough to wean off the tranquilizers. Her stomach rumbled, reminding Avery that she, too, had weaned off the strongest painkillers, and thus her appetite had returned.

She rummaged in the picnic basket, fingers grazing a loaf of bread, a hunk of cheese, grapes, and finally peering inside. "Oh snap, there's a whole feast in here."

"Told you," Cricket said. "They feel bad."

Avery shook her head, smiling, and pulled out a thermos. She gestured for the camping mugs and filled both with a steaming brown liquid. Cricket took her mug happily, clasping it in both hands, while Avery eyed hers before sniffing.

"Hooooo," she wheezed, eyes watering. "What is this?"

"Apple Jack." Cricket grinned. "Another Mac and Ramble special."

"I'm just going to pretend this is medicine."

"Aw, come on." Cricket sipped her Apple Jack, choking off a cough. "Goes down smooth like a sweet gum spiny ball."

"You are a disaster." Avery set her mug down and grabbed the bag of peach rings, pinching one between her fingers and offering it to Cricket. "And cranky. Here, have a peach ring."

Light sparkled deep in Cricket's eyes. She leaned over the picnic basket to take the offered gummy in her teeth, lips closing around Avery's fingers. A curl of heat shot straight to her belly, unfurling as Cricket's eyes fluttered closed, and she let out a decadent moan.

"Okay, yeah," Avery panted. "Starting to understand why they packed what they did in this basket." She offered another peach ring to Cricket, who took this one with her fingers and popped it into her mouth, chewing loudly.

Music drifted to them on a breeze, a guitar chorus from one of the campfires. A horn joined in, a saxophone, and soon the night was full of song as the stars twinkled overhead.

They sat, shoulder to shoulder, sipping Apple Jack and munching on grapes, bread, and cheese. After a time, Cricket shifted, speaking into the dark, "You gonna go home?"

"No," said Avery. "Not yet."

"End of the summer then?" Cricket's ears twitched and she sat up straighter.

Avery shook her head. "End of *next* summer."

Cricket stared at her, face blank. "What do you—"

"My mom is going to lease an apartment in Elkins. It'll be easier that way, I think. Somewhere to set up as a home base. And she's coming back tomorrow with my siblings. They all play instruments, so I'm going to show them the camp and borrow the Gator to show my mom the undeveloped land around the perimeter."

"Okay, so now I'm super lost. Why?"

"For your family." Cricket stiffened beside her, ears twitching. "We can't clear the land, something about a sound barrier with Green Bank so close, but mom has some ideas about shelters and running water and power to—"

"What?" Cricket's ears jolted upright, and she twisted to face Avery, looking so stunned she couldn't help but laugh. "Wait, hold up, *what?*"

"My mom's family owns a construction company in Pittsburgh," she explained. "They're looking for a 'philanthropic endeavor'"—she lifted her index finger from the mug, crooking it at the words—"and when she learned what my dad was doing … and then I told her about your family."

"Aves," Cricket breathed her name. Goosebumps rose along her arms, and she watched the faun out of the corner of her eye.

"As long as Mac runs the camp, as long as this camp exists, the land can't be sold or developed. No one can force them out, and they can integrate as far as they're comfortable. My mom called my grandmother before she left, and she's going to work on the board, but they've never been able to say no to her." She grinned, her cheeks aching and eyes raw from the tears of shock and joy she had already shed. "And Mac is going to need help, renovating an entire camp, overseeing new construction, it's a big job. She'll need her assistant director around to…"

Cricket blinked, and in the low light, Avery realized the soft down beneath her eyes was damp. "You're not leaving?"

"I'm not leaving," she confirmed. "At least, not until Carnegie at the end of next summer. I hope."

Cricket rubbed the heel of her palm under one eye, the other, then turned the full brunt of her wide, watery gaze on Avery. "I really want to kiss you right now."

"So why don't you?"

Cricket wasted no time, closing the slight distance between them. Her lips pressed against Avery's as her arms banded around her shoulders. A light, chaste press of her lips that Avery chased, angling as best she could on the stairs to fit her body against Cricket's. She flicked her tongue along the seam of her lips, and the faun opened to her immediately.

She swept her tongue in Avery's mouth, kissing her in a slow, drugging way Avery was coming to love, luxuriating in the kiss as if they had all the time in the world.

And with the sound of laughter from the campfires and the stars twinkling overhead, Avery realized—they did.

— · —

EPILOGUE

"ARE YOU READY?"

Cricket looked at Avery, her blue eyes bright and hopeful. Her stomach twisted with nerves, and she grabbed Avery's hand. "No."

"Come on, it can't be that bad."

Cricket huffed, ears flicking. "You've never met my father."

"No," she conceded and squeezed back. "But compared to mine, how bad can a Deer Daddy be?"

"Oh, my Gods, I will pay you to never refer to my father as 'Deer Daddy' ever again."

Avery giggled, and the joyful, bubbly sound settled Cricket's nerves.

It had been a surprise, that giggle. So different from the self-deprecating huffs and tiny smiles Avery had shared with her at the start of the summer.

As the weeks passed, and the phone calls from policemen and federal agencies tapered off, that giggle had grown from a tiny snort to a burble of glee. And then her mother's lawyers had called, reporting that Meander's had responded to their subpoena, and that Avery's signature on the receipt matched the forged signature on that last batch of sales.

Cricket had no head for the intricacies of human law, but the phrases "conclusive evidence" and "irrefutable innocence" were thrown around, and Avery had burst out laughing. The same joyful, bubbling giggle she let out now.

Cricket held her breath and faced her parent's dwelling, exhaling as she raised her hand to knock on the birch door. It flew open immediately, and her mother, Thistle, rushed out.

"My baby!" She enveloped them both in a tight hug. "My sweet doe."

Cricket and Avery were half drug, half escorted into the dwelling where her father, Bosk, loomed in the center of the room. The ceiling was highest here, able to accommodate the spread of his antlers without the points scraping the thatch. Parcels and filled baskets lined the walls, and what little had accounted for decoration had been removed and wrapped in linen, ready to be moved.

"Cricket." Bosk nodded, his deep basso rumbling through the room.

"Hey, Dad." Arm tight at her side, she waved her fingers in his direction, feeling every inch the doe her mother had called her, and not a grown faun. "I, um, this is Avery."

It was a cheap trick, she knew it, but it didn't stop her from pushing Avery in front of her. By Avery's own admission, her dad was way worse than Cricket's. And she was a big girl. She could handle herself.

"Hello, Cervid Bosk," Avery said without missing a beat.

Every faun in the room blinked in surprise at her use of the proper title. Thistle recovered first, patting Cricket's shoulder and whispering, "Well done."

"I didn't—"

A wink from Avery shut her mouth. Of course, she'd learned the proper way to address the faun. The real surprise here was that Cricket hadn't assumed that she would.

Pride bubbled in her chest, giving her the courage to step beside Avery as she explained why they'd come. "The camp owns the land," she finished. "As long as Elkwater is open, there's a permanent place for your family. With electricity and access to running water, and—"

"I am sure my daughter has told you already," Bosk cut her off, "the faun have no interest in leaving Green Bank."

"Then don't," Avery fired back. "If you want to stay, stay. Keep uprooting your dwellings and your children, but don't hold back the members of your family who want to settle somewhere for more than a week at a time."

"You could not possibly understand—"

"No, you're right. I couldn't. But I'm trying to." Avery squared her shoulders, lifting her chin as she stared down the seven-foot faun looming over her. "There's a whole wide world out there, a world you can be a part of like the wolven and the naga." Bosk scowled, wide mouth twisting down, and Avery shook her head. "I'm not explaining this very well. What I'm trying to say is that there is a place for the faun. *Here.*" She pointed to the ground beneath her feet. "And for those who want to wander further afield, there's room at Elkwater."

"What do you mean 'here'?" Thistle asked. Bosk jerked his head around to glare at his wife, and Cricket stepped forward, grabbing her mother's soft hand before her father could raise his voice.

"Avery owns the land," she explained, then cringed. "Sort of. A lot of it is being held up in court or escrow. Something like that, it's wildly confusing, but what matters is, it's her signature on the property taxes and deeds."

"Forged." Bosk's nostrils flared.

"Regardless, the land was sold through land contracts, which the previous owners are funding. My mom's lawyers can explain it better than I can, but what it comes down to is that the land is being held in trust under my name, and the attorneys are working with the previous owners to ensure nothing like this ever happens again."

"Impossible," he snorted, burly arms crossing over his chest.

"Hardly," Avery chuckled in reply. "You've never met my mom's lawyers."

"How will they ensure the land doesn't sell again?" Thistle asked.

"We're re-drafting the contracts to include an amendment stating that the land cannot be further developed, nor can it be sold for a profit." Avery grinned, glancing from faun to faun. Her shoulders drooped at Bosk and Thistle's blank expression.

"The land stays ours," Cricket explained. "There's a precedent, or something, tied into the property laws governing the camp. Avery, or rather, Payne Properties, can't develop the land, and they can't sell it for a profit."

"But what we *can* do," Avery said, "is sell it to you. For a dollar." Bosk's wide eyes blinked. His stern mouth fell open, and Cricket grinned. "I can't promise that every seller comes on board, land contracts are tricky, but the people of Green Bank respect the faun. We've already secured twenty-five acres, including the land your dwelling is on, and I'm hoping we can—"

"And the hollow? By Deer Creek?" Bosk asked.

Cricket glanced at Avery. She worked her jaw, eyes narrowed in the way they did when she was thinking hard. "I'm not ... I'm not sure? But I can check. As shady as the whole thing was, Lunar Asset Management kept a clean paper trail; we should be able to locate the owners easily enough."

"You secure the hollow under Little Mountain," Bosk said, "and the faun will be your allies for as long as we roam this world."

"Yikes, dad, calm down." Cricket laid her hand on her father's arm and smiled up at him. "But, you mean it?"

"The hollow is all that matters." He nodded and extended a hand for Avery. She took it without hesitation, her long pianist's fingers dwarfed by the length and breadth of Bosk's own.

"Then I'll have my mother's lawyers start there." She pumped his arm once, and in the tight nod and gleam in her eyes, Cricket saw a shadow of Nathan Payne. His determination, grit, and charm. But where Nathan was all smooth edges buffed to a shine, Avery's shirt, tucked into denim cut-offs, was wrinkled and bore faint, muddy stains. Her fox-fur hair was frizzy and wild, and she'd never looked more lovely.

Bosk released her hand and regarded Avery for a long moment before his nut-brown gaze landed on Cricket. One ear twitched, the corner of his mouth curled, and he pulled her into his side, knuckling the top of her head. "I can see why you like this one."

"Dad."

"Only, I wonder what it is she sees in you."

"*Dad.*" Heat rushed into Cricket's cheeks, and she pushed against him, attempting to wriggle free. But Bosk kept her hugged in tight, spinning Cricket around and calling for Avery to follow. "Dinner is already in the pot, young lady, and my wife's acorn stew waits for no faun or human."

A light haze rose from the forest floor, braiding through the trees and dissipating in the fields where fireflies danced to a soundless tune. Glimmers of warm, yellow lights bobbed and weaved, rising high enough to obscure the line between earth and sky.

Avery and Cricket had left the dwelling after dinner with her parents, both of them flush with laughter and acorn whisky. Without any particular heading in mind, Cricket led her human through the woods.

One glade melted into another. The deer trail she followed took them over a stream, through a cluster of blackberry bushes, and out into a field. On they hiked, chasing the last of the setting sun. She hadn't planned to catch that magical hour of twilight when the fireflies danced and a cool breeze teased mist from the creeks running into the valley, but Gods be damned if she wasn't going to take advantage of it.

Stars twinkling overhead, and a pretty girl holding her hand? Yeah, Cricket was absolutely going to take advantage of *this*.

"Where are we going?" Avery huffed. A light sheen of sweat coated her skin, giving her freckles a luster that shone in the moonlight.

"No idea." Cricket pantomimed scanning the wood, and thrust her arm in an arbitrary direction. "There!"

"What?" Avery stopped short, peering in the direction she pointed. "I don't see anything."

"There, castle," Cricket drawled, then cackled when Avery playfully smacked her arm.

"How the heck have you seen *Young Frankenstein*?"

"How have you?" she retorted. "It has a man playing God and boob jokes. Isn't your dad, like, super Evangelical?"

"It has boob jokes," Avery leveled in a flat tone. "And in case you haven't noticed"—her mouth curled wickedly, and she tugged Cricket's arm, drawing her in close—"I happen to have a thing for boobs."

That said, she brushed her knuckle over the curve of Cricket's breast. She sucked in a breath, ears flicking as an accompanying shiver ran down her spine. "You're feeling bold."

"Acorn whisky," Avery mumbled, her eyes dropping to Cricket's mouth. "Pretty company."

"Pretty?"

Avery flicked her gaze up. Moonlight reflected in her eyes, twin pinpricks ringed in blue, bright enough to hold even the strongest faun captive. That knuckle trailed lower, brushing the row of her nipples, one by one, through her thin cotton tank.

"Beautiful," Avery whispered and closed the distance between them. Her lips brushed Cricket's in a soft kiss, less than the brush of a butterfly's wing, and somehow, it was more than any deep sweep of a tongue or tangle of limbs could ever hope to be. In that brush was a wish and a promise. It was a statement, hopeful in its brevity and everything Cricket could have asked for.

She wrapped her arms around Avery, refusing to let any space between them, and returned the kiss. Soft against her cheekbone, a dusting on the tip of her nose, and then she caught her mouth, swallowing the moan that rose in her throat at the taste of strawberry chapstick.

Time fell away, the meadow and the stars vanishing as Cricket's world became the human in her arms. She chased every sensation brought on by the heat of Avery's mouth, the slide of her tongue, and the deft caress of her fingers. The soft curve of her shoulders and hips, how Avery's body melded into her as if she'd been made to fit every one of Cricket's hard angles.

Warmth pooled between her legs, every swipe of Avery's tongue and tease of her fingers feeding the low, steady throb in her groin. With shaking hands, Cricket tugged her shirt from her shorts, sliding her palms up Avery's waist to cup her breasts and groaning at the soft weight.

"Gods." She broke away from the kiss on a pant, sweeping her thumbs over hard nubs. "Aves, you're so—"

"Shh." Avery pressed a finger to her lips, smirking at Cricket's wide eyes. She trailed the shape of her mouth, the touch as soft and teasing as the caress of her nipples had been. It was a subtle sort of magic, this light caress, hauling every nerve ending to life and drawing all of Cricket's attention to the so-soft-she-thought-she-imagined-it touch.

Her lips quivered in the wake of Avery's finger, chest heaving as she cupped her breast and swept the nipple, pinching lightly before moving lower. Again and again, teasing every one of Cricket's nipples until the muscles in her stomach were tense, her body a tightly wound spring.

Her ears stood fully erect, the soft breeze tickling fine hairs. A shudder built in her core, and with a groan, she chased Avery's mouth. Slipping her hands up, she cupped her cheeks and held Avery in place, nibbling and sucking her lower lip before delving deep to swallow the tiny whimpers clawing up from her throat.

Gods, this human. Avery. Her Avery. In a matter of weeks, she'd driven Cricket wild with lust and met her every step of the way. She'd never known the magic of her home world, and she had never known what it was to feel the flow of healing power through her limbs, but she imagined it would feel a little something like this.

Avery was pliant beneath the force of her kiss, letting herself be walked backward and grunting softly when her back hit a nearby tree. She squirmed against Cricket, and half a thought later, her hands were in Cricket's hair, tugging the curls and—

"Oh, Gods." Her legs trembled as Avery circled the base of her ears, squeezing gently before rubbing her thumbs up the inner curve. "Fuck."

"That's the idea," Avery murmured against her throat, hot breath raising goosebumps beneath the down. Her nails scraped down Cricket's ears, and a warble of pleasure dribbled into her core.

This was it. This was how a human bewitched a faun and turned her into a puddle of goo. A gentle stroke, a scrape of nail, and that plush, plump mouth sucking on her pulse.

A throaty moan escaped, and Cricket buried her face in the crook of Avery's neck, trying and failing to think clearly enough to reciprocate. But what were thoughts when her brain was boiling and her pussy throbbing?

"Avery, please," she managed, kissing the words into the sweet salt of her skin. "Please touch me."

"Where?" Her nails scraped again, and Cricket twitched against her, pussy clenching.

"Anywhere, sweet girl." Her hips twitched, bucking against Avery as if they could demand her fingers.

Avery laughed a throaty chuckle and worked her leg between Cricket's thighs. Hot breath teased Cricket's ear, and she moaned, bending her knees to grind against Avery's thigh as she continued groping and stroking her ears, pinching the tips and rolling them between the pads of her thumbs. It was mind-melting and maddening and everything and nothing. Cricket needed more. She needed those fingers inside her, needed Avery's mouth on her throat, her nipples, her navel her—

"What do you need, baby?"

"You," Cricket panted, rolling against Avery as she chased release. Her body flashed hot, each breath coming in tiny tight pants. How the *fuck* did she do this to her so easily? A wink and a smile, the feel of her soft skin, and Cricket was drooling like a satyr at the Bacchanal.

"Where?" Avery pulled her face away, head thudding lightly against the tree trunk. Her eyes searched Cricket's face. She drew a line with the edge of her fingernail down the side of one ear. "Here?" Cricket's heart skipped a beat and Avery continued the path down to her temple. "Or here?" That lovely mouth pursed, and mischief sparked in her eyes. "Certainly not here." She traced Cricket's mouth and slipped her finger inside, wetting the tip.

Cricket's eyelids fluttered closed, as did her lips. She sucked on Avery's finger, thankful for the reprieve and furious all the same. She'd been so close, and Avery—Gods-blessed Avery—had known and chosen to tease instead of please.

Cricket wasn't sure if she loved her or hated her for it.

So she swirled her tongue around Avery's finger, watching that mischief deepen into desire. Her lips parted, and over the thrumming of her heartbeat, Cricket caught the tiniest, most innocent little "Oh."

An innocence that was far too quick in passing.

Avery's brows lowered, and her mouth curled wickedly. "I see."

"Hm?" Cricket cocked her head, lips pursed around Avery's finger.

She withdrew, eyes flicking low, and before Cricket could decipher that look, Avery pulled her hand away, cupped Cricket's pussy, and pressed her palm against her clit. "Somewhere wet, then."

"Oak and ivy." Cricket slammed her hand against the tree trunk as her knees buckled to keep from falling. The calm she had managed vanished beneath a wave of pleasure, and instantly she was panting and fighting off a rising bleat in her throat. "A-Avery."

"Cricket." She lowered herself to the ground, bringing Cricket with her.

Or maybe she chased her down, refusing to let that delicious touch leave her center. Not that it mattered who led whom, but if it did, Cricket was all too happy to admit she was currently being led along by her nose.

Or her pussy.

Whatever.

"Can we try something?" Avery asked as Cricket settled on her lap. Those strong, steady fingers curled against her center, palm pressing and releasing in a slow tempo—enough to have Cricket panting but not enough to send her over the edge.

"Anything," she said, barely able to catch enough breath to do so. Avery hummed her pleasure, squeezing Cricket's hip as she wriggled lower. Hooking two fingers in the waistband of Cricket's bike shorts, Avery tugged them down.

"Help me?"

No faun ever kicked off lycra so quickly. The shorts landed with an unceremonious whump somewhere behind her, and a half-second later, Avery gripped Cricket's thighs with both hands and kissed her navel.

"I've never—"

"It's alright," Cricket promised. And *GODS*, was it alright. It was damn near celebrated.

"Not never," Avery amended. Her words hummed into Cricket's lower abdomen, joining the curdling pleasure deep in her core. Her legs were already trembling, caught up in a whirlwind of anticipation and need. "Just not with an inhuman."

"S'not so different." She cupped the back of Avery's head, pressing gently to get her to look up. "You don't have to."

"I want to." She squeezed Cricket's thigh in emphasis. "I really, *really* want to."

"Oak and ivy, Aves." If the angle had allowed, Cricket would have kissed the human girl senseless.

"Guide me?"

All Cricket could manage was a nod and then a breathy moan as Avery pressed a warm, wet kiss to her pussy. And again, following the line of her lips and lingering at the peak. Almost shyly, her tongue darted out, catching on Cricket's clit. A flash of pleasure and surprise shot her eyes wide. She dropped her head back, fingers still tangled in Avery's hair. Encouraged by the response, Avery flicked her tongue out again, stroking her in a steady, maddening tempo.

"Aves," Cricket moaned, her hips twitching in time to each pulse of sensation shivering up from her center. "Fuck, you don't need any guidance."

That earned a chuckle, and the vibrations stole Cricket's breath. Oak and ivy, she couldn't see straight. That metronomic pace consumed all of her, adhering her body to the cadence of Avery's softly stroking tongue.

Cricket cautioned a glance down, and the sight of blue eyes watching her intently nearly ruined her. Her hand flexed at the back of Avery's head, and she closed her eyes, soft pleasure easing her features as her tongue stretched along the line of Cricket's lips, parting her with a steady sweep.

One of them hummed, or both of them, what did it matter, and the buzzing filled Cricket from slit to scalp. She rocked her hips against Avery's tongue, no longer in control of herself. She belonged to this human and her bewitching song. Belonged to her every breath, her every smile. Belonged beneath her hands and her mouth.

A hand slipped from her thigh, clumsily reaching between Cricket's legs, and that hesitance filled her heart to bursting.

Her determined Avery. So brave in taking what she wanted, in grasping life by the antlers and bending it to her will. Not that Cricket had antlers, but damn if her human wouldn't take them in both hands and *tug*.

A finger pressed against her, shattering Cricket's last remaining thoughts as it plunged deep. Avery increased the tempo of her tongue, alternating between sucking on Cricket's clit and flicking the bud. Her finger crooked on the alternate beat and it was all Cricket could do not to cry out and startle the moon itself. She fisted her hand in Avery's hair, bleating as the human began to hum.

"Aves—" A shiver rolled up her spine. Her ears swiveled to catch the sound reverberating in her core as another finger pressed within her, filling Cricket until all she could do was moan. With each stroke and the relentless flicking and sucking of her clit, the last shreds of control she'd desperately hung onto dissipated like the rising mist in a breeze.

What had been a slow-building fire in Cricket's belly transformed into an inferno. She cried out to her Gods, called out to the oak and the ivy and the faeries tucked into the trees, riding Avery's face and her hand until stars burst beside her eyes. Pleasure erupted, rushing up her front, and Cricket threw her head back, unleashing a deep, rasping cry that startled the birds above.

Avery worked her through her orgasm, only ceasing the pump of her fingers and the Gods-blessed pace of her tongue when Cricket sagged forward, catching herself on her elbows. Avery pulled her hand away, and Cricket's pussy clenched one last time, missing the stretch of those glorious fingers. She collapsed onto her side, tongue all but lolling out of her mouth as Avery propped herself up on an elbow, gazing down at Cricket, her lips swollen and mouth glistening.

"You said ..." Cricket panted, "you'd need ... guidance." Avery grinned and nodded. "Liar."

"I also said I'd done that before." She wiped her mouth with the back of a hand. "Just not with an inhuman."

"Avery Payne, ladies and gentlemen. One shot wonder." Cricket rolled onto her side, draping her arm over the curve of Avery's waist and scooting closer. "There should be some sort of scout badge you can earn for that."

"Badges?" Avery cocked her head, narrowing her eyes. "We don't need no stinking badges." Cricket stared at her long enough that Avery's smile faded. "*Blazing Saddles*?"

"No, I know." Cricket nodded. "They show it at the Green Bank library twice a year. But how do *you* know what *Blazing Saddles* is?"

Avery chewed her lower lip, eyes dropping. Heat bloomed under Cricket's palm, and it took her a moment to realize that Avery had broken out in a full-body blush. She mumbled something under her breath that had Cricket leaning closer.

"Come again?"

Avery glared at her. "I *said*, 'Madeline Kahn.'" Heat darkened her cheeks. "I don't know what counts as an awakening in Green Bank, but for me, it was Madeline Khan."

"Ah, yes." Cricket slipped her hand under the hem of Avery's shirt, wriggling closer as she drew the cotton shirt up to reveal a soft pink bra. Avery hissed quietly as cool evening air caressed bare skin. "Madeline Kahn. I think she was an awakening for a lot of us."

Her fingers followed the swell of Avery's breasts, eyes intent on her face to ensure she didn't miss a single quiver of lips or flutter of eyelashes. She hooked her finger into the cup and tugged it down. Soft flesh spilled out, warm and inviting. Cricket ducked her head low and laved the flat of her tongue against an erect nipple. Avery gasped, arching into her touch. Her hand came up to cradle the back of Cricket's head, holding her face against her breasts.

"What was the line?" she murmured into Avery's skin. "'What knockers.'"

"Teri Garr."

"Hm?" Cricket angled her face up, questioning.

"Inga." Avery's fingers pressed into Cricket's skull as if she could force the faun back to her breast. "Dr. Franken-stein"—Cricket pinched her lips in a smile at her pronunciation: Fronkensteen—"says it to Inga. Teri Garr."

"Right, Teri Garr." She raised her head, loving the disappointed sigh that escaped Avery.

A disappointed sigh that cut off as Cricket slung her leg over thick, luscious thighs and rolled Avery onto her back.

"What do you say, Avery?" She grinned, letting all of the heat and desire she felt for this human show in her face, and in the warmth of her voice. "Would you like to go for a roll in ze hay?"

Join my
newsletter
to read
their story ⟶

Acknowledgments

With every manuscript that makes it to a published work, the list of people I have to thank grows. This is exactly the sort of problem I love to have. Writing is sometimes solitary, but bringing a world and characters to life takes a village. This is my village:

Oliver — You told me to "shut up and write" without truly understanding what you were unleashing. I love you for that and so many other things.

Ana — The World's Best Hype Woman™. Thank you for listening to me ramble over uncountable glasses of wine and charcuterie boards. I am the luckiest person to have you in my corner.

Molly — Thirty+ years of friendship, and all you got was this faun smut.

Kel — MA'AM. You're the best thing TikTok has ever put on my fyp. I am so sad our paths did not cross when we lived in the same city, and so grateful fate saw fit to throw us together on the internet.

Newport Sea Base, Mountain and Sea Adventures, and the Girl Scouts of America — for the best summers of my life.

The Ladies of Fort Smut — I could not ask for better company on this writing, retreating, and charcuterie-eating life. Over the years, we have added four tiny humans, survived a pandemic, group-read numerous terrible and not-so-terrible books, and crafted the most rewarding and routinely hilarious group chat. Sorry for all the TikToks. I love you all. Where are we going next?

My Beta Team, Amazing ARC Readers, and the divinely talented authors of *Blood and Pulp, NC Indies* and *FaRo*.

You — you lovely, lovely human being who read this book. We frequent the same corners of the internet. I feel like we could almost be friends. I hope you stick around for more.

ABOUT THE AUTHOR

B.L. Brown writes about messy characters solving their problems through banter and questionable choices. Her debut novel, *Shady Depths*, released in April 2023, and her follow-up novel, *Ritual Income* won second place in the Spring 2024 Bookfest Awards – Paranormal Romance Genre. Her short fiction can be found in *Tails, Trysts, and Tentacles: One Monstrous Summer*, *Fireside: Modern Legends and Lore*, and *The Future of Us, A Moms Who Write Anthology*.

Twitter: @brittabrau

Instagram: @brittawritesthings

TikTok: @brittawritesthings

Join her newsletter at www.brittawritesthings.com